OTHER BOOKS BY KATE L. MARY

The College of Charleston Series:
The List
No Regrets
Moving On
Letting Go

Zombie Apocalypse Love Story Novellas:
More than Survival
Fighting to Forget
Playing the Odds
The Key to Survival

Anthologies:
Prep For Doom
Gone with the Dead

SHATTERED
WORLD

Book Two in the *BROKEN WORLD* Series

KATE L. MARY

Twisted Press

Published by Twisted Press, LLC, an independently owned company.

Copyright © 2014 by Kate L. Mary
ISBN-13: 978-1500775360
ISBN-10: 1500775363
Edited by Emily Teng
Cover art by Jimmy Gibbs

For everyone who read *Broken World* and helped make the release such a success!
Thanks for loving Axl and Vivian as much as I do!

CHAPTER ONE

So this is the end. Mitchell — the bastard — promised us a safe place. Instead, he's left us out here to die. I'm not that surprised, really. Axl and I suspected this would happen. But we didn't expect what came next. We're in the middle of nowhere. The damn Mojave Desert! Who would have guessed the dead would find us out here?

Moans fill the silence as we stare at each other, trying to decide what to do. Staying to fight could mean death, but running will lead us to Vegas. Not an ideal place to take refuge. We've already killed dozens of the undead. We're all out of breath. Sweaty and shaking. Terrified. But no one wants to abandon our supplies. No one suggests that we run away like cowards.

Axl's eyes meet mine. My stomach clenches, and all the things we've left unsaid flash through my mind. I owe him so many thank-yous. No one has ever been as kind and thoughtful as he has. I regret all the missed moments. All the times I could have told him how much I cared, but I let them pass. If only there was more time.

Time is something we'll never have again, though.

"Then we fight," Axl says.

I swallow and nod with the others as I grip my gun tighter. My heart pounds, and adrenaline courses through my veins. A warm breeze blows across the desert, catching my hair. It brings with it a sprinkling of sand and the pungent odor of death. This could be the end for us, but I guess I'm okay with it. It's not like I'm leaving a lot behind. Emily is gone, and this thing with Axl may not have ever happened, anyway. I'd rather die fighting.

We turn back to face the horde of bodies at the fence just as the door to shelter opens behind us. I spin around with my heart in my throat, frozen in my tracks. No one speaks, and the night seems suddenly silent. Blood pounds in my ears, and I'm breathing heavily, but it's like everything moves in slow motion as a woman steps out of the building.

I blink three times as if doing that will somehow cause what I'm seeing to make sense. I know her. She's thin, the kind of thin only Hollywood can produce. Her hair is strawberry blonde and silky smooth. It goes just past her shoulders. It's too dark to get a good look at her eyes from here, but I know they're green without even having to see them, and that she has a splash of freckles on her nose.

"Holy crap! That's Hadley Lucas," Al says excitedly. Of course he'd be the first one to snap out of it. Teenage hormones and celebrity worship go hand in hand.

Hadley's body is tense and her eyes dart to the dead moaning behind us. Her expression is so familiar. Am I really here, or am I sitting in some movie theater somewhere watching this all happen? I almost reach for my popcorn. Then the stench of death hits my nostrils and I'm jerked back to reality. You can't smell movies. Even though I've seen Hadley Lucas in dozens of movies over the years, this isn't one of them.

Hadley's eyes move back to the fence while she frantically motions for us to come into the building. "What are you waiting for? Get a move on!"

People take off toward her, but my feet stay rooted to the ground. We can't just run off and leave everything out here. If the dead rattling that fence manage to break it down, we'll never be able to get our supplies. We need to take them now.

Axl takes a step forward, but I grab his arm. "What about our stuff?"

His gray eyes move toward the fence, and I follow his gaze. A tremor of terror moves through me like a snake swimming through my veins. The moans are louder now. The dead howl and shake the fence frantically. Desperate to get in. It's holding, but who knows for how long.

Axl must be thinking the same thing, because he doesn't run for the building. He turns and takes off toward the Nissan. "Everybody grab your gear!"

I shove my gun in the waistband of my pants as I jog to the car and pull out my own things first. Then toss them over my shoulder to free up my hands. I want to be able to carry more. The bags I grab are full of weapons, so they're awkward and heavy. The nylon straps dig into my arms, but I do my best to ignore it. We need to get as much in as possible before that fence collapses.

I glance toward the building just as Joshua and Arthur run out. Joshua's expression is tense when he stops next to me and starts pulling things out of the car. Arthur is right behind him. He's in his sixties and his arms are so thin he doesn't look strong enough to carry much, but he grabs a huge box. Guess looks can be deceiving.

Joshua flicks his brown hair out of his face, and his eyes meet mine. He gives me a smile that doesn't reach his eyes, then grabs a few bags out of the Nissan. "Sorry it took so long."

The smile I give him is strained but genuine. I'm too relieved the door is actually open to complain. Does he really think any of us could blame him? When Joshua went inside with that asshole, we had no reason to think he would be able to get the door open, but he did. Whether it took minutes or hours, he worked a miracle in my book.

"Don't apologize." I grimace when the nylon straps shift on my arm. It's like getting rug burn. "I'm so happy to see you that I'd kiss you if my arms weren't full."

Joshua flashes me a real smile and we head for the shelter. Moans from the dead follow us into the small, concrete building. Everyone huffs and puffs from exertion. Like the big bad wolf, trying to blow the house down. We all barely fit with our bodies loaded down with boxes and bags of supplies, and we bump into one another as we try to squeeze in. I should be relieved when the door shuts, cutting off the sounds and smells of the dead. But it's stiflingly hot and a tight fit. So many people bang into my arms and legs that I'm sure I'm going to be covered in bruises. I'll be alive, though. That's the important part.

The door leading into the shelter is wide open, and Hadley Lucas stands next to it. I'm one of the closest people to her. She smiles, revealing those famous dimples, and actually takes two bags out of my hands before heading down the stairs. I didn't expect a Hollywood star to come to my rescue today. Or ever, for that matter.

The stairwell is narrow and awkward to maneuver with an armful of bags. I'm right behind Hadley, and the footsteps of the others echo on the stairs at my back. No one talks. The panic and exhaustion from before hangs over us like a mushroom cloud. I haven't been able to completely relax yet. Maybe I'll never be able to relax. Even underground, the future is uncertain. We'll always feel trapped and cornered as long as those things are out there, waiting to rip into us.

Somehow, I manage to make it down to the next floor without tripping over myself or anyone else. I drop my things as soon as I'm off the stairs and take deep, soothing breaths while I try to calm my pounding heart. It doesn't work. I half expect Mitchell to pop out and shoot me in the head. Or the dead to come charging down the stairs behind us. No way we're really in this shelter. No way we're safe after the hell we've been through the last several days.

Others file in, and for the first time, I get a really good look at the group. Everyone is covered in dirt and sweat, and several people still gasp for breath. There are tears in Jessica's eyes as she leans against her father. Trey and Parvarti hug. Anne rushes forward and throws her arms around Jake. Even Angus's face is more relaxed, though he does his best to keep his jaw tense and his eyes hard. Classic Angus. Al, oddly enough, is drooling over Hadley. Teenagers.

My eyes meet Axl's, and I have the sudden urge to reach out and hug him, but I hold back. The corner of his mouth pulls up just a tad. He's filthy. Even more so than the rest of us, for some reason. His dirty blond hair drips with sweat. It clings to his forehead in clumps, making the strands look darker. My fingertips tingle with the desire to brush it off his face. I give him a tentative smile as my heart pounds harder. It was just slowing, but one look from him has sent it into overdrive again.

We're alive. More than that, I have a second chance to make things work with Axl. To figure out what all this stuff between us really means. It's more than I'd ever hoped for.

People start to relax. To talk. To cry. The air is thick with relief as the tension melts away. We are not going to die tonight.

Sophia clings to Ava, and when our eyes meet she releases her daughter long enough to run to me. She throws one arm around me and another around Jessica, hugging us at the same time. There are tears on her cheeks. "Thank God you're okay," she says over and over again.

Anne hasn't stopped hugging Jake. There's a look of pure joy on her face that tugs at my heart so thoroughly I'm certain it's going to explode. They didn't even know one another a few days ago, but they belong to each other now.

5

That's what happens when you find yourself in the middle of a zombie apocalypse, I guess. Trying to mend your shattered life with pieces you find along the way. It's what we've all seemed to do.

Emily's brown eyes flash through my mind. My chest aches where my heart used to be. It's raw and painful, and I have to look away. I'm too emotionally exhausted to deal with it. After all the drama, I could crumble to dust at any moment.

We're in a hall. A very industrial-looking hall. The walls are made of cement blocks and the ceiling is unfinished. It's lined with steel beams, exposed wires, and pipes. It doesn't look anything like the luxury condo described in the brochure Mitchell passed around.

There's an open door to my right. The room contains a desk with a few keyboards and the wall is covered with buttons and blinking lights. Lined with television screens. This has to be the control room for the facility. The dead are visible on the screens, lined up outside the fence. Still shaking it. I wonder if they'll stop now that we're gone or if they'll keep shaking it until the whole thing collapses.

To my left is a dark room that has an odd-looking shower, and I have a sudden flashback to my high school chemistry class. I vaguely remember something about a decontamination room in the description of the facility. This must be it, although it doesn't look as high-tech as I expected. It's a good thing this is a zombie apocalypse and not a nuclear bombing. No way that little shower would do us any good if we had to rinse off nuclear waste.

There's a third door in front of us, but it's closed. A small, square keypad is on the wall next to the door. I'm not sure what could be behind that door. Whatever it is, it must be important if you need a code to access it.

"I'm so sorry it took us so long!" Sophia cries, breaking the silence. "We were watching on the security cameras and arguing with Mitchell, but he just wouldn't give in!"

"Thankfully, Hadley stepped in and took the matter into her own hands," Arthur says. His mouth turns up when he flashes a smile at Hadley, making his cheeks look hollow. His skin is an unhealthy color. Maybe it's the fluorescent lighting, or maybe it's the cancer. It's possible it's worse than he's been letting on. "It was looking pretty serious out there."

I glance at Hadley. Even at the end of the world, she looks like she just stepped out of a salon on Rodeo Drive. I swear, there isn't a hair on her head out of place. "You let us in?"

Hadley is—was—a pretty big movie star. I never would have pegged someone from Hollywood as being all that compassionate, especially not her. To be honest, I was never a big fan of her or her movies. Something about Hadley always rubbed me the wrong way. It's odd being face to face with her now that the world as we knew it has come to an end.

"I'm not going to just stand by while people get killed," she says flatly, arching a perfectly sculpted brow at me. Her sparkling green eyes narrow on my face and I squirm. It's like she can read my mind.

"What about Mitchell?" Winston asks.

Hadley rolls her eyes and cracks her knuckles like she'd love nothing more than to punch him in the face. "That prick can go screw himself. This place was made to sustain fifty people for five years. There were four of us before he got here. I think we're going to be just fine." Her tone is blunt. Oddly enough, it reminds me of Axl. Maybe she isn't the entitled bitch I've always imagined her to be.

"He around?" Angus asks, trying to sound casual. His face is hard and his jaw tightens. He cracks his knuckles just like Hadley did, and I find myself smiling.

When it comes to Angus I feel bipolar, constantly going back and forth between hating him and finding him amusing. I guess he's the kind of guy that grows on you. Of course, he's such a prick there's no way those old feelings will ever go away. I can't imagine being with him for more than an

7

hour and not wanting to kick him in the balls.

Hadley's laugh is an oddly familiar sound. It takes me back, and once again I feel like I'm in a movie theater. That's something I'll never get to experience again, though. "He ran to his condo to hide. I think he was a little scared of what would happen when you guys got in here."

Angus runs his hand over his short brown hair and grunts. I'm one hundred percent positive Mitchell was right to hide. Angus would beat the shit out of him if he were here right now. Mitchell better hope he doesn't bump into Angus when the two of them are alone.

A man steps out of the control room to my left. He leans against the doorframe while somehow managing to stand tall. Shoulders back, head raised. He's average all around. Average looks, average height, middle-aged, brown hair and brown eyes that leave little to no impression. The kind of person you meet and forget in ten minutes' time. He doesn't appear high-class like Mitchell and Hadley. Before I even see the company logo on his polo shirt, I know he's an employee. Something about the authoritative way he carries himself.

"This is James," Hadley says. "He worked for the company that built this place. Hitched a ride here with the helicopter pilot right at the end to make sure everything was ready for inhabitants. Of course, the pilot got sick and couldn't get him back out…" She shrugs like it's no big deal, but her eyes give her away. They're full of sadness and pain. She's not that great of an actress. "Well, I guess I should give you all a tour. Feel free to leave your things here and come back for it later or take it with you. Whichever you feel more comfortable with."

I can't fight back the smile that spreads across my face when I grab my stuff and sling it over my shoulder. I don't bother with the guns and other supplies I carried down. We can fool with them later. After we've all had a shower and a little rest.

Hadley leads the way, talking over her shoulder as she

heads toward a set of stairs that descend even further underground. "There's plenty of space for everyone since most of the condos are empty. There are one, two, and three bedroom units, so we'll just split people up as we go down. Luckily, James was able to locate the master key. They're all stocked with food from the company and clothing from the owners, so I guess it's finders keepers now." She pauses for a moment and shrugs without looking back. I'm right behind her, and even though her voice is even and steady, there's a slight droop in her shoulders. This is affecting her more than she wants to let on.

Al's right on Hadley's tail and I'd be shocked if his eyes weren't glued to her ass. But when we step into a much nicer room that has a few desks and computers, Al actually manages to rip his eyes away from the walking wet dream in front of him. The kid was a computer nerd or something in his school, so he's been dying to get his hands on one. Looks like he's in luck.

Hadley pauses long enough to point toward one of the computers. It looks expensive, not that I would know anything about that. The trailer park I grew up in didn't have Wi-Fi, and when I ran out on my dad, a computer wasn't really a priority.

"This is the media center that has all the computers and stuff," Hadley says. "Not that it matters much anymore, there's no Internet or anything."

Al's face falls and he stares at the computers like his puppy just died. He doesn't even move when Hadley starts walking again. Poor kid. Guess he'll have to find something else to occupy his time. Maybe Angus can give him one of his *Penthouse* magazines.

Hadley heads down a poorly lit hallway that ends in a decked-out common area. There's a fully stocked bar to the right and a pool table in the center of the room. Couches and chairs are arranged on the other side, gathered around a few coffee tables. Everything is sleek and modern. Expensive. It's decorated in bright reds and blues that were probably intended to combat the gloom of being underground.

"Here's one of the shared spaces. The theater is through that door over there." She waves across the room to a set of double doors. They're open and the room is dark, but I can just make out a few cushy-looking leather chairs. "There's a pretty decent selection of movies, it looks like. Plus, I'm sure you'll find more in the individual condos. People brought all the necessities for the end of the world." Her tone is biting and she rolls her eyes just a little when she says it.

Hadley sounds oddly sarcastic for someone who bought one of the condos. Maybe she's just bitter? Or maybe she never really thought she'd need the place and reality is a lot scarier than she expected it would be. It could be dozens of things. The end of the world brings about a whole range of emotions. It's not like I can really blame her for being upset about the turn of events.

She shakes her head and turns toward the stairs. There's an elevator, but no way we'd all fit inside. I follow her without a word. Not that I could get one in. She doesn't stop talking for even a second.

"The next level is split in two. Half is a clinic and the other half is set up as a classroom. You'll be able to find books there too if you need something to read. Levels three through eleven are living quarters, you'll find the pool and gym on twelve. Thirteen is where the gardens are. There's some crazy aquaculture thing set up so they can grow fresh vegetables and fruit down here. I'm not even going to pretend to understand it." She reaches the next level and stops, then turns to face us. "The bottom level is storage. Extra diesel and any supplies you may need. There are also weapons down there, although James has the key to that. I know you have your own, but they're there just in case."

The hallway we're standing in is small and there's a door right in front of us. It's crowded with all seventeen of us standing around, and when I glance over my shoulder, I notice some people are still on the stairs.

"Okay. So, I'm on this level and I'm all alone in a three bedroom condo. It's ridiculous and lonely, and I think a roommate would be great. Any volunteers?"

I look around and my eye catches Axl's. It hadn't occurred to me that we wouldn't be together until now. We've been sleeping side by side for what seems like years. Would it be presumptuous to think he wanted things that way? We've only kissed once, back in San Francisco when Emily was with us. He wasn't too thrilled about it the next day, though. He even said some harsh things about women attaching themselves to him just to get through a rough patch. I don't want to be that woman. I'm stronger than that. At least, I always thought I was.

I tear my eyes away from Axl and step forward. "I'm alone. A roommate sounds nice."

Hadley smiles, and my stomach does a flip flop. Yikes. I'm going to be living with a movie star. No. She's not a movie star anymore. She's just like me now. Only she may not know it. What if she's a bitch? Guess I can always move out.

With Axl...

"Great! You can go on inside and make yourself at home if you want. I'll be back as soon as everyone is settled in." The smile lights up her green eyes and her shoulders ease a little like she's relieved.

Maybe living with her will be okay. How bad could it be? She seems friendly enough, and she sure stuck out her neck for us with Mitchell.

My insides settle just a tad. "That sounds great." The words come out in a whoosh, along with a relieved exhale.

She gives me one last smile before heading further underground. Almost as an afterthought, she calls over her shoulder, "The door's unlocked. My stuff is in the first bedroom. Take any of the other two."

People smile as they walk by and pat me on the back and

the arm. Everyone is so much more relaxed than we've been since…Well, since we met. All the tension is gone, replaced by exhaustion. We're all going to sleep soundly tonight.

Axl hangs back, and I shift from foot to foot while the others disappear down the stairs. My heart is in my throat as I wait for him to talk. Is he going to ask why I'm not coming with him? Doesn't seem like something he would do, but it's possible. Do I want him to? Yes. Yes, I do. I want him to admit he has feelings for me so I can finally get mine out in the open.

"You doin' alright?" he says once we're alone.

He's referring to Emily. My stomach tightens and the hole where my heart used to be aches. I have to look away for a second. Talking about this sucks. Why can't we just forget the past?

My daughter. She was such a brief part of my life, in and out almost before I could adjust to her being here. Why does it hurt so badly, then? Oh yeah, because I failed to protect her when she needed me the most. She was the first casualty in our group, the first one to get bitten by one of the dead and turn. Axl held me back while his brother, Angus, shot her in the head. He had to do it. I know he did. If he hadn't shot her, she would've attacked us. Knowing that didn't make it any easier to watch, though.

"No," I whisper, trying to blink away the tears that sting at the back of my eyes. "Maybe I'll never be, but I'm going to try."

He purses his lips like he always does when he's thinking things through. The fluorescent lights are bright, and the scar on his face is more visible than usual. It goes from the bottom of his chin almost all the way to his bottom lip. A mark left behind by his abusive mother. One of the many things we have in common. Trailer parks and abuse, abandonment and rough lives. We're so alike, he and I.

"Get some sleep," he finally says, drawing the words out. There are miles and miles of space between those words.

I nod and swallow against the lump in my throat. It isn't easy, and it reminds me of when I was sick not that long ago. My throat was so swollen from strep. Axl was so gentle when he took care of me. My body aches for him. Not for sex — although I have to admit that doesn't sound bad — but for his company, his closeness. Too bad those are the very things he was angry about the first time we kissed. So even though I don't want to walk into the condo without him, I don't ask him to come with me.

He turns away. "See you in the mornin'."

I can't force any words out, so I go into the condo. Alone.

CHAPTER TWO

The condo is the most luxurious place I've ever set foot in. Odd how it took the end of civilization to get me out of the low-class life I've always lived. Away from trailer parks and run-down apartments. It doesn't seem right. Or fair. Of course, I was never under any delusion that life was fair.

My curiosity wins out over my exhaustion, and I walk through the condo to check it out. The entire building is circular, so the outside walls are rounded. It almost feels like a dream. Like the tunnel vision that sometimes accompanied my dreams of Emily.

Just like the common area, the furnishings are fashionable and modern, but the decor in here isn't as bright. The condo's decorated in warm, neutral colors. Hardwood floors run throughout the living room and kitchen, which is equipped with stainless steel appliances and granite countertops. Something I've only seen on TV.

I find the first bedroom and peek inside. Hadley's stuff is strewn about the room — she's clearly not a neat person — but it still looks rich and expensive. The second bedroom is just as nice, but much smaller. I don't care, though. I'm exhausted, and all I want to do at this point is shower and crawl into bed.

I strip down, right in the middle of the bedroom, and stand there naked for a moment while I try to decide what to do. All my clothes are dirty. Hadley's comment about clothes in the condo comes back to me, and I open the dresser. It's full and everything still has the tags on. Bras, underwear, and silky pajamas that no one could possibly need when the dead are banging on your front door. All there just waiting for me. Will Hadley mind? My fingers brush against the elegant lace thongs, and I shrug. Who cares? I'm filthy and all I want is to put on a clean pair of underwear and get in bed.

So I grab a pair, along with a pink nightie that is a lot less over-the-top than the other stuff in the drawer, and head to the bathroom to get clean.

WHEN I OPEN THE BATHROOM DOOR AFTER MY shower, I almost bump into Hadley.

"Hey," she says with a friendly smile. "I realize I didn't even get your name earlier."

"Vivian," I say, playing with the lace hem of the nightie I'm wearing. Is she upset I took it? She doesn't seem to be. The smile on her face is warm and open, and she's barely even glanced at the clothes. "I'm sorry. I borrowed some things from the dresser. I hope it's okay. All my stuff was dirty."

She shrugs and slouches against the wall. It isn't casual or relaxed, though. It's more like she's exhausted and finds it difficult to stand up straight. "It's no big deal. None of this is mine."

My eyebrows shoot up and I wait for her to continue.

There has to be a story behind that statement. There's no way she happened across this place accidentally.

For a few seconds she's silent. She leans against the wall and stares at the floor. Her lips are pulled into a hard line, and her eyes blink rapidly. "Jennifer Swanson was my best friend."

The name has a familiar ring to it, but I can't quite figure out why. Swanson...right! The blonde, curvy actress who was constantly on the cover of tabloids. She was a paparazzi favorite.

"She bought this place and this is all her stuff." Hadley laughs a little, but it isn't a happy sound. It's sad and strained. "She was convinced the world was going to be destroyed by global warming. Damn zombies... Anyway, when she got sick I stayed and took care of her. My family was already gone by then. Ohio got hit pretty early on, so I didn't have anywhere else to go. When she got close to the end and realized I was going to make it and she wasn't, she told me the code and who to call for a ride. I was the last one here. The helicopter pilot was already sick when he picked me up. I was terrified he'd die before we made it." She lets out huge sigh, and I imagine it traveling through the halls of the condo, filling the rooms with her pain.

"I'm sorry."

I am sorry. Not just for her, but for everyone. For myself and women like me who lost children. For Sophia and the baby growing inside her who will never know a world without fear. For Jessica's lost fiancé, and Parvarti's and Trey's dead families. For all the bodies mindlessly walking the earth at this moment, searching for food or peace or who knows what.

But I'm also exhausted. My legs are like half-cooked noodles, and there's a deep ache in my bones that makes it difficult to breathe or stand or focus. "I need to get some sleep." It's all I can say, because everything is suddenly just way too heavy and painful to bear.

"I know. I just wanted to say hi and make sure you had everything you needed. Help yourself to anything."

She's so insistent when she says it. So sincere. Who knows if her fame and money had made her selfish before all this bullshit, but it's certainly gone now. She isn't like Mitchell. She knows the end is here and everything has changed. And I like her for it.

"Thank you."

She smiles one last time before heading back to her room.

I drag myself into my new bedroom and crawl into the king size bed, pulling the blankets up to my chin like I'm snuggling into a cocoon. The sheets are soft and warm and probably the best thing I've ever experienced. Even better than the shower, because in this bed I can drift off and pretend everything is okay and nothing hurts. I can imagine Emily didn't come into my life just to shatter my world, and that all there is in my future is sleep and relaxation.

WHEN I WAKE UP, THE FIRST THING MY EYES FOCUS on are the green numbers announcing it's 10:23. A clock. How strange to know what time it is again. It doesn't feel even a little reassuring or normal, though. Too much has changed for that.

How long did I sleep? It had to have been late by the time we got into the shelter. By the time we got away from those monsters on the surface. It felt like we were up there for days. If I had to guess, I'd say it was close to midnight when I crawled into this bed. Although, it could have been much earlier. That means I got at least ten hours of sleep.

If only my body wasn't still tingling with exhaustion. Sleep didn't bring me peace or comfort the way I'd hoped it would. All it brought me were images of the dead and Emily.

I shiver and stumble out of bed, suddenly desperate for company. Hopefully, Hadley's here so I don't have to go looking for it. If only Axl were with me. But I don't even know what floor he ended up on. That's something I need to find out.

I exhale when I step into the kitchen. Hadley sits at a small round table with a cup of coffee in front of her. She's already dressed for the day, and she smiles when I walk in. "Morning."

I nod and mumble a few sounds that are supposed to be a greeting. They're nothing but gibberish, so I close my eyes and take a deep breath before trying again. "Coffee."

She laughs and gets to her feet, banging around in the kitchen as she makes me a cup of coffee. She's loud and cheerful, and every sound she makes pounds against my temples from the inside out. It's like I'm hung over or something. Probably from all the stress.

"Thanks," I say when she sets the cup in front of me. I pick it up and wrap my hands around the ceramic. It's hot and stings a little, but I don't loosen my grip. I need to wake up.

"I take it you didn't sleep well."

I shake my head and take a big sip of coffee. It's bitter, but rich. So much better than the Folgers I always had to buy. "This new reality has done a number on my dreams. Try getting a good night's sleep after fighting off a horde of the undead."

She laughs, but it's tight. "I can't imagine. God, when Mitchell showed up down here screaming about zombies, I thought he was insane. I was sure he was playing some trick on me. You know, because of that movie I was in."

I vaguely remember a movie about zombies she was in years ago before she really made it big. I think it was called *Zombieworld*. She looked different then, not as thin. What is it about female celebrities that makes them think they need to waste away to nothing once they become famous? She did it, and I remember a few others. They usually looked better before the weight loss. Hadley did.

"Anyway, Joshua and Sophia convinced me he was

telling the truth and then the sirens went off. We all ran up to the control room, and there they were. Zombies, right outside the fence. That bastard Mitchell just wouldn't give in! What kind of a person leaves others to die when they have the ability to save them?"

"You'd be surprised," I mutter. "I grew up with a mom who abandoned me and a father who beat the shit out of me whenever things didn't go his way. The shitty things people do doesn't really surprise me a whole lot."

Hadley's mouth pops open in surprise. She's going to ask questions. It's obvious by how tense her shoulders are and the way she tilts her head to the side. Not a road I want to go down right now.

"So you had no idea about the dead coming back until we got here?" I ask.

Hadley shakes her head, and her body relaxes. Odd how talking about the dead coming back to walk the Earth is less stressful than talking about my crappy childhood.

"No. I was the last one here, and that was a week ago. We kept waiting for someone else to show up. All these condos, and only three of the owners were able to get here. It seemed nuts."

"Who else is here? We met James last night, but what about the other two people?"

"Lila Quinton was the first one here. She's seventeen and a spoiled rich kid who called the helicopter the second the virus got bad. She was here two weeks before me."

"Where are her parents?"

"They were in Europe and couldn't get a flight home since all travel was suspended. The last time she talked to them, the virus had just broken out there. That was right before I got here, before the Internet went down."

"So she has no idea if her parents are alive or dead." My stomach clenches yet again. Must be awful to be a teenager at the end of the world and have no idea where your parents are.

"Nope. But she doesn't seem all that torn up about it. She says she rarely saw them anyway." Hadley lets out a bitter laugh. "She actually seems to be having a good time. She's really been enjoying the bar and the pool."

Great, more snobby rich people.

I take a sip of coffee before asking, "Who else?"

"Victor Gates. He's a doctor from Beverly Hills, only not the useful kind like Joshua. A plastic surgeon to the stars. He's the person everyone went to when they needed a little Botox or a face lift. He's a nice enough guy. But his wife died, and I think he's a little depressed."

"Who isn't?"

She lets out another big sigh. "I'm glad you all showed up, to be honest. I would have let you in regardless, but the thought of being stuck down here with these people for the next five years was starting to make me depressed."

I laugh and shake my head in amazement. Just give her a few days with Angus and we'll see what she has to say then. "Maybe you should get to know us before you say that. We've got some interesting people."

Hadley leans forward like she's telling me a secret. "Like the redneck brothers? The older one offered to keep me company if I got lonely. I'm not going to lie, it wasn't even a little tempting." I start to laugh, but it's cut short when she says, "The younger one though..."

My insides twist, but I try not to react to her words. I force out another laugh. Hopefully, it isn't obvious how hot my face is, or how much I suddenly want to hurl. The laugh comes out strained and too loud, though. Hadley must have noticed, but she doesn't even blink.

There aren't a lot of women who could make me feel insecure, but Hadley does. How could she not? She was famous and widely lusted after by most of the men in America. I never understood what the big deal was, but I don't have a dick. Axl does.

The urge to get away from her is suddenly so strong that

I jump to my feet, almost knocking my coffee cup over in the process. "I think I'll head back and get myself dressed. Um, I'm probably going to have to borrow some clothes. Mine are all dirty."

She waves her hand in the air dismissively. "Whatever you need. And if you want to throw your clothes in the washer, we can do that too. Seriously, make yourself at home."

I do my best to return her smile. I like Hadley, I really do, but the fact that she's already thinking about jumping Axl's bones makes me want to bitch slap her.

After I'm dressed, I throw myself on the couch in the living room. Hadley's reading a book and I briefly consider going upstairs to get one, but to be honest, I'm just too tired. There are way too many stairs between me and the common area.

Hadley looks up from her book and gives me a hopeful smile. "You want to go to the pool or something?"

I lay my head back and close my eyes. "I'm exhausted. Maybe later."

She doesn't answer and I'm just too tired to open my eyes, so I let it go. Instead, I try to relax. My mind is buzzing but my limbs are heavy, and it doesn't take long for me to get that weightless feeling that proceeds sleep. I exhale slowly and give into it.

I've just started to drift off when there's a small knock on the door that makes me jump. My eyes fly open and I bolt upright, letting out a little yelp that sounds like a frightened animal more than a person. Hadley arches an eyebrow, and my cheeks grow warm. I'm jumpy as hell. Side effect of the dead walking the Earth, I guess.

"You okay?" she asks as she gets to her feet and crosses the room, studying me calmly.

I nervously play with my hair, twisting a chunk of it around my finger like you see little kids do when they're sleepy. I used to do it all the time when I was little. Would do it all night long and wake up with giant knots in my hair. My mom would cuss her head off while she tried to brush them out. I haven't done it in years, though. I'd actually forgotten all about it. Why the hell did it come to mind now?

I try to push the thought of my mother out of my mind as I follow Hadley to the door. That bitch is the last thing I want to focus on. Mostly because there's a small part of me that wonders if she's still alive. If she's immune, or if she lived long enough to get eaten. Which way do I want it to be? Sometimes when I picture her dying a horrible death—either from the virus or from one of the dead eating her—a sliver of satisfaction shoots through me. Like she finally got what she deserved. But other times, it just makes me all the pain and sadness swimming through me more intense. I'm tired of feeling sad.

Hadley opens the door, and Parvarti stares back at us. She tugs on her black hair, and her dark eyes get huge when they rest on Hadley. They dart around to meet mine and she relaxes a little, but not much.

"What's up, Parv?" I say, calling her by the nickname Trey's been using. Hopefully, it will help her relax. She's so tightly wound I'm afraid she's going to burst into tears at any moment. I don't have a clue why, though.

She tugs harder on her black strands and shrinks about three inches while she stares at the ground. God, she reminds me of a kid, standing there in what has to be Trey's Cornell sweatshirt and a pair of yoga pants that are way too long for her.

"I was wondering…" She doesn't look up, and her cheeks turn so red that it's visible even on her dark skin. "I just wanted to know if you had—"

Hadley looks at me and raises an eyebrow. She does that a lot. I shrug and look back at Parvarti, waiting for her to continue. But she just keeps pulling on her hair and beating around the bush. I have the sudden urge to yell at her, to tell her to just spit it out. She obviously needs something she's embarrassed to ask for. It's probably tampons or something.

"Parvarti," I say firmly.

She looks up.

"What is it?"

Her cheeks get even redder. "Condoms. I need condoms."

Oh. *That's* why she's acting so uncomfortable.

She looks back at the floor, and I fight the urge to laugh. I don't want to scare her off or freak her out. I take a deep breath and work on keeping my voice level. "You don't have to be embarrassed to ask for condoms, Parv. It's not a big deal."

She looks up and finally smiles. It's still strained. "I just hate announcing to the world that I'm going to have sex. It's not really how I imagined my first time..."

My mouth drops open, and her cheeks gets even redder. I'm not sure if it's because of my shocked expression or the little sound of surprise that popped out of Hadley's mouth.

I force my mouth shut and take a deep breath. "First time? You mean for you and Trey or..."

She shrugs and kicks at an invisible ball on the floor, making her look even more like a child. "Both. Trey and I...We didn't really get much of a chance before now. Sleeping in the motel with Angus, being on the road with you guys, just finding out our families had died. It never really seemed like the right time, you know?"

I do know. Axl and I actually had the chance—more than once. But the timing sucked. I'm not really surprised she never did it before, either. She always struck me as the type of girl you'd find at the library on a Friday night more than the type you'd catch doing keg stands at a frat party.

"Don't sweat it. You don't need to be embarrassed. We're not going to tell anyone." I look over my shoulder at Hadley, who nods in agreement. "You got any condoms?"

She shakes her head but turns toward the bathroom. "I doubt it, but I'll check."

She walks away, and I cringe inwardly. There's one place I can find condoms for sure, but I don't want to go down that road if I can avoid it. Hopefully, Hadley finds some. I want to help Parvarti out. Lord knows the girl deserves to get laid after surviving the end of the world. But asking Angus for condoms would really suck.

Hadley's back in less than a minute, empty-handed and frowning. I turn back to Parvarti, who looks like someone just killed her dog. Shit.

I sigh and look up, like I'm asking God why. It occurs to me that God—if he does exist—may not be able to hear us at this particular moment. Several floors underground with a horde of zombies above us...seems unlikely.

"I know where I can get some," I say. "I'll get them and bring them to your condo."

When I look back, Parvarti is actually smiling. The first genuine smile I've seen on her face since we met. It almost makes the task of going to see Angus endurable. Almost.

"What floor are the 'redneck brothers' on?" I ask Hadley.

"Eleven."

I return Parvarti's smile as I head to the elevator. She's right on my heels. "I'll bring it to you. What floor are you guys on?"

There's no way in hell I want her going with me to ask for condoms. Exposing her to Angus right now could scar her for life. Then she may never end up losing her virginity.

"We're on five."

I tense up the second we step into the elevator. What's causing me more anxiety, asking Angus for condoms or seeing Axl? After Hadley's comment—and my insane reaction—I really wanted some time to figure out what to say before I see him again. Guess that isn't going to happen.

Parvarti hops out at five, practically skipping, and I ride the elevator down to eleven. It seems to take forever. Being claustrophobic down here would suck. Normally, I'm not even a little concerned about tight spaces, but even I get a little antsy when I think about being so far underground.

When the elevator stops, I step out. There are two doors on this level, one to my right and one to my left. I have no idea which one the brothers are in or who might be in the other, so I decide to play eenie, meenie, miney, mo. My finger stops on the door to my right. I knock and cross my fingers.

Angus answers, and I let out a sigh of relief even though my body tenses at the smile on his face. "I don't remember askin' for a booty call, Blondie, but if you insist." He wiggles his eyebrows, and his smile widens. Of course, he's staring at my chest. Damn fake boobs. They were an asset in the club, but now that the world is over they may end up being a liability.

"In your dreams, Angus." He opens his mouth to say something that I'm sure would make me gag, but I don't give him a chance. "I came to get some condoms. I know you have them."

Angus purses his lips and leans against the doorframe. "You hookin' up with somebody?"

Irritation prickles up my spine and I press my lips together, fully intent on not answering him. I don't want to give him the satisfaction. But my eyes go past him to where Axl is standing, his shoulder resting casually against the doorframe. His gray eyes are expressionless as he watches me. Waiting for me to answer.

The words come out before I even have a chance to think about it. "They're not for me."

"Who they for?"

Angus doesn't make a move to get them, even though we both know he has some. We took them when we were at Walmart stocking up on supplies. Before we even knew about all this undead nonsense.

"None of your business. Someone was looking for them and I said I knew where I could get them."

Angus frowns, and his eyes narrow. "Can't help ya. Lost

'em," he replies just as Axl pushes himself off the wall and says, "I'll get 'em."

Angus spins around and glares at his brother, but Axl just shrugs and turns away. He heads through the doorway he was just leaning against. I smile at Angus when he turns back to me. He glares at me like he's ready to wrestle me for the condoms. He'd just love that.

Axl comes back with the box and holds it out.

Before I can take it, Angus rips it out of his hand. "Don't give 'em all to her!"

He tears the box open and pulls out the string of packets, ripping a few off and tossing them my way. They hit my fingertips and bounce off, almost falling to the floor. I manage to save them, though. Once they're safely in my hand I look down. Three. He gave me three condoms.

I look up at Angus with a teasing smile on my face. I can't resist. "Seriously? Three condoms out of twenty-four? You must really think the end of the world is going to get you lucky."

He isn't one to be deterred, though. He smiles right back and stuffs the remaining condoms in the box, puffing his chest out as he raises his head. "Never know. Women might start gettin' desperate real soon here. Want to be prepared." He wiggles his eyebrows again.

I laugh despite myself. "I'm not going to, if that's what you're thinking."

"You ain't the only one here."

I shake my head and turn away, yelling over my shoulder as I head toward the elevator. "Thanks."

The elevator opens as soon as I push the button. I walk in and push the button for five before leaning back against the wall. Just as the door starts to slide shut, Axl ducks in. Casually. His expression is blank, and he's just as laid back as always as he pushes the button for the pool.

"Going swimming?"

He nods while his eyes sweep over the numbers. They

focus on the small number five, lit up on the control panel. He clears his throat, trying to act more casual than usual. "Trey and Parvarti?"

"Did you think I was lying?"

He looks down, and something flashes in his stormy eyes. That's it. I hit the nail right on the head! He got in the elevator so he could see where I was going, because he didn't believe me.

An odd sense of pleasure surges through me, and I have to resist the urge to smile. It takes a lot of effort to maintain a straight face. The muscles in my mouth twitch. "You going to swim in your clothes?"

He looks down, and his cheeks turn a little red. I caught him. I almost laugh.

He clears his throat and meets my gaze, just as cool as always. "Don't like to swim, just thought I'd check it out."

The elevator dings and the door slides open on the fifth floor. I step out. "Sounds good. Maybe I'll head down there after I drop these off." I hold up the condoms and give him a flirty smile. "If you decide to make use of the ones Angus kept..." I time it so the door shuts before I can finish the sentence.

I didn't get to see the expression on Axl's face, but I laugh anyway.

I pause outside the condo door and stare at the three condoms in my hand. Two should be good, right? We can find more. I rip one off and stuff it in my pocket before knocking

CHAPTER THREE

gape at the little strings spread out on the bed in front of me. Hadley has to be kidding. "These are the only swimsuits she had here?"

I may have been a stripper, but when I went to the pool I always wore a sensible bikini that wasn't going to leave my ass — or tits, for that matter — hanging out. The things laying on the bed in front of me will probably do both.

Hadley shrugs and sorts through the bikinis, holding them up individually so she can get a better look. "Guess she wanted to make sure the men had a good show when the world ended."

I snort and a smart-ass comment goes through my head, but I think better of it since she was Hadley's best friend. And she's dead now. I should be respectful.

Hadley holds up a red bikini that must have come from a trashy lingerie shop. "At least they'll look good on you. You have curves. Can you imagine my skinny ass in this thing? It will probably fall off!"

Hadley shakes her head and starts undressing. When she's naked, she grabs the least revealing swimsuit. If she's going to tough it out, I guess I can do the same. I strip down to nothing without even batting an eye and pull a hot pink *string* bikini on. Once it's in place, I study myself in the mirror, turning so I can get a good look at every curve. I could have danced in this thing and gotten plenty of tips without even having to take it off. The bottom barely covers my ass and the top is just two tiny triangles that were never intended for my double D's. I hope Al's not at the pool. The poor kid will probably have to run for cover. On the flip side, I'm kind of hoping that Axl *is* there.

"Damn," Hadley says with a shake of her head. Her eyes go up and down my body, and my cheeks actually heat up under her scrutiny. "A few years down here and you won't be able to leave the condo in that. You'll get attacked."

I laugh and despite the joke, a little thrill goes through me. Thinking about Axl being down there, about being attacked…doesn't sound half bad.

I do my best not to stare at Hadley when we head out of the condo. She's so thin. They say the camera adds ten pounds, but this is the first time I've really believed it. I've seen her in movies and always thought she was skin and bones, but in person, in a swimsuit, she's thinner than skin and bones. If there is such a thing. Why do actresses think — thought — that being this thin is what men want? It sure as hell isn't sexy.

The elevator door opens on level twelve, and I'm hit in the face with steam and laughter. Almost everyone is at the pool, and the sound of people enjoying themselves is relaxing. Wonderful, really. For just a second, I pretend I'm on vacation at some fancy resort. The pool is in front of us and the wall behind it is painted in a huge mural. A beach and palm trees, blue skies and puffy, white clouds that make it almost seem like you're outside. Plus, the ceiling down here is higher and painted blue. It's peaceful, and I let out a sigh as I walk forward with Hadley. I need some time to relax, to forget about everything on the surface.

People turn our away when we walk in and I have the sudden urge to cover up. Their eyes bore into me, and it makes me want to run back to the elevator. I'm not used to being self-conscious like this. Why am I embarrassed? Being naked in front of other people was what I did for a living.

I scan the crowd, and my eyes land on Ava and Jake splashing around in the shallow end of the pool, and Arthur sitting in a lounge chair chatting with Anne. It hits me. This is like being naked in front of your family, which is not a comfortable feeling at all.

I almost go back to the elevator when Sophia notices me. She lets out a little whistle, and my cheeks get even hotter. "Holy cow, girl! That's some bathing suit!"

A laugh bubbles up inside me. Her expression isn't judgmental or catty. She's honestly teasing me, and it helps my insides settle a little. Anne and Arthur turn my way, and they join in the laughter. Their attitudes are just as casual as Sophia's.

"All the swimsuits in our condo were like this." Hadley lifts her arms and spins in a circle like she's modeling the damn thing. She looks more like a skeleton than a model, though. "At least Vivian fills it out. I look like I'm twelve years old."

After that, it doesn't take long to really, truly relax. The threat is still here, but it's miles above us and I'm able to push it to the back of my mind. For once in my life, I want to take it easy and enjoy myself. I've never been worry-free before. But at this moment, I am. The emotional turmoil is still present. My heart still aches and I still feel like a part of me has been ripped away, but I can deal with it later. For now, I want to pretend the last few days never happened.

I laugh with the others and listen to Hadley's friendly chatter. She's cheery. Happy. Like someone who will throw out a joke to ease the tension in the room. It will be a welcome addition to our group.

My cheeks ache from smiling. It makes me laugh even harder and I shake my head. I actually like her. It's not something I was expecting.

Everyone else seems to like her too. Sophia and Anne ask her about her life like she's a regular person, and she describes in detail growing up in a middle class family in Ohio. Then she starts telling us about moving to Hollywood and auditioning for movies. About eating crackers and bologna for dinner while she was waiting for her big break. She makes it all sound light and casual. I constantly have to remind myself that she was rich and famous just a few short weeks ago. It isn't uncomfortable being around her at all.

A high-pitched squeal of delight breaks through the air. I look toward the pool to find Ava being thrown around by Jessica and Winston. The little girl giggles and squeals with delight. Jake is next to them. He jumps up and down excitedly with a huge smile on his face. The sight of the kids tears at my heart just a little more. If things had turned out differently, Emily would be here now. She would be splashing around the pool with the other two kids. It hurts too much to think about and I have to look away.

I do my best to tune out the children's laughter as I study the room. There's a teenage girl, who I can only assume is Lila, on the other side of the pool. Lying on a lounge chair like she's getting a tan. She's beautiful, even from a distance. Her long, dark hair is silky and shimmers under the lights. She has olive skin and the perfect body of a girl who grew up with money. And probably a personal trainer.

Al sits in a chair next to her, desperately vying for her attention. I guess he found something to distract him from the lack of computers. Lila plays at being annoyed. She gives him smoldering looks from time to time, but I know teenage girls. She's loving the attention. If she didn't, she wouldn't arch her back the way she is or adjust her bikini top quite so often. And Al is playing right into her hands, hanging onto every look she gives him.

I laugh quietly to myself and turn back to the others. That girl is trouble, and Al is already caught in her web.

"What's so funny?" Sophia asks.

I tilt my head toward Al and Lila. "He's a goner."

"She's something else," Arthur says. He looks even unhealthier in this light. Like he's inches from death's door. "He's been drooling over her since she came down."

"Someone needs to teach him how to play it cool." Hadley glances at me and arches a brow. Her eyes sweep over my too-small bikini. "You should go over and talk to him."

I throw my head back and laugh. I can just imagine Al running off toward the elevator, holding a towel over his crotch. He turned about six shades redder just from hearing that my boobs were fake. It seems like such a mean thing to do, though.

"Poor Al," Anne says. "If you walked over in that tiny little thing he'd probably have a heart attack."

"It would distract him from the she-demon at least," Arthur says.

Even he's grinning at the idea, so it must not be too mean. In fact, getting him away from Lila and talking a little sense into him might actually be nice. He's going to make a fool of himself if he keeps acting like that.

I watch Al for almost a full minute, and he doesn't take his eyes off Lila once. At this point, she could probably snap her fingers and he'd do anything she wanted. And she knows it, too. Yes, it would be a very nice thing to distract him from that girl.

"I'm going for it." Sophia starts to protest, but I shake my head. "Just to get him away from her for a few minutes. Someone needs to have a serious talk with him about playing it cool. If he keeps throwing himself at her like that, she's never going to respect him." I like Al too much to let him make a fool of himself.

I adjust my teeny bikini as I head to the other side of the pool where Al sits fawning over Lila. When I get closer, I have to resist the urge to roll my eyes. Al is talking about computer stuff, rambling on and on without even pausing to take a breath. He must be a nervous talker, because nervous he is. He keeps biting his lower lip and reaching up to rub the back of his neck awkwardly. He's clearly smart and comes from a nice family, but he must have no experience with girls whatsoever.

"Al," I call out cheerfully when I'm about three feet away from them.

Both teens' heads snap up. Lila narrows her hazel eyes on me until they're nothing more than slits. Her expression is slightly evil-looking, but she's even more beautiful up close. Like an exotic porcelain doll. No wonder Al's attached to her side.

Al's chatter stops and his mouth drops open. His cheeks get red and his eyes move to my barely-covered breasts, then up. Poor Al. I can tell he's desperately trying to focus on my face, but his eyes keep darting down and they're so big they look like they're about to pop out of their sockets.

I stop in front of them and give Al a big smile, completely ignoring Lila. "We were talking about computers over there and needed your opinion. You know, since you're so smart and the resident expert on that kind of stuff."

Al stutters for a few seconds, then all sound stops while his mouth keeps moving. He pauses and takes a deep breath. When he does finally manage to make sounds they're not intelligible at all. Just noises that are way too high-pitched to be coming from a seventeen-year-old guy.

"We're kind of in the middle of something," Lila snaps. She flips her hair over her shoulder and glances toward Al like he'll agree with her. He doesn't even glance her way.

I still don't look at her. I just smile at Al and hold my hand out to him. "Come on, you can come right back after you help us."

Al reaches out and takes my hand, and I pull him to his feet. From the way he's staring at his hand in mine, I'd guess he has no idea how it happened. He mumbles something to Lila that sounds a little bit like, *I'll be right back*, and I pull him toward the others.

"Kid, you need to play it cool with that girl," I hiss as soon as I'm sure we're far enough away that she can't hear me.

He looks at me with eyes as big as saucers, but still can't manage to get a sound out. Someone else is going to have to talk some sense into him, because he's become a mute around me and this ridiculous swimsuit.

I shake my head when we reach everyone else and push him forward. His hand falls out of mine, and I force him into a lounge chair next to Sophia. "Tell this kid that drooling all over snooty pants isn't going to do him any favors. He's speechless around me."

Hadley throws herself into lecturing Al on how to get a girl's attention just as the elevator dings behind me. I turn in time to see Axl and Angus step out. I'd be lying if I said my heart didn't jump a little. Angus isn't in a swimsuit, but Axl seems to be. A red and blue floral thing that doesn't fit his laid-back personality at all. It's so comical and out-of-place on him that I actually giggle. Angus frowns. Clearly, he isn't thrilled to be here. As usual, Axl's face is expressionless. They stand by the elevator doors for a few seconds, scanning the area, and their eyes land on me at the same moment.

Their reactions are totally different, though. Angus grins, and as usual, I can read him like a book, and the story within those pages is a pretty nasty one. Just thinking about it sends a shudder through me. Axl, on the other hand, barely reacts. Something that could be called a smile tugs at the corner of his mouth, but it's so brief I have a hard time convincing myself it's real. I want it to be. So desperately it actually, physically hurts. But I'm not sure if it is.

I walk toward them just as they head my way. My heart

kicks up a few notches, pounding against my ribcage like a drum. Angus's eyes move over me like he's trying to memorize every curve. Probably storing it away for later. His gaze never quite makes it to my face, but I do my best to pretend I don't notice.

When I stop in front of them, a slow smile spreads across Angus's face. His eyes are glued to my tits. "If that ain't a fuck-me swimsuit, I don't know what is."

I fight the urge to cross my arms over my chest. If I could somehow block Angus from being able to see me while ensuring Axl still could, I'd do it. "I didn't pick it, Angus," I say flatly. "I had no control over what was in the dresser."

"And I ain't got no control over the pictures in my head neither," he growls. His voice is thick with so much lust and nastiness it makes my stomach turn.

"Shut up, Angus," Axl says. He watches me. Calmly, quietly. No matter how hard he tries to cover it up, the storm in his eyes is unmistakable.

Angus mutters something under his breath and stomps off. I'm not sure where he's going and I don't care even a little bit, because right now I'm in a safe shelter and Axl is in front of me. I'm half-naked — more than half, really — and it's obvious by the desire in his eyes that he only has one thing on his mind. Lucky for me, I'm thinking the same thing.

The corner of his mouth pulls up a little more, and he tilts his head to the side. "So, you was interested in usin' them condoms?"

My body ignites from that grin, and his words make the fire rage even stronger. I return his smile and try desperately to hide my eagerness. To play it cool. He can tell, though. I know he can because he takes a step closer to me.

"I was thinking of some place a little more private." I lean forward and my chest grazes his, sending a shiver down my spine. But I don't want to rush things. I want to draw out the anticipation and have him begging for it before I give in. We've waited too long and been through too much to rush through this. We need to savor it.

His shoulders stiffen at the contact. And probably other things too. "We got lots of privacy now."

I bite my lip in what I imagine to be a very sexy way and move just a tad closer. The heat between us is intense, and all I can think about is closing the gap so I can drape my entire body over his. Giving him every last inch of me.

"We do," I whisper. "Your place or mine?"

I expect him to jump at the invitation. What man wouldn't? Even if the world hadn't gone to shit and I wasn't mostly naked. But he stays as calm as ever. "You know everybody can see them nipple rings through that fabric?"

I almost laugh, but I bite it back. Maybe he has the same idea about drawing it out as I do. Maybe he wants me to grab him and pull him toward the elevator. To take control.

But I don't want to do that.

"I was going to hit the sauna." I give him a little smile, then walk toward the back of the room without a backward glance.

The sauna is empty when I open the door, just like I was hoping. When I step in, the air is thick. It makes it difficult to breathe. I lower myself onto the hard bench right across from the door and wait for him. He'd be a fool not to come, and Axl is no fool.

Less than a minute later, he's standing in the doorway. The steam rises up around him, and a thrill shoots through my body when he shuts the door and walks toward me.

"Never understood saunas," he says as he takes a seat next to me.

I ignore his comment because I can't think of a damn thing to say. Axl sits *so* close to me. The heat between us has nothing to do with the steamy room. All I want is to touch him. To think of a legitimate reason to have my hands on his body. He's still wearing his shirt, which gives me the excuse I'm looking for.

I get to my feet and stand in front of him. "Getting rid of

this will help," I say, grabbing the hem of his shirt.

I pull it over his head and his eyes follow my every move. When I toss it aside, he's just as calm and relaxed as always. Sitting there in the steamy room, staring up at me with what can only be described as a steamy expression on his face. I take the initiative and step forward, standing above him with one leg on either side of him. Straddling him.

The corner of his mouth pulls up ever so slightly. Desire and lust surge through me, and I can't hold back any longer. I grab his face between my hands and press my lips to his. Gently at first, waiting to see how he's going to respond. Then his hands move up my thighs, sliding over my ass to my hips, and I lose control. The kiss deepens, and he pulls me onto his lap. He forces his tongue into my mouth in a powerful, sexy way. A surge of desire shoots through me, swirling around in my stomach for a few seconds before moving lower. I pull him closer and press my body against his. His hardness rubs against me, and desire ignites in my veins. I moan against his lips. He makes a sound that's somewhere between a groan and a growl, and kisses his way down my neck. To my chest. His hands are still on my ass, and he pulls me closer. He grips the small triangle of fabric with his teeth and yanks it aside, taking my nipple in his mouth. I cry out when his tongue flicks against my nipple ring. I rake my fingers down his back just as the door to the sauna opens.

CHAPTER FOUR

"Fuck," Angus growls. "We got a room, you know."

Axl pulls away from my breast and replaces the swimsuit so fast that if it wasn't for the wetness between my legs and the pounding of my heart, I might think I imagined the whole thing. He climbs to his feet, taking me with him, and absentmindedly rearranges himself as he faces his brother.

"You need somthin'?" His tone is rough. I've never heard him speak to Angus like that before, but I guess I can't fault him for that.

"We got a problem," Angus says, jerking his head toward the door.

Axl sighs but walks to the door anyway. He grabs my hand almost as an afterthought. I'm hot and so horny that there's a part of me that doesn't give a shit if everything on the surface has suddenly been blown to a million pieces. All I want is for Axl to throw me down and ravage me. But the rational part of my brain knows I need to find out what's going on. So, I do the right thing and follow the brothers, checking to make sure I'm properly covered as I go.

We head back out to the pool, where everyone is standing around looking terrified and worried and even furious. Joshua, who wasn't here a few minutes ago, stands in the center of the group. His expression is darker than I've ever seen. There's talking, but it's scattered. Clipped and anxious, angry but quiet. Everyone is tense. So tense that my heart suddenly starts pounding for reasons that have nothing to do with Axl's body being so close to mine.

"What's wrong?" Axl asks before I have a chance.

The muscles in Joshua's face tighten, and he runs his hand through his hair already messy hair. "I was in the clinic. I wanted to check things out, see if there were prenatal vitamins for Sophia and what kind of meds they had stocked the place with. But I couldn't find anything. Not even a bottle of Tylenol."

I want to shrug his words off. Tell him it's okay because we took all that stuff from Walmart before the dead even came back. But I can't, because it's obvious by the expression on his face more is coming. And it's worse than a few missing drugs. Axl's body tenses, and he squeezes my hand so tight I wince. I want to tell him to stop, but I'm afraid if he does I'll start to panic.

"What else?" Axl asks. He must realize more bad news is coming, too.

Joshua sighs and pinches the bridge of his nose like he has a headache or something. His shoulders slump, and it makes him look shorter than his actual six foot seven inches. "It got me thinking. The cabinet I got food out of in my kitchen this morning only had a few meals in it. I figured it was no big deal, that there were more in a pantry or closet, or in a storage area in another part of the shelter." He shakes his head, and my heart almost stops. "I searched the entire condo and then went down to the storage area on the bottom level. Nothing. No extras anywhere. So I came down here to check with everyone else and found out the other condos are all the same. Almost no food."

"He's right," Sophia says. "I noticed it this morning when I grabbed one of the prepackaged meals for breakfast."

My stomach tightens, and I grip Axl's hand harder. "How much do we have?" I manage to get out. I'm sure they've talked this through before Axl and I got here, but I need to know how long we have before we starve.

"If we gather all the packaged food and ration it, cutting down to one or two meals a day, we'll have enough for about two weeks." Joshua can't even look anyone in the eye when he says it, as if it's somehow his fault.

"Okay, but we still have the gardens," Hadley says calmly. "At least we'll have some fresh fruit and vegetables."

Joshua nods but his face is still tense. He's still having trouble meeting our eyes, and my stomach sinks even lower. All the way to the bottom level of the shelter like it's trying to reach the pits of hell. That's stupid though, because I'm pretty sure this is hell. Or something like it, at least.

Axl purses his lips, then lets out a deep breath. "But there's more?"

This time, I'm the one squeezing his hand so hard that I grind the bones together. Of course there's more bad news. Why wouldn't there be?

"The fuel for the generator." Joshua keeps his eyes on his feet. "I don't know without looking at it closely, but there's no way it's enough for five years."

"What about the wind turbine?" Anne asks.

We all saw it when we arrived at the concrete building above ground. A huge, white wind turbine about a football field's length away from the fence. It has to be for the shelter. There's nothing else out here.

Joshua shakes his head and finally looks up. "No idea. I don't know enough about this thing to even venture a guess, but I do know that the diesel is low. I mean really low."

"Fuck!" My whole body jerks when Angus yells. His

voice echoes through the room. He picks up a lounge chair and hurls it through the air, right into the pool.

Little Ava squeals, and Jake holds onto Anne. The echo of the splash takes over as Angus's curse fades away.

When Axl lets go of my hand, hurt and disappointment twist at my already ravaged insides. But he puts his arm around my waist and pulls me close. It isn't like him, showing affection in front of all these people, but I guess after the sauna the secret is out. And I'm thankful for it, because right now I'm pretty sure I'd fall to pieces if I didn't have someone to lean on.

"Where's that guy?" Jessica asks. Just like the little kids, she seems to be clinging to her dad—not that I have any room to talk.

Winston rubs her back absentmindedly and nods. "Yeah. The one who worked for the company."

Joshua sighs and shakes his head. He acts so guilty. Like all of this is his fault. He takes too much responsibility for things he has no control over. If he's not careful, he's going to end up with an ulcer. "Couldn't find him. He's not in his condo or the common area. I have no idea where he is."

"Did you check the control room?" Hadley asks. Her features are relaxed, unlike everyone else. But she *is* an actress. Anything could be going through her head. "That's where he usually hangs out. I think it's a comfort to him, feeling like he still has a job to do."

Joshua shakes his head, and people immediately head to the elevator. But we can't all fit. Only six or seven of us will be able to squeeze in there at a time. We're twelve levels down and I don't want to take the stairs. Or get left behind. I pull away from Axl and grab his hand so we get to the elevator at the front of the pack.

We make it in, and I find myself squeezed in the back corner with Axl pressed firmly against me. Angus is here, along with Hadley, Winston, and Joshua. None of us talk as the elevator moves up. I'm not even positive any of us are breathing.

We find James in the control room with his eyes focused on the screens. There are bodies outside still, hanging around the fence. They aren't shaking it anymore, but they haven't given up completely. Their presence suddenly makes me feel even more claustrophobic than being twelve stories underground did.

James turns when we walk in. It must feel like a mob descending on him, the way we all rush into the room. Angry and terrified. But he doesn't seem concerned, and he doesn't even look surprised to see us. He simply pushes his chair away from the desk and leans back. He crosses his arms over his chest and stares at us silently. Waiting.

"What the fuck is goin' on here?" Angus growls before anyone has a chance to ask a reasonable question.

I'm all prepared to tell Angus to shut up so someone with a little sense can get a word in, but James seems to understand. He sighs and shakes his head, then glances at the monitor before turning back to us. "I was waiting for this. Obviously, I knew it wouldn't be long before you all noticed things weren't quite right."

He's so calm and laid-back, which blows me away. We're facing starvation and being trapped underground with no power, but he doesn't even seem worried about it. Maybe he's already dealt with it. Already faced the fact that this is the end for him. It sure was nice of him to let us in on the secret. I hate that I got my hopes up for nothing. Seems luck will never be on my side.

Winston walks forward, actually daring to step in front of Angus. He always seems to be the voice of reason. "You think you can tell us what exactly is going on here? Give us some clue as to where we might find more provisions?"

James shakes his head and lets out a long breath that sends my stomach plummeting all over again. "You can't. They're long gone."

"What do you mean, 'long gone?'" Winston asks between

clenched teeth.

"The people who started this company were members of a society that believed the world was actually going to end on December 21, 2012," James answers calmly.

Joshua sighs and slumps against the wall like he knows what James is talking about and where this whole thing is going. I have no clue what's going on, though. I catch his eye and shake my head slightly.

"The Mayan calendar," he says before James can speak again. "It ended on December 21, 2012, so a lot of people thought the world was going to end that day."

That's right. It inspired a crappy movie, and there was a bunch of stuff on the news about it that December. I'd forgotten all about it. I'm still not sure what any of this has to do with the lack of supplies, so I look back at James and wait for an explanation.

"Yeah," James says with another big sigh. Bigger than the one before. "Well, these guys were fanatics. They preached it like it was the Bible and recruited members and built these shelters and filled them with all the people they talked into believing that nonsense. They were all here that day. Sitting in their condos, waiting for the world above them to come to an end in a big fiery ball."

"But it didn't," Winston says. He sounds defeated and tired. I can't blame him, because we all know where this story goes and what it means for us.

"No, it didn't. Unfortunately, the company was in the middle of renovating a fourth silo shelter. When the world didn't end, a lot of their investors pulled out of the project. People who had been talked into spending millions on a shelter filed a lawsuit, and the company started to struggle financially.

"The lawsuits had no basis, everyone knew that. No one forced these people to purchase condos. But fighting it cost money, and things were already tight." James stops talking and studies the back of his hand intently. Like there's something on it he's never seen before.

"So they sold off the supplies?" Hadley asks.

James sighs again and flexes his fingers. "That's what I heard." He looks up and shakes his head a little. "I'm nobody important, so I don't know all the details. I only know what I overheard, really. From what I understand, the medical supplies went first. They knew the condo residents would be less likely to notice that, and they were really hoping that would be all they had to sell. That things would get better and they'd be able to replace them. They started talking about global warming in their sales pitches, changed the websites, and kept moving forward. Things got a little better, but not enough. So they started selling off other things."

"Let's just get down to it," Winston finally says. "What are we looking at here? We already know we're low on prepackaged food, but we have the gardens."

James laughs and finally looks up, narrowing his eyes on Winston. "Have you been to that floor? Have you really looked things over?"

My stomach lurches, and I'm suddenly in real danger of hurling. Which would suck, because I can't afford to lose any nourishment. Food is going to be tough to come by real soon here. I swallow and glance around the room. Everyone is shaking their heads. Of course no one has been down to check out the gardens. Why would we?

"So you're saying there are no gardens?" I manage to get out. It isn't easy. There's a lump the size of Mount Everest in my throat.

"There are, but maintaining gardens takes money. It hasn't actually been a priority on the company's list. You may be able to find some vegetables and fruits that are salvageable, but probably not much. The good news is, if you work at it, things are set up so they will grow. It's just going to take time."

"So we gotta get us some food in the meantime?" Axl says out of nowhere, making me jump.

He's right next to me, but he's been so silent this entire time I had actually forgotten he was here. I glance at him now. He's just as calm as ever, which I just can't comprehend. Even he has to be worried.

James nods, but he's still frowning. "And fuel. They sold most of that off too, as I'm sure you've already discovered."

"What about the wind turbine?" Winston asks. "How much power can we reasonably get from that?"

James shrugs, and he suddenly looks tired. I'm not sure how old he is. Thirty-five, forty maybe. But at the moment he appears ten years older. The bags under his eyes are so prominent it's all I can look at. He's had this weighing on him since he got here, waiting for all of us to figure out that we're not as safe as promised.

"Look, I don't know a lot about the power grid. I've been looking through things and studying the manuals, but I'm still not sure. We get wind out here, so that's good. But there's one wind turbine, and this is a big facility. It isn't going to provide enough energy to power the whole thing. The diesel we have now will be good for three weeks, maybe a month with the whole structure running the way it is. If we cut power on certain levels, we could make it stretch. After that, the wind turbine will be enough to run emergency lighting and the air filtration system."

"We conserve energy," Winston says, scratching his beard. "We turn off the power on any unnecessary levels."

"Yeah, that's right," Axl says. "And we're gonna hafta go out and get us some supplies. Find some food. Some more fuel."

"Vegas is the closest city," I mumble. I'm talking to myself, really. Trying to psych myself up for the trip, I guess. Just the thought makes me more nauseated than before, but there's no doubt in my mind I'm going. I'm a good shot and I'm quick. And I have nothing to lose if I don't come back.

"Shit," Angus growls. That little vein is back on his forehead, and for a moment, I'm pretty sure he's going to punch the television screen next to him.

"We gotta get everybody together and go over plans. Round up the food, put one person in charge of it, and ration it out," Axl says. "And get to Vegas as soon as possible.

CHAPTER FIVE

"Well, you're all just going to have to leave. You didn't pay for one of these condos anyway!" Mitchell yells for what feels like the hundredth time. His high-class demeanor has slipped away and been replaced with panic.

We're in the common area, and he won't sit still. He paces frantically. Like a caged animal. And his eyes are wild. We've been trying to get him to listen to reason for almost twenty minutes, but no matter what we say, it just comes down to one thing for him. He doesn't care what happens to anyone else as long as he's safe. He just doesn't seem to get that even if we leave, he's not going to be okay. That he'll eventually run out of food even if he doesn't have anyone to share it with, and the fuel won't last forever. He's too self-involved to be able to understand.

"Just shut up!" Hadley suddenly screams.

She's been silent this entire time, letting Winston and Axl try to talk some sense into Mitchell. I guess she finally reached her boiling point.

She stands up and crosses the space between her and Mitchell in two quick strides. She's right in his face when she pokes him in the chest with her fingernail. It's perfectly manicured and red. Sharp like a weapon. "You listen here, asshole. You're not better than anyone else! You never were before all this, and now that the world has gone to shit you're about the least useful person here. So if I were you, I'd sit back and keep my mouth shut before everyone here decides to drag your ass to the surface and chuck you over the fence. You hear me?"

Mitchell's eyes get huge and his face turns red. His cheeks puff up like he wants to argue, then his eyes dart around the room to everyone else. No one is happy right now. No one is giving him anything but disgusted, angry looks. He presses his lips together more firmly and throws himself into a chair.

"There!" Hadley says, stepping back. "Now we can make some real goddamn plans!"

The corner of Axl's mouth twitches a little. He looks like he's impressed with Hadley. Despite the tense situation, a pang of jealousy shoots through me like a bullet. Axl's eyes follow her across the room, and my insides tighten. No. This is no time to be jealous. No time for thinking about how close Axl and I came to having sex. Right now, we need to focus on surviving. This thing with Axl is pointless unless we can figure out a way to survive.

"Okay," Winston says, getting to his feet. "First off, the food." He turns toward the three boxes on the floor behind him. They contain all the prepackaged meals we could find in the condos. There isn't a lot. Especially not for twenty-one people. "We're going to try and stretch it out until we can get some more provisions. That means rationing. Everyone is down to one meal a day except Sophia, Arthur, and the kids."

"Why do they get more food?" Lila pushes out her bottom lip and looks toward Al like he'll be on her side. He doesn't even glance her way, which only makes her pout even more. She's been about as helpful as Mitchell so far, only slightly less angry.

"Because they're kids," I say, rolling my eyes. "Sophia's pregnant and Arthur is sick."

"I don't need any special treatment," Arthur says, standing up. "I've lived a long life. If I can't get by on one meal a day like everyone else, then it's my time to go."

Winston scratches at his beard. It's thicker than it was a few days ago. I guess he hasn't bothered to shave. "We'll talk about it. For now, this is what we decided."

"Who put you in charge?" Lila asks. "Shouldn't we like, vote or something?"

"We decided as a group." Winston doesn't even look at Lila this time, and his jaw tightens. I can tell he's fighting the urge to yell at her. "Now back to the food. We're going to get a group on the gardens right away. Sophia, Jessica, Parvarti, and Arthur are going to go down there to see what they can find that's still good. After that, they're going to do some reading and figure out what we need to do to get some more crops growing. Everyone will get fresh food in addition to their one packaged meal. Sound good?"

Everyone nods, and not even Mitchell or Lila dare to argue. Which is good. The vein on Angus's forehead pulsates every time he looks at Mitchell. I know he's just itching to get his hands on him. I wouldn't stop him, that's for sure. The prick needs to be put in his place.

"In addition to that, we're going to shut off the power on all the levels that aren't completely necessary. That includes the pool—sorry, kids—and the theater is off limits." Mitchell grumbles and Lila whines, but Winston doesn't give them a chance to get any real words in. "We have to keep the power as low as possible until we get some more fuel." He stops talking and nods at Axl. "Now for your part."

Axl stands and looks calmly around the room. "We gotta make a run to Vegas and get us some supplies. It's gonna suck and people might die. Who's in?"

The speech is so Axl that I almost smile. Short and sweet. "I'm going."

He nods and doesn't even glance my way as more people volunteer. Eight of us in all. Angus and Axl, me, Trey, Winston, Anne, James, and surprisingly, Hadley. Eight of us ready to risk our asses in Vegas. I can't help feeling that we've all volunteered to shorten our lives. Even if we get through one trip okay, there will be more. I don't know how this walking dead shit works, but I'm pretty sure they aren't going to die anytime soon. They're already dead.

With that decided, people start to wander off to whatever tasks they were assigned. Mitchell, who was given nothing to do, hurries off to his room like he's afraid he's going to get jumped. Lila huffs and grabs a drink before following him.

The eight of us that volunteered to head to Vegas gather together around the bar to make plans. It's tough to tell what everyone else is thinking, but the idea of heading to Vegas makes me want a drink, so I start pouring shots.

"We ain't sendin' everybody out at once," Axl says.

He throws back a shot, barely reacting to the alcohol, then sets down the glass. When I offer to pour him a second, he shakes his head. He isn't a big drinker, due to an alcoholic mother, so I'm not surprised. Probably just wanted to take the edge off before heading to the slaughter.

"I'm thinkin' a group of four to start off, that way if they don't make it back we can send more people out later."

"Makes sense," Winston says. "Who's going out first?"

Axl looks everyone over while he drums his fingers on the counter. "Not Hadley. She's gotta learn to shoot before headin' out. Angus, you're gonna hafta stay behind to teach her."

Axl purses his lips when his eyes land on Anne. It's

obvious why. She's a good shot—used to be a cop—and she'd be useful, but she's got Jake. He's not her kid. She found him wandering the streets after his parents died from the virus, but he's her responsibility now. Axl doesn't want to put her in danger, and I can't blame him.

"I'll take Trey and Winston with me...and Vivian." He winces when he says my name, like he doesn't want me to go. Probably just being protective. It has a strange effect on me. I have the urge to tell him to shove his overprotective bullshit up his ass and rip his clothes off at the same time.

"Sounds like a plan," Winston says. "When do we leave?"

"In the mornin', I suppose. Better get our shit together and figure out how we're gonna get past them bastards outside the gate."

"We still have plenty of ammo up here or do we need to see what they have in storage?" I ask.

"They don't have anything there," James says. "They sold that off."

I can't even look at him. I just pour myself another drink and throw it back. Of course they sold off the weapons.

Anne's frown is so deep that it makes her look more like she's in her forties than her mid-thirties. Her short, brown hair is messy, and she swipes her hand through it nervously, making it even messier. She won't stop looking toward Jake, who's playing on the other side of the room with Ava.

"Since I'm not going tomorrow, I'm going to head out. Get Jake and Ava downstairs and ready for bed."

Axl nods, and his lips are so tight I'm surprised he can talk. "Sounds good. We'll use you next time."

Anne's eyes move toward him, and the smile she gives him is quick. She rushes away like she's afraid Axl will change his mind. I know her type. She's not scared of dying. She's afraid of leaving Jake alone. Who can blame her for that?

Hadley exhales and clinks her glass against Trey's before

doing a second shot. I can't help wondering if it's a good idea. As skinny as she is, her tolerance can't be that high.

She pushes her strawberry blonde hair off her forehead and closes her eyes. "I guess it's a good thing the pilot died before he could get more people. It doesn't seem like we're much safer here than we would be out there."

I nod and throw back a shot of vodka. It burns going down, and I squeeze my eyes shut. When I open them, my gaze focuses on Axl. His lips are pursed, and the expression on his face is confused. I stand up straighter. "What?"

"The pilot died."

It isn't a question, so I'm not sure how to respond. Hadley nods slowly. She looks as confused as I feel, but Winston's eyes are big and round. Even Trey looks like he just saw a ghost.

"Here?" Winston asks.

Dread comes over me, and I suddenly have the urge to slap myself in the forehead. Hadley told me the pilot died here. More than once! Why didn't I think of it before now?

"What'd you do with the body?" Angus asks.

Hadley's eyes get big, and James starts to sweat. They hadn't thought of it before now, either. Why would they? Before we showed up they didn't have a clue about the undead, and since then it's been so crazy.

"Bottom level," James says. "There's a freezer."

"Damn." Angus throws back yet another shot. He's been hitting it pretty hard. "Bastard's probably down there runnin' into the walls, trying to get out."

"Maybe not," Trey says hopefully. "What if the cold prevented him from coming back? What if the freezing temperatures stopped him?"

Axl hops up and shakes his head. "Guess we'll find out. If it does, we might wanna think 'bout headin' up north come winter. We ain't gonna get no freezin' temperatures out here."

Winston nods and pulls himself up. "Only one way to

know for sure."

All seven of us head to the elevator even though it isn't necessary. I'm unarmed, but Angus flips a giant knife between his fingers like it's his favorite toy. It reminds me of the one from *Crocodile Dundee*. Axl has a knife too. The same one he always carries. The blade is smooth and shiny, and the handle is brown. It kind of looks like it's carved from wood. He's had it since before the dead came back. He cleans it every night religiously, like it's a prized possession. Maybe it is.

We're silent as we squeeze into the elevator, and no one utters a word on the way down. I find myself leaning against Axl like he's some kind of support. A pillar of strength holding me up, keeping me from collapsing in on myself. Maybe he is. I don't know if I would have wanted to go on after Emily's death if he wasn't here.

I lace my fingers through his and the lower we go, the firmer my grip becomes on Axl's hand. Winston's face is tense like being so far underground is uncomfortable for him. I hope not. If so, the next few years are going to be rough.

The door opens on the twelfth floor, and my legs turn to stone. Everyone else steps forward, but I can't make myself move.

Axl's hand is still wrapped around mine, and when I don't follow he looks back. "You okay?"

"Yeah." I nod and swallow when the words get stuck in my throat. "It's just—I know what we're going to find down here. I didn't expect it, you know? Not in the shelter. We were supposed to be safe."

"Ain't no place safe no more," Angus says.

He spits on the floor. James glares at him, but Angus meets the angry look with one of his own. It's a hell of a lot more intimidating than the one James gave him.

Axl ignores his brother and gives my hand a little squeeze. "This ain't nothin' we can't take care of. Right?"

I nod.

"We been through worse."

I nod again. He's right. A body locked in a freezer? It's child's play compared to what we faced in San Francisco. To what we'll face in Vegas.

"You're right."

I squeeze his hand and step out of the elevator. Everyone is standing in front of the freezer now. Like they're waiting for us. I feel like I should thank them, except it would be the most awkward thank you in the history of the world. Thank you guys for waiting until I'm next to you to let the dead man out of the freezer. Right.

Axl drops my hand as we move closer. His grip tightens on the knife. Why don't I have a weapon? How stupid!

It's one of those industrial freezers you see in restaurants. It reminds me of watching *Hell's Kitchen*. Stainless steel with a thick door. Walk-in. We'd never be able to hear it if something was banging around inside.

Hadley takes a step back to stand at my side just as Winston reaches for the handle. He looks over his shoulder at the rest of us. No one nods, but no one tells him to stop. I guess he takes that as a signal to go ahead, because he pulls the door open.

Every muscle in my body tenses. Angus and Axl step forward since they're the only two who are armed. The door slowly eases open, and a mist of frozen air puffs out. I hold my breath, but nothing happens. It's dark in the freezer, so it's difficult to see in, but as far as I can tell there's no movement.

Hadley lets out a sigh of relief just as Trey shrugs and says, "Maybe he didn't turn."

Winston mimics his shrug. James shakes his head like he thinks we're all a bunch of morons prone to overreacting. Who knows? Maye we are.

Axl's arm relaxes. "Guess not."

A high-pitched scream fills the room, and every hair on my body stands up. Something runs toward us, faster than any of us can react. James jumps back three feet, and Winston's hand slips off the handle when the door bursts toward him. Axl steps in front of me and Hadley while bringing his knife forward.

He ends up pushing me to the side and I stumble back, tripping over my own two feet. The smell hits me just as I slam against the floor. It's muted, thanks to the freezer, but it's still death. Like an animal rotting on the side of the road as you drive by in a car.

The pilot rushes forward. He's coated in a layer of ice. Like the first frost that covers your grass in the fall. His skin is blue instead of the usual gray, and the rotting is minimal. But his eyes are still milky and wild as he charges at Angus.

Luckily, Angus is ready, and for once his rage is useful. He actually has a smile on his face. The dead pilot runs toward him with his mouth wide and his arms reaching, and Angus steps forward to meet him. He brings the blade of his knife down so hard that the crack of bone vibrates through the room. The body drops to the ground, and black goo oozes from the cut. The smell is so rank that my stomach lurches uncontrollably.

Hadley coughs and covers her nose, and for a moment she looks like she's going to hurl. I crawl back a few inches to get out of the way.

"Guess cold don't stop 'em," Angus says. He spits, and a drop of brown liquid lands on the pilot's back. His clothes are crisp from the freezer, making the circle of saliva stand out.

"At least we know," Winston says, and Trey nods.

James stands to the side with his mouth hanging open. He doesn't even blink. The expression on his face reminds me of the way I felt when I realized the dead were walking the Earth. This was his first opportunity to get up close and personal with one of the bodies. He looks like he might be a little in shock. I'm glad he isn't going with us tomorrow.

I'm still on the floor, and when Angus turns, he flashes

me one of his signature monkey grins. "While you're down there, Blondie..." He motions toward his crotch while my insides convulse.

I blow the hair off my forehead and push myself up. "Keep dreaming, Angus."

"I plan on it." He shoves the knife back in its sheath.

I feel like I need to wash my brain out with soap and water.

Axl glares at his brother, then focuses on me. "You okay?"

"Other than the giant bruise that I'm sure to have on my ass? Yup."

"Sorry. Instinct." He shrugs, and doesn't look very apologetic.

"Don't worry about it."

Trey cracks his neck, and I cringe. I hate that sound. "Guess we better bury this guy."

Hadley's face is white, and I'm not sure she would survive a trip to the surface right now. Plus, I feel like I'm covered in a layer of slime after Angus's comment. I grab Hadley's arm and turn to the elevator without even looking at anyone else. I need a shower. "We're going to head back to my condo. Have fun with that."

CHAPTER SIX

"Are you scared?" Hadley asks.

I look up from the dresser and sink my teeth into my bottom lip. She stands in the doorway of my bedroom while I dig through the closet and dresser. Her skin is still pale after her first encounter with the undead, and her eyes look too big for her face. She reminds me of a frightened child.

"I don't know." I bite down harder on my lip and think about going, about facing a city full of those monsters. About the possibility of not coming back. Of someone else not coming back.

I look away from Hadley and stare at the carpet. The tightness in my stomach when I think about something happening to Axl tells me exactly what I'm afraid of. I don't want to lose anyone else, especially not him.

"You scared of losing him?"

It's like she's reading my mind. When I tear my gaze away from the floor, her emerald eyes are calmer. Curious, even. She studies me like she'll be able to read my mind if she looks hard enough.

She walks in and sits on the edge of my unmade bed. "You could have just told me this morning that something was going on between you two."

"Nothing is." I sit next to her. "Not yet, anyway."

"That isn't what it seemed like when you two came out of the sauna."

"It's complicated. Axl is complicated. This thing has been hovering over us since I got sick."

Hadley's eyebrows shoot up. Oh yeah, she doesn't know about that.

"We were traveling. We'd just picked up Joshua and just learned how bad the virus really was. Axl, Angus, and I were waiting to see if we'd catch it. We didn't know if we were immune." I stare at my hands as the memory presses down on me. I'll never forget how hopeless I felt when I thought I was going to die. "I woke up one morning sick and we thought it was the end. Angus wanted to ditch me, but Axl wouldn't let him. He took care of me. Better than my own mother ever did."

"You should go to his condo, have some time with him before you head out. What if one of you doesn't make it back?"

My whole body tenses, and I can't take my eyes off my nails. The red polish is chipped now, probably from fighting off the dead. I guess having nice nails is a thing of the past. I should peel them off. They're not real, anyway. Not much of who I was before all this started was real. Not my nails, not my hair, not my boobs. Not even my personality. When I stole all my dad's cash and ran out on him, I did everything in my power to change who I was. Worked on dropping my low-class dialect, took a few college courses, bought nice clothes. I wanted anyone who saw me to think I was someone, because I had always felt like nothing. It was all just a show, though. At the end of the day, I still went to a club and danced naked for cash, then crawled home to my hole of an apartment.

It wasn't until the virus hit that I started to feel like I belonged somewhere. How pathetic is that?

"Are you still here?" Hadley asks.

I look up and let out a tense laugh. "Yeah. Kinda. Just thinking things through."

"It's obvious you want to be with him, so do it."

I swallow and nod slowly, but I'm not sure. Which would be worse? Having one night with him and watching him die, or never having a night with him at all? "Maybe that will make it harder. Being there in the middle of all that, trying not to focus on him."

"You should at least talk to him."

She has a point.

I jump off the bed and take a deep breath like I've decided what to do, even though I still feel as lost as I did the day my mom walked out on me. "Well, I'm going to have to go somewhere, because there is nothing in this condo I can wear." I glare at the closet. I've been searching for something suitable to wear while killing the living dead. There's nothing, of course. I'd be set if I were getting ready to walk down the red carpet, though. "Did your friend think she was packing for the Academy Awards or what?"

Hadley laughs and shakes her head, but her expression is pained. It's going to be a while before any of us can think about the past without being sad. "That's just how she was. She loved being the center of attention."

I snort. "I can relate." It's usually a trait people use to cover up insecurity, but I don't say that to Hadley. No reason to trash her friend. It's not like she's coming back. Well, she probably did, but none of us will ever be back in Hollywood to know for sure.

IT TAKES ME THREE TRIES BEFORE I GET UP THE

NERVE to knock on the door, and even then my hand shakes. Why am I so nervous? I wasn't nervous in the sauna earlier so it just seems stupid now.

Angus answers the door, of course. Luck has never been on my side.

He purses his lips and crosses his arms over the chest, then leans against the doorframe like he wants to prevent me from going in. "You come for more condoms or to fuck my brother?"

I roll my eyes and fight the urge to punch him. It isn't easy. "God, Angus, can you ever just be normal? I came to see if there are any women's clothes in this condo. There's nothing but evening wear and lingerie in mine."

He grunts and pushes himself off the wall, then steps aside so I can walk in. "In the back bedroom."

"Thanks," I say as I head back.

I push the door open without knocking. Angus didn't indicate that anyone was in the room, so it's a bit of a shock to find Axl standing there with his back to me. His hair is damp like he just showered. Probably had to after dragging a body to the surface. He's shirtless, and his pants sit low on his hips, revealing the waistband of his boxers. God, he's sexy.

He turns around, and my heart pounds when the corner of his mouth twitches just a bit. I've come to love that little half-smile. "Don't you knock?"

"I was looking for some sensible clothes. Jeans and a t-shirt. Mine are all dirty," I blurt out.

I realize it doesn't answer his question, but at the moment I'm too focused on his bare chest to think straight.

He tilts his head toward the dresser. "There're some in there."

He's as laid-back as usual, but I don't get how he can be after that moment in the sauna. It's doesn't make sense. My legs wobble as I walk across the room, and my heart races whenever I look at him. But he just watches me, as calm as always.

I open the dresser and dig through it, doing my best not to look back at him. It doesn't really work, though. He hasn't put a shirt on, and I'm distracted by it. I'm having a difficult time holding back.

Even with the distraction it only takes a moment to find a pair of jeans and a t-shirt that will work. Nothing warm, though. No sweatshirts or jackets. That may be a problem. It's warm now, but this is the desert. The nights will be chilly, and who knows how long we'll be out there. I want to be prepared for anything.

I jump when Axl's hands touch my shoulders. He brushes my hair aside and runs his fingers down my arms. When his lips skim the back of my neck, my legs almost give out. It's so soft and tender, so sensual. I turn to face him, and his stormy eyes search mine. Then he kisses me.

I close my eyes and it takes two seconds for me to forget all my doubts and worries. I run my nails down his bare back while his mouth attacks mine hungrily. Like he's trying to devour me. I run my tongue over his lips. The subtle taste of vodka is still there from his earlier shot.

He nips at my bottom lip, then kisses his way down my neck. Thanks to the ridiculous wardrobe Hadley's friend left behind, I'm braless and the dress I'm wearing is low-cut. He takes advantage of it. I gasp when his hands cup my breasts and he runs his tongue between them.

He pinches my nipples, and I gasp again. I open my eyes, and my gaze lands on the pile of clothes sitting on top of the dresser. The clothes I'm going to wear to Vegas. To kill the dead.

No. This is a bad idea.

I step back on wobbly legs. My dress is pulled down, exposing my breasts. I cover myself and shake my head. "I'm not sure if this is such a good idea." It takes everything in me to get the words out, because I want to be with him, I really do. But I'm afraid it might make things too difficult when we're in danger.

He swallows and stretches his neck like he's in pain. I almost give in when the muscles in his shoulders flex. I love strong shoulders. They make me feel safe, like he can handle anything.

"Sure would complicate things," he whispers.

I swallow and try to take a step back before I attack him, but the dresser is behind me. I end up bumping into it. He's so close and his shirt is still off and he looks so amazing and my brain is still fuzzy from kissing him. I need to focus on something else.

I take a deep breath. "Why did you pick the three of us to go with you?"

He frowns and steps back, then scratches his chest and sighs. "Didn't think it'd be such a great idea to have Angus out there with Winston and Trey."

Winston and Trey are both black, and Angus has a history of being racist. Makes sense.

"And me?"

He winces, and his eyes flit away. "Wanted to keep an eye on you."

My heart constricts, and the urge to attack him returns full force. I've never had anyone want to look after me. Not my parents or the endless line of losers I dated. Only Axl.

He looks up, and we stare at each other for a few seconds. There are a million things I could say, but I don't speak.

After what seems like forever he says, "Was brave of Hadley to volunteer. She's somethin'."

My insides tighten. That look on his face when Hadley yelled at Mitchell... Was it just admiration? "Men do seem to love her."

His gray eyes search my face, and he presses his lips together. Not his usual expression, something different. "Not me," he says slowly. "She ain't my type. I'd be afraid she'd break in half."

I laugh, and my muscles unravel like a ball of yarn. "So what's your type?"

"I always liked curvy girls myself."

He takes a step closer. His hands rest on my hips for a second before moving up. They caress every curve and my cheeks heat up. My blood still simmers from a few seconds ago, and now that his hands are on me again, it starts to boil.

His hands stop on my cheeks, and he pulls me forward. Then his lips are on mine, and everything fades away. The kiss is softer this time. Sensual and slow.

I want him so bad that my body hums at his nearness. But waiting would be better. Wouldn't it? My heart pounds when I pull away. "Would it make things too complicated in Vegas if we slept together now?"

His hands drop to his sides, and he sighs. He swipes his hand through his dirty blond hair. "Probably," he says. "We should hold off for now, wait 'til things have settled down a bit."

"What if they don't?" My voice is breathless, almost desperate. That's how I feel. Like if I don't have him now I'm throwing away my only chance at happiness.

He gives me a half-smile and shrugs. He doesn't seem to have an answer to that question. Then again, neither do I.

CHAPTER SEVEN

There's a good size group of people to see us off when we meet in the common room at six in the morning. Hadley and I are the last to stagger in. It was a rough start for me. I took a sleeping pill—courtesy of Joshua—so I could get some real rest before we left. I'm sure I'll feel more rested later, but at the moment, I'm walking through a fog.

"'Bout time," Axl snaps.

I'd be offended if I weren't used to it. I give him the finger and lean against the wall. Hopefully, the dead trying to get at me through the fence will wake me up. The coffee and cold shower sure as hell didn't work.

"You going to be okay?" Hadley chews on her lip while her green eyes swim with worry.

I wave a hand at her and nod. "I'll be fine. I just need some time to snap out of it."

"If you say so," she mumbles.

"Let's head out!" Axl calls.

We walk as a group to the hall outside the control room. James is already there, watching the monitors closely. It's stupid, but I look away. I can't focus on the dead, or I'm afraid it will make me too nervous. Like seeing them will make them more aggressive or dangerous.

"What's the plan?" I ask Axl as he studies the screens.

"First we're gonna get to the car. Once we're in, Angus is gonna throw a flare over the fence, away from the gate. Hopefully, that'll draw them away, so's he can get the gate open. Anne and James are gonna cover him." His voice is tighter than usual, and when he turns to face me, his jaw twitches. "You ready?"

I nod and try to hide the fear that creeps up inside me. When those doors shut behind us just two days ago, I really thought we were safe. Now we have to go back out there and not only face the dead surrounding the fence, but the ones in Vegas too. I can't believe it.

I double-check the knife at my waist and make sure my gun is loaded for the hundredth time this morning. My pack feels heavy, and the straps dig into my shoulders. I'm not sure why. There isn't much in there but a few bottles of water and some more bullets. I adjust the straps, but it doesn't do any good.

"Be careful," Hadley says. I'm more than a little shocked when she pulls me in for a hug. "I saw this lying on the floor in your room. Thought you might want it." She slips something in my back pocket, and when I pull back, she flashes me a grin.

I give her a questioning look and shove my hand in the pocket. The plastic condom wrapper crinkles when I touch it. "Seriously?"

She shrugs and shoves me toward the stairs. "You never know. Just want you to be prepared for any scenario."

"Thanks." I roll my eyes, but she's behind me now so she can't see.

James drags himself out of his chair and heads for the

door. He types in the code, and the little red light on the keypad goes out and the green one next to it lights up. He glances over his shoulder at Axl, then nods once before pulling the door open to reveal the dark staircase.

Axl starts up, and I follow him on shaky legs. I grip my gun tighter. I'm ready. Or as ready as I'll ever be, anyway. Can anyone ever really, truly be ready for a zombie apocalypse? I don't think so.

When we reach the top of the stairs, Axl pauses and looks back at us. He's carrying his own pack as well as a bag of guns, and he adjust them while his eyes hold mine. They dart away, and he takes a deep breath. "Y'all ready?"

Winston and Trey are next to me, with James, Angus, and Anne at the back. They all look as tense as I feel. The three of us going nod. Axl takes another deep breath, then pushes the door open and charges out of the building.

I'm out the door behind him before he's taken two steps. The sun isn't up yet, and the air is still cool. There's a slight breeze, and it blows my hair into my face as I run to the car, bringing with it the stench of death. The smell is so much stronger than it was two days ago. I gag, but I can't afford to waste any time throwing up. I swallow down the bile and focus on Axl's strong shoulders.

Winston and Trey's footsteps mingle with the moans of the dead. The more time that passes the louder the wails get, growing more and more frantic with each step we take.

I'm panting by the time I reach the passenger side of the Explorer. I'm pretty sure it's more from fear than exertion. The good news is, I was right. Facing a horde of the undead sure did wake me up.

I rip open the door and climb inside, slamming it behind me just as Trey and Winston climb in the back. Axl is busy with the wires under the dash, trying to get the car started. We don't have a key since we stole the thing, and he has to hotwire it to get it going. Luckily he's experienced, and in less than a minute, the engine purrs to life.

"Seatbelts," he says tensely when he puts the car in drive.

He can't move since the fence surrounding the small building is shut tight, and we all wait in silence as Angus runs toward the fence with a flare held tightly in his hand. He hurls it over, and I let out a sigh of relief when the dead actually go for it. Once they've moved a safe distance, Angus runs to the gate with Anne and James right behind him. It takes him a few seconds to cut the zip tie holding the gate shut, and as soon as he does, he throws the gate open and Axl hits the gas.

We fly through the gate, and Axl doesn't slow down for even a second. I twist around in my seat and stare through the back window. Angus has the gate shut and is working on getting it secured while Anne and James shoot the approaching dead. The flare didn't distract them for long. When he's gotten it shut, the three of them run back toward the building.

"They made it," I tell Axl when I turn back around.

"Knew he would," he says.

Every inch of his body is tense, so I put my hand on his leg and lean closer. "Relax," I whisper in his ear.

The corner of his mouth twitches, and he puts a hand on top of mine. Slowly, he starts to relax.

"So what's the plan?" Trey calls from the back. "If the stores we looked up are no good?"

"No idea 'til we get there. Like to avoid the Strip if possible. Maybe find a more residential area. Hafta wait an' see what we can find."

We're about an hour from Vegas. Probably less with the way Axl is driving. The sun is just now coming up, and the horizon is painted a brilliant shade of yellow and orange in the distance. It will be early morning by the time we reach the city, which will be convenient. I want to be able to see when a body tries to eat me.

The city's going to be crawling with them, there's no doubt about it in my mind. Vegas was a vacation hot spot, virus or not. I can't imagine how many people were crowded into those hotels when martial law was declared and travel was cut off. They stopped air travel pretty early on, too. Thousands of people were probably stranded. Eighty-five percent of which died from the virus and rose again. It's staggering.

But what about the others? People who were immune. People who have managed to stay alive. Some are going to be dangerous, but some are going to be like us. Just looking for a way to survive.

"So what happens when we come across other survivors?" I ask suddenly.

"Who says we will?" Trey says from the back.

I glance over my shoulder. Is he kidding? He's the one who thought we were overreacting to the virus in the beginning, who pointed out that four million people surviving a deadly virus is still a lot. Now he thinks we won't find any other survivors?

"You think we're the only ones who've managed to make it?"

He shakes his head, but his eyes are flat. "No. I think others survived the virus, but I think they either got eaten by the zombies or got the hell out of the city. Who would be stupid enough to hang around?"

"There are bound to be people trapped in the city," Winston says. "Vivian brings up a good point. How's everyone going to feel if another group comes back to the shelter with us? We barely have enough to live on as it is. Are people going to be mad if we bring someone else back? Five someones? It's something we should have discussed before we left."

Axl snorts and shakes his head. "No need to discuss it. We ain't leavin' people to die if we can help 'em. Hadley coulda left our asses in the desert to get eaten by the fuckin' zombies, but she let us in. Same goes for us. If we can do somethin', then we're gonna."

It never occurred to me that we might abandon people, so I'm glad to know Axl's on board. I glance back at Winston and Trey, and they're both nodding in agreement. I guess they feel the same way Axl and I do.

"Okay, then. If we see people, we save them," I say.

We reach the outskirts of Vegas just after the sky is fully lit by the sun. It's totally residential, though. No stores, no gas stations, nothing but cookie cutter houses in neat rows. And the dead walking the streets. There's plenty of that. The bodies react to the sound of the car the same way a dog would react to a canine whistle. They can hear us coming from a mile away. They're ready for us before we even turn onto a street, waiting for us to show up. It's eerie and terrifying, and I have no idea how we're going to get out of this car alive, let alone make it through the city.

I'm on map duty, and the further we get into the city the more I struggle to find us on the atlas.

"Where do I go?" Axl asks me for the millionth time.

"I don't know!"

"Let me see," Winston says, reaching forward and yanking it out of my hand.

We'd looked up a few addresses the night before, courtesy of a Las Vegas phonebook in the control room, and found several addresses for Sam's Club warehouses in the area. They seemed like the perfect places to stock up on supplies and possibly gas up, since most have gas stations these days. Only I apparently can't read a map.

It only takes Winston a minute of searching to figure out where we are and tell Axl where to go. Before I know it, a sign for the warehouse is looming in the distance.

"Everybody grab your shit and be ready," Axl says through clenched teeth.

I get my pack and sling it over my shoulder, hitting my head on the dashboard as we roll over more bodies. This is insane and beyond dangerous. And hopeless. Did I mention hopeless? We aren't going to make it out of this car alive.

Why the hell didn't I just go ahead and screw Axl last night like I wanted to?

"This isn't going to work." I grip the *oh shit* bar as the wheels of the car thump over more of the dead.

There's just no way to avoid them. They charge us, completely oblivious to the fact that they're no match for the Explorer. The terrifying thing about it is that there's nowhere we can stop to be completely free of them. They hear the car. They want the car. And they are more than willing to throw themselves in front of the car. They'll be on us the second we stop, and then there will be no escape.

"We need a distraction," Axl mutters as the wheels bounce over yet another body.

He purses his lips, and his gray eyes search the road in front of us. He's thinking, and there's no doubt in my mind he'll find a way to get us the hell out of this situation. Axl is smart.

Just as we're passing a car parked on the side of the road—a BMW that looks brand new despite the thick layer of desert sand settled over it—he swerves to the right. He barely touches it really. Just a tiny ding that probably did minimal damage to either car. But it's enough to set off the alarm on the Beemer.

Even in the Explorer we can hear the high-pitched alarm that goes off. It's the same annoying pattern I've heard hundreds of times throughout my life, but this time it's like music to my ears. Suddenly the dead are no longer interested in the purr of the Explorer's engine. They hear a much tastier-sounding treat coming from the Beemer. Every last body in sight heads in the direction of the car alarm. Mindlessly walking toward the sound of the dinner bell that shrieks through the air. It's amazing and wonderful and so much of a relief that I'd lean over and kiss Axl if the situation still wasn't so dire.

"Are they goin'?"

I nod and reach over to squeeze his leg. "They are

going!"

He smiles—an actual, real smile—right before he jerks the wheel hard to the left and pulls into the parking lot of the Sam's Club, skidding to a stop in front of the door. Axl turns the car off, but none of us move. There are still bodies milling around the store. But just like the others, they're on their way to the BMW wailing down the street.

"You're a genius," I whisper.

He gives me a quick smile before growing serious. "We're gonna wait just a couple minutes. When I say go, I want you to get out and run toward them doors as fast as you can. Stay close, keep your weapons out, and try to make as little noise as possible. Once we're inside, we gotta get that door secured. But stay alert. There are bound to be some of them fuckers inside, too." He pauses and glances out the window, scanning the parking lot.

My right hand is on the handle and I clasp my knife tightly in my left. They shake from anticipation, nerves. Fear. I chew on the inside of my cheek while I wait for Axl to give us the go ahead. There's a raw spot, like I bit it in my sleep or something. The more I gnaw on it the more it hurts. I bite down so hard that the sharp, coppery taste of blood fills my mouth.

The parking lot is pretty clear. There are a few stragglers left, but the alarm is still blaring in the distance and they're slowly making their way toward it. It's amazing how decayed they look at this point. Their skin is so dark gray that there'd be no way to mistake them for the living, and it hangs on the bodies like tissue paper. It's probably just as thin. They have open sores and cuts and tears on every visible part of their bodies. And the black goo that flows through them in the absence of blood seeps out of every opening. From cuts, from their eyes, from their ears. They're covered in the stuff.

"Now!" Axl hisses, breaking through my thoughts.

I was so intent on watching the lumbering bodies closest

to us that it almost catches me off guard. But my hand was already on the handle, and it only takes a second to collect myself. I shove the door open so I can hop down. The smell hits me as soon as I'm out. The rancid scent of decay is so strong that my eyes water and my stomach lurches. I focus on not breathing through my nose and shut the car door as quietly as speed will allow before taking off toward the store. Winston and I have to run around the side of the car to reach the door since we're on the opposite side, and Axl has it open by the time we get there.

I rush inside, joining Trey in the darkness. He has a flashlight in his hand and he's standing in the doorway with it shining into the store, keeping watch for anything that might be lurking between the shelves. My hands shake as I fumble in my pack, searching for my own flashlight. Why hadn't I thought to get it out in the car?

Breathing in and out is difficult. The stench inside the store is strong. The smell of rotten meat and produce, on top of the dead that are most certainly wandering the aisles, has mixed together to create an odor so strong and unique that there's no way to even describe it. It makes my eyes water. Even breathing through my mouth doesn't help. I can taste it. It leaves a film in my mouth that feels thick and sticky. Rotten. I pull the collar of my t-shirt up over my nose and mouth, desperate to diminish the stench.

Axl and Winston join us after moving two rows of shopping carts to block the doors. The tension between us is as strong as the smell in the store. It's dark in here, and there are almost no windows to help us see. The further back we get, the more dangerous things will be.

"Now what?" I ask. Even though I whisper, the sound of my voice cutting through the silence makes me jump.

"We should do a sweep first, Winston whispers. "Try to hunt any down so we can load up on goods without any surprises."

"Yeah. That sounds good. That way we can check out the

other doors too. Make sure nothin's open." Axl's still nodding in agreement when he steps forward. "Stick together."

I swallow and follow him with my shirt still up over my nose. I have no intention of wandering off.

We make it halfway through the store—to the center where all the clothes are on display—before we spot the first body. Its back is to us, but it turns as soon as the beam from Winston's flashlight is on him.

It used to be a him, anyway. Now he's a mindless body with only one eye. He opens his mouth and chomps at us as he walks forward. He's wearing a short-sleeved shirt and there are bite marks on his arms. He must have gotten bitten and came in here to hide. Maybe he was like us and hoped he wouldn't turn from the bites. That this outbreak of the living dead was nothing like the ones Hollywood had depicted over and over again. He was wrong, of course, just like we were.

The body stumbles a little as he walks forward, almost falling down. But he rights himself and raises his arms. His hands grip the air as he moves forward. Reaching for us. Axl doesn't let him get close. Without saying anything, he walks over to meet the body, swiping his hunting knife through the air and sinking it into the skull. It squishes in, spewing out black stuff that splatters onto the table of shirts next to them. The body collapses, and Axl uses the clothes to clean the blade of his knife before turning back to us.

"They're decaying fast," I say through the fabric of my shirt. "Maybe they'll just waste away?" It comes out as a question. Like I want someone to reassure me that everything will in fact be okay. As if they know more than I do.

"We can only hope," Winston mutters as he starts moving forward again.

We head to the back of the store as planned. We don't encounter any other bodies along the way, but the place is huge. We could have missed them. I just hope we don't have any surprises down the road.

The back room is packed to the ceiling with the store's excess inventory. Just the sight of it fills me with hope. If we can find a truck, we can load it up with canned and boxed food, and we'll be set for years. They have everything we need at Sam's.

It's bright, but it takes my mind a minute to register why.

"Door's wide open," Axl says before I have a chance.

He's right. The door to the delivery bay is open, filling the room with light. It's one of those huge, silver, metal doors that slide up on a track. It's electric. Is it even possible to get it shut when the power's off?

Axl walks over to inspect the door, and we follow him. I'm gripping the handle of my knife so tight my hand aches, but with the door open like this, I'm nervous and jumpy. Every little sound makes my heart race even faster, and right now there are a lot of them. Birds outside chirp, and a can blows across the empty parking lot. What sounds like a flag flaps in the distance. It's all causing my anxiety level to shoot through the roof.

"Shit! Take a look at this," Axl calls out.

I almost jump out of my skin, and I swear my heart actually stops beating for a second, but I tell myself to cool it and walk closer to him. He isn't looking at the doors anymore. He's staring outside, and when I get next to him I see why. There's a truck. A delivery truck with its doors wide open. It's already half full.

"What do you think the odds are that it has gas and keys?" Winston asks with a huge smile on his face.

"Don't know," Axl says as he jumps down. "Only one way to find out."

We all follow him, and I glance around nervously once we're outside. We're at the back of the store and it seems clear. No bodies and very little stench. I rip my shirt off my nose and take a deep breath. There's still a hint of decay in the air, but it's faint. A hell of a lot better than it was inside.

I follow Axl to the front of the truck while Winston

climbs in the back to check it out. Trey hangs back, scanning the area with a tense expression on his face. The driver side door is wide open. Axl pulls himself inside, while I stay below to keep a lookout. It would be too good to be true if this thing was gassed and ready for us to drive back to the shelter. Much too good.

I wait for Axl to tell me what's going on, nervously shifting from foot to foot. My eyes never stop moving. Never stop scanning the area. I find myself sniffing the air. If they're coming, the smell will give them away.

"Somebody's lookin' out for us," Axl says.

I look up at him, and he's got a huge smile on his face. He holds up a set of keys, and I want to jump for joy.

"And the tank's full," he says, hopping down.

"Can we drive it? I mean, don't you have to take a special class to drive a truck like this?"

"We'll figure it out. Not like we're gonna hit traffic."

He has an excellent point. Right now, I'd try to fly a rocket if I thought it would get us to safety.

We head back toward the store and find Trey and Winston waiting for us.

"Keys and gas," I tell them.

Axl jingles the keys. "Don't suppose either of you knows how to drive a semi?"

Winston nods, and I feel like kissing him. "I worked for the San Francisco Fire Department for over twenty years. I drove the truck."

"Told ya somebody was lookin' out for us," Axl says, winking at me.

CHAPTER EIGHT

I shove a mass of damp hair out of my face and wipe my brow. My body is covered in sweat. At this point, I probably smell as bad as the store. It's late morning now, and the Las Vegas sun is sweltering despite the fact that it's fall. The smell in the store gets more intense as the minutes tick by. More than once, I've had to stop because my stomach keeps threatening to empty all its contents onto the floor.

We're moving as fast as we can. Working in teams of two, filling wheeled flatbeds with boxes of cereal and cans of soup. We've gotten everything from huge bags of flour to packs of toilet paper. Anything we may need in the near future. We've been at it for hours, although it feels more like days. The truck is nearly full now. My arms ache from loading the carts and pulling the flatbeds, and my neck is tense from constantly looking over my shoulder. Amazingly, we haven't come across any other bodies.

I pull the cart toward the dock, trying to ignore the sweat that trickles down my back. The cart is loaded down with stuff I found in the baby aisle. It reminded me of Sophia when I saw it. Wipes and boxes of diapers in every size are crammed on. After this, I'm going for the clothes. She'll need all of it in about six months.

Axl is right next to me, lugging a cart full of canned goods. It probably weighs twice as much as mine.

"Truck's getting pretty full," Winston says when we finally get to the back.

"We can get still get more," Axl says.

He's so determined. I admire it.

I shift from foot to foot while the men unload the flatbeds. I can go get more. We should stick together, though. It's stupid to wander off. But we've been in the store for hours. If there were other bodies walking around we'd have seen them by now. Right?

"I'm going for clothes," I say. "For the baby and the kids. They'll need new stuff, and the condos don't seem to have a whole lot."

"You shouldn't go alone," Axl says, but he barely pauses. He's dripping with sweat, and his face is streaked with dirt from handling all the boxes. I probably look the same.

"I'll be okay. This place seems pretty clear."

Axl shakes his head, but he keeps unloading the cart. Trey's on the ground, and he takes the box from Axl before handing it to Winston, who is in the truck. They have a nice rhythm going, and it's pointless for me to just stand here watching.

"I'll be careful," I whisper.

He pauses for just a second and purses his lips. "Promise me."

The words wrap around my heart and squeeze it so hard that I almost have to gasp for air. I have the sudden urge to kiss him, but he's back to unloading the cart before I can even respond. His eyes are still on me though, waiting for my response.

"I promise."

He nods, and I head back out into the store. I find a shopping cart sitting in an aisle, full of food from the refrigerators and freezers that went bad a week ago. I pick them up and the boxes squish in my hands. They're soft from when the frozen food thawed out, and the cheese is almost completely green. I gag as I toss them aside.

When the cart is empty, I head to the center of the store where the clothes are. They don't have a lot, but I grab as many pairs of infant sleepers as I can in every size they have. They're Carter's brand, covered in things like frogs and hearts, ducks and princesses. They have some other infant clothing too, so I load up on those. Both boys' and girls' clothes, since I have no idea what she'll need. The other side of the rack has clothes for older kids, so I get some things for Ava before heading to the table next to it and pulling out jeans and shirts I think will fit Jake. If only I could do more.

I move my flashlight around and the beam stops on a huge swing set. Toys. They have toys here, too.

Before heading that way, I glance over my shoulder. The store still looks clear, and it's as silent as a tomb. The thought sends a shudder down my spine. I should head back, but it would be so nice if the kids had a few books and toys to play with. It won't take long if I hurry.

I'm rushing when I turn the corner, focused on the swing set looming in the distance. The stench of rot hits me just as my cart slams into the body. My flashlight isn't pointed in that direction, so it catches me completely by surprise. I scream and grope for my knife as the undead man lurches forward. I shove the cart into him as hard as I can, backing away while I desperately try to get my knife free. The damn thing's stuck.

"Vivian!"

Axl's panicked voice echoes through the store. My heart is in my throat, and I can't force any words out. I stumble back and somehow trip over my own feet, falling to the ground just as I get my knife from its sheath. My elbows slam into the floor. Pain radiates up my arms and the knife slips from my fingers. It skitters across the floor and into the darkness.

My elbows throb. The body in front of me gets around the cart and takes a step closer. The pungent odor of the black ooze is so much stronger and more distinct than the stench in the rest of the store. It's too dark to get a really good look at him, but I don't miss the way his hands grope the air in front of me. Reaching for me.

I crawl backward and finally find my voice. "Axl!"

My knife is gone and my gun is in my pack. Back in the loading bay. I'm weaponless, and the body is so close that I get a whiff of his rotting teeth every time he chomps at the air. It takes another step forward, and his foot lands on my toe. I shriek again and jerk my leg back, scrambling further away. My legs won't cooperate, so I can't get to my feet. My heart pounds and my mind screams *run!,* but I can't do anything other than crawl backward.

Axl calls for me again, and my heart pounds harder. He's getting close. I call to him, praying he finds me or I can get my body to cooperate in some way. The dead man in front of me leans down and wraps his bony fingers around my ankle. I scream and kick, and my foot makes contact with his face. It's soft and squishy, and my stomach convulses.

The body loses his grasp, and my leg is free. I move back two more paces and bump into someone behind me. My heart pounds and a sob pops out of my mouth when the body is finally illuminated by the beam of a flashlight. His milky eyes move up. A shot rings out, echoing in my ears, and the head of what used to be a man explodes, spraying black goo and decaying flesh all over the surrounding merchandise.

I shake, and tears stream down my face when I look up at Axl. Only it isn't Axl standing behind me.

The man points the gun at my head. "You bit?"

He's tall and imposing, standing over me with an

expression that could freeze a volcano. He's in his late twenties, possibly early thirties, and he's filthy. His blond hair is greasy and matted, clinging to his scalp. He has a thin, blond beard that has grown out of control.

I shake my head, unable to find my voice, and my eyes flit past him as movement catches my attention. He isn't alone. There are several other people standing in the shadows, but it's too dark to see how many there are.

"Vivian!" Axl is suddenly there, running down the opposite side of the aisle.

Trey and Winston are behind him, and their guns are gripped tightly in their hands. Axl's eyes grow huge when he sees the man holding a gun to my head.

"Get the fuck back!" he yells, raising his own gun and aiming it at the man.

"Not until I know she hasn't been bitten or scratched," the man responds in a tense voice.

Two other men step forward, flanking him on either side. One is in his late thirties. He has a ratty hat pulled down low, covering most of his face. The other is young, probably only sixteen. They're both armed, and their eyes are just as icy as the blond man's.

The men in my group come to a stop next to my shopping cart with the dead body lying on the floor between us.

"We take care of our own," Winston says.

Axl steps forward and holds his hand out to me, but the blond man stops him. "If she tries to walk away, we'll kill her. We don't need any more of those things walking around. We have a zero tolerance policy."

I'm shaking, but I manage to find my voice. It comes out small and squeaky. "I wasn't bitten."

The man doesn't blink, and his finger twitches on the trigger. "We need to be sure. Take your clothes off."

"Like hell!" Axl growls. He steps over the body and jerks me to my feet. "We ain't stupid. You think we're gonna just let you strip search her and not bat an eye? You ain't touchin' her!"

The blond man shakes his head and doesn't lower his gun. "I won't touch her. I won't take a step closer to her. I just want to be sure she's clean. We've been fooled before."

I'm shaking and Axl is gripping my arm so tightly that he's sure to leave a bruise, but it's clear this guy is serious. He fully intends to kill me if I try to walk away. Maybe he's making it his personal mission to clean out the city, or maybe he's just seen too many people ripped apart by the undead to stomach seeing someone else turn. Even a stranger. Either way, he's prepared to kill me in order to stop me from turning.

"I'll do it," I manage to get out. "I'll take my clothes off to prove to you I'm okay."

"No!" Axl says through clenched teeth.

"It's okay." I put my hand on his, the one holding my arm, and slowly loosen his grip until I'm free. "It's okay."

I turn back to the blond man and meet his eyes. "If you move, he will shoot you."

The man nods but doesn't say anything. This isn't some crazy guy out trying to get his jollies. I've seen that type a lot in my line of work. They flock to strip clubs in hordes. This guy just wants to protect his people and probably me. Maybe he's going about it in a crazy way, but I can't fault him for that. This world is crazy now.

I pull my shoes off with shaky hands and toss them aside so I can remove my pants. Once they're off, I pull my shirt over my head and drop it on the ground next to me.

"Put your arms over your head and spin around so we can see you," the blond man says.

I nod and do what he says, raising my arms and turning slowly, giving him the chance to check for any injuries. When my back is to the man, my eyes meet Axl's. They're hard, and his jaw is tense. Anger is visible in every muscle of his body, and the hand holding his gun shakes just a little. I keep spinning until I'm facing the man again. When I stop, he nods and lowers his gun. He averts his eyes like he hates he had to put me through that. I believe he did.

"Put your clothes on," he mutters, still looking away.

The other men in his group lower their guns as well, and I quickly get dressed. No one moves, and the tension surrounding us is so volatile that it's likely to cause an explosion if I don't do something fast.

Once my clothes are back on, I turn to the blond man and give him a smile, hoping to relax him. "Thank you."

His eyebrows shoot up, and even in the dark store the color in his cheeks is visible. He swallows and reaches up to rub the back of his neck. "I'm sorry. It's just—we've seen so many people turn."

I nod and glance back toward the three men in my group. They're still tense, and Axl hasn't lowered his gun yet. "It's okay," I say, nodding to Axl before turning back to the men in front of me.

I glance behind him, trying to get an idea of who else is in his group. He motions for the others to step forward. There are four of them. A woman and three children. They're filthy, and their eyes are wide and full of terror. The woman holds a gun that shakes so badly I doubt she'd be able to hit anything even at point-blank range.

"Are you here looking for supplies? Do you have a safe place to hide?"

The blond man shakes his head and sighs. The sound is worth a million words. "We've been moving around, hiding in stores and homes, trying to stay safe. We were out of food though, so we decided to come here and stock up. We just can't keep running like this. We have to get out of the city."

The men in my group step forward, and Axl places his hand in the middle of my back. It relaxes me. He's still tense though, and he's glaring at the blond man in a way that I know means he'd love to punch him in the face. I give Axl a tight smile and nod to let him know I'm okay. He doesn't relax

"We have a safe place," Winston says.

The blond man tilts his head to one side and looks us over like he doesn't believe it can be true. "Where?"

"About an hour outside the city," I say. "You're welcome to come. We have room."

"Can we trust them?" the older man next to him says, speaking for the first time. He pulls the hat off his head and scratches his scalp. He's slight, and his hair is dark and thinning. The skin on his face sags. He looks weary and exhausted like he hasn't slept in weeks.

The blond guy runs a filthy hand through his hair and sighs again. "Do we have a choice? We're going to die if we stay here. Hell, most of us already have."

He glances behind him at the woman, and she nods. Her eyes are huge, and there are tears on her cheeks. She looks just as exhausted as the man.

He turns back toward us and nods. "I'm Nathan, and this is Brad." He points to the older man on his left before turning to the teen on his right. "And Jhett." He turns around and pulls the woman and kids forward. "This is my wife, Moira, and our daughter Liz."

A jolt goes through me. All three of them survived the virus? It seems impossible that they'd all be immune. "How did you all three make it?" I ask before I can stop myself.

He shakes his head and pulls his family in for a hug. "I have no idea, but I thank God every day that we did. Most of the people we know are dead, and the few people who are left have lost everything. How we got so lucky, I have no idea."

He shakes his head and wipes a tear from his cheek before turning to the two other kids. "This here is Max and Dylan. We found them at the playground right before the dead started coming back. Lucky for them."

I introduce our group since Axl still hasn't calmed down, then turn to the kids and kneel in front of them. "We have a two other kids in our group, and I was just going to get some toys for them. Want to help me?"

Their eyes light up in the way that only a child's can when you mention toys with a dead body on the ground. I motion for them to follow me and head down the aisle, patting Axl on the shoulder as I go by. Moira comes too. She clings to Liz's hand, and I don't blame her for that. If I had been more diligent with Emily, protective the way this woman is being, maybe she'd still be here.

A sharp pain rips through my body. I have to hold my breath and stop walking until it passes. It makes my knees weak. I hide it from Moira by pretending to study the toys in front of me. Really, I'm afraid that if I keep moving, I'll collapse from the pain.

"How old are the kids in your group?" Moira's voice breaks through my pain and self-loathing to bring me back to reality.

My eyes are still focused on a display of dolls. Their black, plastic eyes stare back at me. "Ava is five and Jake is eight."

"The boys are nine and Liz is seven."

Liz pulls away from her mother and goes to the display of dolls. Even though it's only a foot away, Moira looks stricken for a moment, like she's missing a part of herself. She bites down on her lip and her blue eyes follow Liz's every move. She's an attractive woman, short and slightly round. Her hair looks brown, but I'd guess that once it's clean it will probably be dirty blonde. Liz resembles her mother a lot.

It doesn't take long for the kids to load the cart full of toys and books. Then we all head back to the loading bay as a group. The kids cling to the cart while Moira pushes it, and the men walk around us in a half-circle. No one talks, and I hold my breath like I'm waiting for a monster to jump out. But we get there without running into any more trouble.

When everything's loaded, Winston shuts the truck's door and turns to face us, frowning. "Now we have to worry about finding a vehicle for everyone to ride in and gassing it up."

I hadn't even thought about that.

CHAPTER NINE

"**Y**ou guys got a car?" Axl asks, addressing Nathan for the first time.

Nathan tenses when Axl looks at him but nods anyway. "Yeah, but it's small. Ours was out of gas, so I took it from a neighbor's house. The tank is full."

They have a full tank of gas and they're still in the city? What the hell were they waiting for?

Axl shakes his head. He's thinking the same thing. I know him. "Why the fuck didn't you get outta here if you got a full tank of gas?"

Moira and Nathan both give him disapproving looks, and Moira pulls Liz close to her. They're annoyed that he's cussing in front of their daughter? Seriously? The dead are walking the Earth, intent on eating us all, and they're worried about a little cussing? Seems stupid to me.

Axl ignores their expressions and turns to Winston. "We gotta gas up the Explorer, then we'll be good. We should split up, make sure there's at least one of the four of us in each car."

"Good thinking. If we get separated somehow, there will be someone in each car who knows how to get back to the shelter." Winston looks at the newcomers. "I'm driving the truck back, and I can take one person."

"I'll go with you," Brad says, stepping forward.

"The kids are riding with us," Moira says defensively. She holds Liz tighter, like she's afraid we're going to try and steal her.

"Then Vivian can ride with you too," Axl tells them.

"No. I'm staying with you."

Axl shakes his head and turns to look at me, his gray eyes intense. "They got a full tank already. They can get outta here even if I don't got time to siphon the gas."

"I don't care," I say firmly. "Trey can ride with them. I'm staying with you."

Axl sighs and runs his hand through his hair, but he nods in agreement. "Alright then."

"What about Jhett?" Nathan asks. "We can't take him if Trey's with us, and he's just a kid."

Jhett doesn't really look like a kid with the way he handles that gun, but he's young. His face is marred by acne, and his dark, shaggy hair is so greasy it sticks to his scalp. His teeth are crooked when he grins at me. His parents should have gotten him braces.

"We can fit three," Winston says. "It'll be tight, but it's no problem."

I expect Brad to step forward and say he'll give his seat up for the kid, but he doesn't. He just stands back and presses his lips together, letting everyone else decide what's going to happen now that he has a seat to the shelter. Something about the look on his face bugs me. He seems like an ass, to be honest.

"It's just you and me, then," I say tensely.

Axl glares at Brad. He's probably thinking the same thing

I am. We always seem to be on the same page. "Now we just gotta create a distraction, so's I can siphon some gas."

"There was a car alarm going off down the street when we got here," Nathan says. "They were all over it. Sounds like it's off now, though."

"Axl did that," I tell him. "To draw them away from the store."

Nathan nods appreciatively, but Axl's hard stare doesn't soften even a little. "Nice job."

Axl just grunts, and it reminds me of Angus. That's a pleasant thought.

"Got any ideas?" Winston asks him.

"Not particularly."

Winston looks over toward the truck. "How about you try to sneak out nice and quiet and siphon some gas? I'll pull the truck out and keep watch, and if things get hairy we can fire some bullets in the air, draw them our way. That thing's huge. Even if they surround us we'll be able to get out."

Axl purses his lips. "It's better than anythin' I can come up with." He turns and looks at Nathan and Moira. "You parked out front?"

Nathan nods.

"Why don't you come on out with Vivian an' me and pull the car 'round here? That way the kids don't gotta go out there at all."

Nathan nods again, but Moira grabs his arm. "You can't leave us!"

"I'm not leaving you. I'll be right back, I promise." He pulls her against his chest, hugging her tightly for a brief moment. He kisses the top of her head before he lets her go.

I throw on my pack and tuck my gun into my belt. I'm not making the mistake of leaving it behind ever again. My hand brushes my sheath. It's empty. Shit. I never found my knife. I'll have to get a new one. Axl had a whole bag of weapons in the car. There has to be one or two in there.

"Ready?" Axl asks Nathan.

He nods and gives his wife a worried glance before he heads to the front of the store with Axl and me. We don't talk. Axl's still pissed, and Nathan's too tense. I'm caught somewhere between terror and dread. I hate that I lost my knife, but I try not to let it bug me. No way am I going back to that aisle to crawl around in the darkness looking for it.

When we get closer, I notice that a front window is broken and a row of carts has been pushed in front of it. That must be how Nathan and his group got in. It's sloppy, though. Anyone can see that the bodies could have gotten through it if they'd really wanted to. How the hell have these people survived this long?

Axl and Nathan pull the carts aside with very little effort, and we look through the hole before stepping out. The sun is pretty high since it's well into afternoon, and it takes a few seconds for my eyes to adjust to the light. Once they do, I'm surprised to find that the parking lot is pretty empty. There are a couple stragglers at the far end of the lot, but it seems like most didn't come back this way after the alarm went off.

A black sedan is parked half on the sidewalk right in front of the hole like the driver was in a hurry. It wasn't there when we got to the store, so I can only assume it belongs to Nathan and his group. It's in good shape. Not very old. I still can't figure out why the hell they're still hanging out in Vegas when they have a car that will get them out of here.

"You go first," Axl whispers to Nathan. "Get to the back and get everybody loaded up."

Nathan nods and steps through the hole, ducking so his head doesn't hit the jagged glass at the top. Every muscle in my body tenses as he runs to the sedan. I keep a close eye on the few bodies stumbling around about twenty feet away. They don't seem to notice Nathan until he starts the car, and as soon as he drives off they head after him. The car's too fast for them though, and Nathan loses them before he turns the corner.

"Ready?" Axl asks.

I nod even though the answer is no. It will always be a firm no when someone asks if I'm ready to head out to face the dead. I go back to chewing on the inside of my cheek despite the fact that it already hurts.

Axl dashes out into the sunshine, heading to the Explorer. Even though the fear of being eaten is still very present in my mind, I breathe a little easier the second we step out. It sure smells better than in the store. The scent of decay is still there, especially whenever a breeze blows, but it's nothing like it was inside where there's no ventilation.

Axl jumps into the driver's seat and has the car started before I'm even to the passenger side. I hop in and shut the door just as two bodies notice us and head our way. There are only two, so it doesn't really worry me. I can take two. It's the possibility of running into a horde that has me worried.

We drive over to a group of cars at the opposite side of the parking lot, and Axl pulls right up to them. "Keep watch," he says as we climb out.

I don't respond. I just keep my eyes open and circle the car while he gets gas cans out of the back and gets busy. The two bodies that noticed us are still about fifteen feet away and moving slow, so I keep an eye on them while I watch for any others. So far there aren't any, I relax even more when the two that were headed our way change direction as Winston pulls around the building in the semi. Nathan and the others are right behind them in the sedan, and I tap my toe nervously when a few more bodies on the other side of the parking lot head that way. They need to keep back. The semi can withstand a horde, but I doubt the smaller car could.

Axl works fast, draining all four of the cars around us in what seems like minutes and transferring the gas to the Explorer. "That's all I can get, but it should be enough. Let's get the hell outta here."

We climb back in the car and Axl puts it in gear, signaling to the others to get moving. It looks like we made it

Kate L. Mary

in the nick of time, too. Six of the dead are circling the sedan, getting more aggressive by the minute. Trey's in the driver's seat and he takes off, leading the way. Winston falls in behind him while Axl and I bring up the rear.

The air in the Explorer is almost as ripe as it was in the store, but when I look at the window, it's closed tight. I sniff my shirt, and my nose wrinkles in disgust. I smell as bad as one of the bodies, thanks to the black goo from the dead man who tried to take a bite out of me, and the sweat soaked into my skin.

"I can't wait to get back to the shelter," I say. "I need a shower."

The corner of Axl's mouth twitches, and he glances over at me. His face looks even dirtier now that we're in the sun. "I was meanin' to talk to you 'bout that."

I slug him in the arm playfully. "I wouldn't talk if I were you! You smell worse than one of the dead."

He chuckles and flashes me such a relaxed grin that it totally lightens the mood in the car. I lean back in the seat and close my eyes, then let out a big sigh as tension rolls off me in waves. I won't feel really comfortable again until we're out of the city, but at least we're on the road. And with a full truck too. This should tide us over for a while.

"Shit," Axl mutters a few minutes later. "Why the hell's he goin' this way?"

My heart jumps to my throat at the panic in Axl's voice. I bolt upright and my eyes fly open. Axl rarely loses his cool, so whatever it is, it must be important. At first look, nothing seems different, though. We're still in Vegas, the street is clogged with zombies. Normal. Or as close to normal as we can come these days. Then I catch sight of a few casinos in the distance, the sheer number of bodies in front of us hits full-force, like a tidal wave. It must be thousands.

"Are we on the main strip?"

Axl's hands wring the steering wheel. "Never been to Vegas, but that's what it looks like."

94

All the tension that had just disappeared is suddenly back, and my shoulders are in knots all over again. The streets are so crowded with the walking dead that it reminds me of Time's Square on New Year's Eve. The truck in front of us slows down, probably because the sedan is having a difficult time getting through the throng of bodies, and Axl is forced to slow too. I glance at the speedometer nervously. We're not even going thirty miles an hour.

"This was a bad idea," Axl mutters, gripping the wheel even tighter than before and leaning forward.

The bodies swarm us and slam into the sides of the car. Their rotting fingers rake against the glass, scratching at the windows. I swear one loses a couple nails. A few bang their heads against the car, leaving splatters of black goo on the glass. Axl has to slow even more until we're down to fifteen miles an hour. It doesn't even feel like we're moving at this point.

"Shit!" Axl slams his hand against the dashboard.

It startles me more than the dead trying to break into our car, and I almost jump out of my skin. The fact that Axl's worried makes all of this so much more frighteningly real that I start to sweat all over again. My heart kicks up about ten notches, and I dig my nails into the palms of my hands to stop them from shaking. It doesn't help. Nothing can, because when you face thousands of bodies intent on eating you, you're pretty much in a helpless situation.

I do my best to shove the fear down as I lean forward and try to get a good look at the sedan through the mass of bodies in front of us. That's who we should be more concerned about right now, Trey with Nathan and Moira and the kids. They're vulnerable in that small vehicle, while we may be able to take a beating and squeeze out of this alive. I strain my neck and twist in my seat, but no matter which way I turn, I can't see a thing. My eyes land on the moon roof, and I climb to my feet.

Axl watches me push the button that opens the small

window above us. "What're you doin'?"

"I want to see what's going on."

I pull myself through the window and into the blinding Vegas sun. The stench is so strong it singes the hairs in my nose. It's like thousands of rotting corpses baking in the sun, which is exactly what's happening. But it's so bright that it takes a moment for my eyes adjust. When they do, I wish I'd stayed inside. Bodies rush toward us like a tsunami, ready to wipe us off the face of the Earth. Their moans and cries fill the air, and it's so loud that I almost clamp my hands over my ears. It's earth-shattering and so unnatural that the hairs on the back of my neck stand up. I shiver despite the scorching Vegas sun pounding down on me from above. This just can't be real.

Almost worse than the dead walking around are the signs that the living were once here. There are splatters of blood on the cement and sides of buildings, bloody trails that lead to mangled masses of flesh and bones. Things that used to be human lie discarded and rotting in the hot sun.

I try not to focus on it, try not to think about how awful it would be to have these monsters' teeth sink into my skin. Try not to think of Emily.

Instead I look ahead and try to find the sedan. It's barely visible. Only the smooth, black top peeks out of the mass of dead. It's so surrounded that it's moving at a snail's pace now. The undead pound on the windows, and as I watch, a few climb onto the hood, making their way to the windshield. It won't be long before they manage to break the windows.

I pull myself back inside the car and shut the moon roof. "We have to do something. They're right on top of the sedan!"

Axl swears again and turns the wheel. He keeps swearing as he maneuvers around the truck, accelerating through the mass of bodies. It's slow going, though. Even in this big vehicle. The dead bump against us, leaving trails of black ooze on the windows. They bang against the doors like they're trying to get in. It's unreal how many there are.

We pull up beside Winston in the Sam's truck. His expression is tense when he looks down at me. I wave, and for some reason it feels final. My chest tightens as we pull past and move up behind the sedan. I have a strong suspicion that I just said goodbye to Winston.

My throat is thick. "What's the plan?"

"Gonna try and draw them away." Axl's voice is so tense it doesn't sound anything like him.

A sick feeling enters my stomach. What we're doing is going to be the end of us.

I could slap myself. I'm such an idiot! Why the hell didn't I sleep with Axl when I had the opportunity? How many chances at happiness have I had in this life? Just that one, and I let it slip away. We could have had one amazing night before everything went to shit again. Just one. It's like I'm my own worst enemy.

"Are we signing our own death warrant by doing this?" I say between clenched teeth.

He gives me a tense smile. His knuckles are white from gripping the steering wheel so tight. "Does it matter?"

I laugh as tears come to my eyes. God, we are so much alike. "Not really. Those kids deserve a shot more than I do."

His jaw tightens as he finally moves up beside the sedan. I glance at Trey, and our eyes meet. Hopefully he knows to just leave, to get the kids out of here safely. He nods. Of course he understands. My stomach contracts, and his face blurs. I give him a little wave as Axl pulls ahead.

Axl moves off to the side of the road and slows down, then puts the car in park next to the Paris casino. There's a road up ahead. If we can distract the bodies long enough, Trey and Winston will be able to pull off the main strip and out of the city. Hopefully they make it, and we aren't sacrificing ourselves for nothing.

"Here goes nothin'," Axl says, echoing my thoughts.

He leans down and fools with the wires under the steering wheel. The dead bang against the car, but even more have surrounded the sedan. I dig my nails into my legs while I wait for Axl to do whatever he has planned. He grunts, and a few sparks fly. My entire body jerks when the deafening sound of the alarm rings through the car.

The world around us explodes. The bodies go crazy and converge on the Explorer, banging on it with their hands, their bodies, their faces. They leave thick smears of black on the windows as they desperately try to get in. The door handle rattles, and some even climb on top of the car.

They're wild and frantic. It's so terrifying that for a moment I can't remember exactly why we decided to do this. My heart pounds and I cover my ears, trying to block out the sounds of the hammering and the alarm. Trying to keep the terror at bay. All I want to do is run, but there's nowhere to go. The realization that we're stuck hits me so hard I start to shake.

Then the sedan drives off. It turns the corner with the truck close behind it, and I relax just a little. They're going to make it. Nathan and his wife, their daughter. Two other little boys who have years ahead of them. Trey can get back to Parvarti and Winston to his daughter. They will have food and safety. That's why we chose to commit suicide in this horrifying way.

Axl pries my hands away from my ears and pulls me against his chest. He wraps his arms around me as the pounding continues. He doesn't say anything, and neither do I. All I can do is watch silently as the truck pulls out of sight.

After a few minutes, he turns the alarm off, but the damage is already done. They know we're in here, and they won't give up until they've broken in. A crack starts at the corner of the windshield and travels across. Then another. A dead man hurls himself against the glass and pounds his fists. Hundreds of cracks fan out across the windshield in a frightening web pattern, and I have to stifle the urge to scream. It's safety glass, so it doesn't give. At least not yet.

"I won't let them get us." Axl's lips brush against my head, and strands of hair fall into my face. They tickle my nose, but I can't find the motivation to move them aside.

I nod and swallow against the lump in my throat. He doesn't mean he won't let them get in, because we both know there's nothing we can do about that now. Surprisingly though, I'm okay with it. A bullet to the brain sounds a lot better than being ripped apart by the undead.

The glass behind us shatters. Axl's arms loosen. We both turn to see the first body pull itself through the back window. He's so thin he resembles a skeleton, and the skin on his face and scalp is ripped to shreds. His face is streaked in black goo. He howls at us as he pulls himself forward. His fingers are black, and two are missing. More pull themselves through the opening behind him. They're crawling over one another as they try to get at us. Their high-pitched screams and rancid smell are even more intense in the small space. And more terrifying.

My hand shakes as I pull out my gun and face the screaming bodies. Axl pulls the trigger first, and the gunshot is so loud that it makes my ears ring. He takes the closest one out, and I aim for the one behind it. Black liquid sprays the inside of the car when my bullet pierces his skull, coating everything in its rancid scent. I gag when bile rises in my throat, but I have to swallow it down as more and more bodies find the opening and pull themselves in. Crawling over their fallen brethren. Reaching out to us with decaying hands.

We continue to fire, but no matter how many we take down, more find their way in. I blink and clear my throat and focus on the dead. But nothing I do can stop the tears that stream down my cheeks.

"Save one bullet," Axl yells over the screams and pounding of the dead.

His words are like a knife in my stomach. A dose of

reality. We are really and truly screwed. I pause to check my ammo anyway, because he's right. I need to save one if I don't want to end up being eaten alive. My hands shake when I pull out the clip. Four bullets left.

Three for the undead and one for me.

"I'm down to four," I say as I take out another. "Three."

Axl fires twice in quick succession, taking out two more. "I got two."

He fires one last time, then puts the gun down. Seeing the gun in his lap is so final that a sob forces its way out of me. My whole body shakes. I take my time with my final shots. Partly because my hands are unsteady and partly because the bodies are moving slower than before. They've piled up. New ones have trouble getting through the back. They've stopped pounding on the other windows and are now focused on just the one small opening.

My hand trembles so much when I fire my last shot that I'm surprised it hits something. It rips through the temple of a putrid man. His head explodes, and the car vibrates. Or maybe that's my body. I lower my gun. This is it. I have nothing left. Not even my knife, because I lost it in the store. We have more weapons, but they're in the back of the car where they do us no good at all.

One body makes his way toward us. A chubby man who was almost bald in life. His scalp is torn now, probably from the broken glass of the back window. Black goo seeps from the wounds, flowing down his face. Into his eyes and mouth. He moans and grabs at us, stopping every few inches to reach toward us before moving forward again. My heart pounds and my body quivers. This is the end.

Axl pulls me against him. His eyes look stormier than the clouds that follow a tornado, and my own eyes are filled with tears, making his face blurry. I wipe them away so I can focus on him in my final moments.

"Shoulda slept with you last night," he says.

My heart leaps, then twists painfully. I start crying all

over again. "I was thinking the same thing." I can barely get the words out between sobs, but I *need* him to know.

He lets me go and raises his gun, pointing it at his head. "You ready?"

I nod and lift my own gun. Trying to block out the moans coming from the back of the car and the smell of decay surrounding us. Trying to focus only on him. "On three?"

He nods, and his Adam's apple bobs like he's trying to swallow down the tears. "One."

"Two," I say between sobs.

He opens his mouth, and my body trembles. My finger moves to the trigger. Do I close my eyes or focus on him? His lips move again before I've had time to decide, and he must say three, but the word is cut off by an explosion so loud it vibrates through the car.

CHAPTER TEN

My heart stutters and my finger twitches on the trigger. Axl's eyes hold mine. We're both frozen with our guns held to our heads. My breathing slows, and I blink. Am I going nuts, or has the pounding on the car lessened?

Another explosion rips through the air, followed closely by a third. The car shakes again. My hand drops to my side just as Axl lowers his gun. The pounding has stopped almost completely now.

"Are they leaving?" I ask, trying to get a glimpse of the Strip through the black goo smeared across the shattered windshield.

Axl shakes his head. The dead man crawling toward us moans. Without blinking, Axl rips out his knife and slashes it toward the body. The blade strikes the man in the side of the head, and the body collapses.

Axl pulls the knife out and wipes it on the seat. "It's quiet."

"You think Winston or Trey did that? Blew something up to try and draw them away from us?"

"It's a good guess. I know I woulda done somethin' to help out if the situation was reversed." His eyes dart to the back of the car, but no other bodies have crawled inside. He takes a deep breath and says, "I'm gonna check it out."

He reaches for the button to open the moon roof, and my heart pounds. We might be okay. I exhale and say a silent prayer as he pulls himself through the window. Religion has never really been my thing, but if there's ever a time to ask God for a break, this has to be it.

Axl ducks back inside the car seconds later. His face is still tense, and I can't read his expression. My heart pounds, and I grab his arm. My nails dig into his flesh. "What?"

He shakes me off and starts gathering his things. "There are still a few 'round, but there ain't many. There's a fire one street over and they've hauled ass in that direction."

"What do we do? We can't drive this thing. We can't even see out the window."

Axl reaches back and rips his pack out from under a few bodies. He shoves his things inside. It's covered in the rank, black liquid. "Get your shit. We're makin' a run for it."

I do my best to ignore my pounding heart as I throw my pack over my shoulder. It doesn't work. Where the hell does Axl plan on going? I'm all for getting out of this car, but the uncertainty scares the shit out of me.

He presses a button on the door, and the locks click. "Ready?"

I take a deep breath and shove the door open, stumbling down and running around the front of the car. The Strip is amazingly empty considering how full it was just a few minutes ago. There are still a few bodies milling around nearby, and masses in the distance, but it seems like most of the dead that were trying to get to us a few minutes ago have headed toward the fire. There's a huge, black pillar of smoke floating up toward the sky in the distance.

I reach the other side, and Axl grabs my hand. He pulls me toward the front door of a casino as the few bodies still lingering around shuffle our way. A replica of the Eiffel Tower looms over us, blocking out the sun. It's the Paris Casino.

We dodge a rotting cocktail waitress as we duck inside. The interior is dark, and the outline of slot machines lined up throughout the room reminds me of headstones in a cemetery. In the distance, something moans, but it isn't close.

"Where are we going?" I ask as he pulls me through the dark.

We dodge slot machines and stools that have toppled over, not slowing for even a second. A body lurches toward us and Axl swipes at it without pausing. The blade cuts into its skull, and the dead man hits the ground right at my feet, almost tripping me. I manage to jump over it at the last second.

"Stairs," Axl says between breaths.

The stairwell is right in front of us, and the green sign above it still glows despite the lack of electricity. It must run on batteries.

Axl shoves the door open and rushes into the stairwell. The door slams behind us, and he drops my hand. I can hear him fumble around in the dark, but I'm not sure what he's doing until he flips the flashlight on and shines it up the stairs. We don't need it to know the stairwell is clear, though. The air lacks the stench of decay everything else in the world now seems to have.

I lean against the wall and take a few slow, deep breaths. "Do you have a plan?"

Axl nods, but he's breathing heavily. It takes him a few seconds to gather himself. "Roof," he finally says.

Is he nuts? "Roof? That's your plan?"

He grabs my hand and pulls me with him as he starts up the stairs. "Gotta get a better look at what's goin' on out there. Try an' figure out where to go from here."

It makes sense. Just taking off down the Strip is a bad idea and not something I even want to attempt. At least from the roof we'll be able to see if there's a car we can use and the best way to approach it.

When we reach the end of the staircase, Axl shoves the door open. We burst out onto the roof, and the sun almost blinds me. We're not all the way at the top, though. It takes my eyes a moment to adjust because it's so bright. So much brighter than the Strip, thanks to the sunlight reflecting off the shimmering water of a pool.

Axl chuckles and drops my hand. He brushes the sweaty hair off his forehead. "Didn't expect that."

I laugh too, and even though it feels out-of-place it eases something inside me. Dread maybe? "No kidding. I had no idea there was a pool up here."

I exhale and slump against the wall. The wind blows and the sun beats down on my head like it's trying to burn me alive. My skin is moist, and even though the air on the roof is clear, all I can smell is death. It's like the stench has coated my skin and seeped into my pores. I'm not sure I'll ever be able to smell anything else.

"What now?" I ask.

"Let's get this door blocked off just in case, then do a quick sweep of the area. Make sure nothin' else is up here."

"I only have one bullet and I lost my knife at Sam's."

Axl curses and pulls his backpack off. "Think I got an extra knife."

He digs for it while I nervously study our surroundings. There's nothing moving, and it's amazingly quiet up here. Still, I won't be able to relax until I'm armed again. There are cabanas and a few other structures on the other side of the courtyard where dead things could be lurking.

Thankfully, Axl finds me a knife. He hands it to me, and I tuck it in my sheath. It's smaller than the one I lost, which isn't great, but it's better than nothing. One bullet isn't going to get me far when a horde charges us.

We get busy trying to find things to pile against the door. Unfortunately, there's nothing but chairs and a few small tables on the roof. It won't really keep anyone out, but if someone—or something—opens the door, we'll know. It will give us some warning at least.

Once that's done, we head to the other side of the roof and check out the cabanas. There's nothing moving around, living or dead, but the cabanas do have small refrigerators stocked with bottles of water.

"Let's load up," I say, pulling off my pack. I hold it open while Axl piles them in. The water is hot, but water is water.

Getting to the edge of the roof so we can look over isn't easy. The cabanas are in the way, with very little space between them. Beyond that, the edge of the building is lined with shrubs. It's a tight fit, and the branches scrap against my arms when I squeeze back, but we manage to make it. When I look over, my heart sinks. The fire has just about died out at this point—and from up here we can see that it was a gas station—and the bodies seem to be heading back toward the Strip. Why they're gravitating this way is beyond me. Maybe there's something leftover in their brains that tells them the Strip is the place to be, or maybe there's some noise down there that we can't hear from this high up. Either way, we're screwed.

I can't look anymore, so I leave Axl to check out the area while I head to the bar. It's full of booze, but not much food. I find a jar of green olives and shove those in my bag. Something red on another shelf catches my eye, and I almost giggle like a schoolgirl when I pick up two jars of maraschino cherries. My stomach growls, and for some reason the thought of having the cherries to eat makes me feel better. One last treat before we meet our final end, or something like that.

I shove the cherries in my bag and head for the pool. The water is slightly murky since the electricity has been off for a while now, but it still looks nice. And sparkling. Probably cool. My skin itches to be clean. I'm sweaty and my clothes stick to me in places I don't even want to think about. I didn't pack much, so I don't have any clean clothes. A dip in the pool sounds amazing, though.

Axl walks over and plops down in the lounge chair next to me. He doesn't look happy. Great.

"See anything?"

"Whole lotta shit."

"No cars? No way out?"

He shakes his head, and my heart sinks all the way down to my stomach. "Now what?"

"Well, seems like we got two options. First, try an' make a run for it. Hope that we can distract 'em somehow and find a car."

Sounds like an excellent way to get ourselves killed. "Or?"

"Sit tight." He puts his hands behind his head like he's out relaxing by the pool, not hiding from flesh-eating undead.

I have the sudden urge to hurl. "What's that going to do?"

"We're pretty secure up here. We got water, probably a little food in that bar over there." I pull the jar of cherries out of my bag, and he grins. "If we wait it out a day or so, Angus'll come lookin' for us. No way he'd leave us out here."

Axl's right. Angus is a prick who doesn't care about many things other than himself, but there's one thing he just might care about a tiny bit more than his own ass. That's Axl.

I exhale slowly and focus on the water in front of me. Waiting it out sounds like a good plan. No way will Angus walk away from his brother. No way. "Yeah. That's the way to go." I put the cherries back in my bag and drop it to the ground next to Axl. Then I flash him a big smile and tilt my head toward the pool. "Is it bad to worry about being filthy in the middle of all this?"

"Naw. Only natural. Go 'head, jump in."

There's still a little uncertainty in me, though. It isn't easy to relax when there are bodies walking the Earth, but Axl knows what he's talking about. The roof does seem secure. The stairwell was empty, and I can't think of a single reason the undead would come up here looking for food. Not when they've had such good luck down on the Strip.

Plus, the water looks so nice and being clean would feel so good.

I'm going for it.

I pull my shirt over my head, and Axl sits up straighter. The way his gray eyes follow my every move makes my legs quiver. My bra is soaked with sweat, so it comes off next. I undo the hook, then slide the straps down. Axl's lips twitch. The filthy bra falls to the ground, and my shorts go next. I pull them down nice and slow. Finally, my experience as a stripper comes in handy at the end of the world. I leave my underwear on. Red and lacy, there's barely anything to them anyway. Axl purses his lips, but I just smile.

My eyes move to the water. I'm already imagining how nice it's going to feel on my skin. "You going to get in?"

"I'm just gonna sit here an' enjoy the view."

I glance over my shoulder. Axl's grin stretches from ear to ear. He reminds me of a little boy in a toy store. It's cute, and it makes my stomach do a little flip-flop.

"You need it," I say. "You're dirty."

He winks at me and smiles even bigger. "You got no idea."

I laugh, then throw myself into the pool. The water swallows me whole. My eyes are squeezed shut and my lungs are full of air, and I stay under. It feels amazing. Like a hot bath at the end of a really hard day. I stay down until my lungs burn for relief, then blow the air out as I swim up. I dip my head back just as I break the surface. The water runs down over my face and back. It isn't particularly clean and I don't have any soap, but my skin already feels less grimy.

I swim to a more shallow area, where the water only

comes up to my waist. The sun is warm against my skin, and I can almost imagine I'm on vacation as I scoop up handfuls of water and scrub my face and arms, making sure all the dirt and stench of death is washed off.

Axl doesn't take his gray eyes off me for a second. They caress me from six feet away as he takes in every move I make, every curve of my body.

"You really should get in." I run my hand down my chest, and Axl squirms in his chair. I have several reasons for wanting him in here, only one of which is getting him clean.

He slips off his shoes, then stands up. My pulse quickens when he pulls his shirt over his head. His muscled chest is filthy and covered in little beads of sweat, but that only makes my heart beat faster. His eyes hold mine as he unzips his pants, and my throat tightens when they fall to the ground. He's wearing nothing but boxers that sit low on his hips. My eyes trace every muscle, then move down, stopping on his happy trail peeking out from the top of his boxers.

Axl heads down the stairs and into the pool. My body is already on fire, and my heart beats like a jackhammer. He's as laid-back as always, though. He dives under and swims across the pool, resurfacing about ten feet away from me. The water glistens on the plains of his chest, and my heart skips a beat. I'm on a roof with Axl, possibly stuck here for the night, and we are both almost naked. I've come a long way from ten minutes ago when I thought we were about to die.

I swim to the edge of the pool and climb out, laying on the lounge chair so I can watch Axl better.

"Done already?" he asks.

"Disappointed?"

"Whatever. Long as you don't put clothes on, I'm good."

He swims to the edge, clean, and climbs out. His eyes move up my body as he walks over, sending a little thrill down my spine. What he said to me in the car comes screaming back, and that thrill turns into an ache. For as long as I live, I will never be able to forget how I felt when I thought I was saying goodbye to him.

He sits in the chair next to mine. I stand up, and he scoots over so I can sit with him. His eyes are serious. Like he can read my mind. It wouldn't really surprise me. He always seems to know what I'm thinking.

"What you said in the car—" The words catch in my throat. I have to pause so I can pull myself together. Facing death isn't an easy thing to talk about, but I need to sort out how I feel about him. And how he feels about me.

He purses his lips, and a storm like I've never seen before rages in his eyes. "I meant it."

I swallow and force the words out. "Me too. Axl, I—" Once again they stick.

Before I have a chance to try again, Axl grabs me and pulls me to him. He presses his mouth to mine, and all the air leaves my lungs. I run my hand through his wet hair and pull myself closer as his tongue explores my mouth. His hands run down my back, burning my skin. They stops at my hips and he lifts me up, moving me over so I'm on top. Straddling him. When he kisses me again, it's more passionate than before, more urgent. Every nerve in my body comes alive. Tingling, begging for more.

I move my hands over his chest, exploring every muscle and dip. My lips brush against the scar on his chin, then move lower. His neck, his collar, his chest, his stomach. Teasing his skin with my tongue. He groans and pulls me up. His tongue moves down my neck to my chest, and his mouth closes over my right breast. I moan when his tongue flicks the small ring that pierces my nipple.

I lose all sense of time as we kiss. Everything fades away. The dead aren't walking the streets, we're not trapped on the roof of this casino. The only things that exist are Axl's hands and mouth on my body and the pleasure he's giving me. All I can focus on are the two of us together and the fact that somewhere between Route 66 and here, I fell in love with Axl. I never even saw it coming.

111

We're both breathing heavily, and I'm once again covered in a layer of sweat. His skin is warm and moist against mine. My hand creeps down his stomach. Under the waistband of his boxers. I tug on them, trying to remove the last bit of clothing that either one of us is wearing. But his hand pushes me back and he pulls away.

Seriously? He's stopping me? After all this he's going to stop? "What are you doing?"

He sits up and runs his hand through his hair. "No condoms."

Thank you, Hadley!

"Is that so?" I say, flashing him a mischievous smile.

"You plan ahead?"

My jeans are crumpled on the floor next to the lounge chair. I scoop them up and dig in the back pocket. Hopefully it didn't fall out somewhere between Sam's Club and here. My fingers brush against plastic and my grin widens. I got lucky, for once. I pull the condom out and flash it at Axl. His smile gets so big it makes him look five years younger.

He snatches it out of my hand and pulls me down on top of him. His mouth covers mine, and heat moves through me. I reach for the waistband of his boxers while he rips the foil packet open. I can't get his clothes off fast enough.

I toss his boxers aside, and he slips the condom on. His eyes search my face. "You're sure?"

"I've never been more sure of anything in my life. If we die tomorrow, I know I'll die happy because I had you."

He pushes me onto my back and leans over me. His lips move against mine as he slides inside me, and I raise my hips to meet his. I dig my nails into his back as he pushes deeper.

"We ain't gonna die tomorrow," he says against my lips

CHAPTER ELEVEN

Axl and I huddle together in a cabana as darkness descends on Vegas. With the sun no longer up, the air has turned chilly, and my body is covered in goose bumps. We've gathered every hotel towel we could find to try and keep warm, but it isn't working. I shiver so hard my teeth rattle together.

Axl wraps his arms around me and pulls me against his chest. "We gotta get you a sweatshirt."

"C-caesar's P-palace, p-please." The words shake like someone put them in one of those old scrambler rides you used to find at state fairs. I press my teeth together to try and stop them from clattering. My jaw still quivers.

He chuckles and rubs my arms. "I'll see what I can do."

Now that the euphoria from sex has worn off, reality has come crashing down on me. It was an amazing distraction while it lasted. It's just too bad it couldn't be forever. The jar of cherries is gone and so are the olives. All we have left to eat is a handful of nuts. I'm not dressed for cool weather, and we're pretty exposed to the sun during the day. We lost almost all our weapons in the car. Things are not looking good.

Who knows how long we'll be stuck in Vegas.

It's eerily quiet on the roof of the hotel, and being up here makes it seem like Axl and I are the last two people on the planet. Of course, that would probably be a welcome alternative to what's really happening. The undead walking the streets below us is much more terrifying than Axl and I being alone for all of eternity.

I shiver, but this time it's not because I'm cold. "All those bodies walking all over the city, maybe forever. It's so depressing."

Axl presses his lips to my forehead. I sigh when his warm breath caresses my hair. "You never call 'em zombies. Just bodies or the dead."

My chest tightens. He's right. I try to keep myself from even thinking the word. It's too scary.

"The word's just too crazy. I can't even bring myself to think it, let alone say it. Like saying it will make it more real or something." I sigh and lean my head against his shoulder. "I don't want all this to be real."

"It's plenty real without sayin' the word."

"True." I whisper, shivering again. "When do you think Angus will show up?"

He sighs, and I can picture him pursing his lips. I've gotten to know him so well. It's like we've been together for years, not weeks. "He probably wanted to run out soon as they got back without us. He ain't one to really think things through. If I had to guess, I'd say Winston or somebody talked some sense into him. Got him to agree to go in the mornin' so they had time to plan. We'll just have to keep our ears open come sunup. They'll come back to the casino to look for us, I'm sure of it."

My chest is tight. They have no idea where we are, and the Strip is huge. What if they can't find us? What do we do then? "How do you know they'll come here?"

"'Cause it's what I'd do. If Winston was the one who got left behind, I woulda come right back to the last place I saw him. Me an' him seem to think alike, so that's what I'd put my money on."

My lips curl into a smile despite the tension in my body. Who knows if Axl ever harbored the same racist feelings as his brother, but if he did, they seem to be wiped away now. I have a feeling he didn't feel that way, though. Maybe he thought he did, but I doubt it was real. Axl's too good to take any of that shit seriously.

I snuggle closer, and his arms tighten around me. I've never felt as safe and secure as I do in his arms. Never had anyone treat me as good as he does either. I dated a lot of assholes, and most ended up being just like my dad. They liked to slap me around when they got mad. Not Axl, though.

Being left behind isn't ideal, but being here with Axl is kind of nice. "Morning, then," I whisper.

"Mornin'," he says, kissing the top of my head.

A cool breeze whips across the roof and seems to blow straight into the cabana. I shiver and scoot closer to Axl. My backside is pressed up against his crotch.

"So we just have to try and stay warm between now and then." I can think of a few ways to achieve that.

Axl chuckles, and his lips brush against my neck. Shivers of pleasure shoot through my body. I wiggle against him, and he groans. He grabs my hips and pulls me closer. He's hard again.

"I hear body heat's good for that," he says against the sensitive skin on my neck.

I twist to face him, and his lips find mine. He pulls my body against his. Within seconds, the shivers are gone and the goose bumps have disappeared. His tongue brushes against my lips, and my blood heats up. It's like he's my own personal electric blanket. Body heat definitely works. Not only am I no longer cold, I'm on fire.

He runs his hand down my neck and over my chest, between my breasts. He pauses just long enough to tease me before moving to the button on my pants.

It takes every ounce of willpower inside me to pull away, and my body is cursing me for doing it. "We can't. I only had one condom, and I don't want to risk it. Not without protection."

"Shit," he mutters.

His hand moves over my back to my ass, and he pulls me closer. I moan when he grinds against me. "What are you doing?" My voice sounds tortured. I feel tortured with him moving against me like that, knowing that I can't do anything about it.

His lips move over my neck to my chest. He pulls my shirt over my head, and his tongue runs over bare skin. I never put my bra back on.

"We can't," I whisper. "I want to, but we can't."

"Don't need a condom." It's too dark to get a good look at him, but the teasing in his voice is obvious. "You got a mouth, don't ya?"

I laugh and shove him playfully. "So do you."

He pauses and pulls away. His eyes glint in the dark cabana. "Damn right I do," he growls.

He flips me onto my back, and before I have a chance to react, my pants are a tangled mess on the floor of the cabana. His hands move up the inside of my thighs, and his lips are right behind them. I throw my head back and close my eyes, tangling my hands in his hair while his tongue moves over my skin.

MY EYES FLY OPEN, AND THE SUN IS SO BRIGHT THAT I'm pretty sure my corneas are toast. I squeeze them shut and cover my face with my arm, trying to register what's going on. There's a shrill howl in the distance. It's vaguely familiar, but I can't focus. My brain is too fuzzy.

Axl bolts out of the lounge chair and I go flying. Our bodies were so tangled that I end up on the floor. On my ass. I crack one eye and rub my throbbing right cheek. That's going to leave a mark.

The cement is cold under my bare butt, but I don't move. Axl stumbles out of the chair, just as naked as I am, and a big grin spreads across his face. My brain finally starts working, and my hand stops moving mid-rub. A car alarm. That's what that sound is. Hallelujah we are saved!

"That's gotta be him." Axl pulls his shirt on while sweeping his boxers off the floor. He darts out of the cabana, still naked from the waist down.

I scramble around on my hands and knees in search of my clothes. My underwear is MIA, so I pull my jeans on without them. My bra's laying at my feet, but who gives a shit about that. I want to get the hell out of this city. I yank my shirt on and run after Axl, grabbing his pants on my way out.

"Fuck yeah!" he yells. He squeezes through the small opening between the cabanas and runs back toward me with a huge grin on his face. "It's Angus! Knew that son of a bitch would be here."

He yanks his pants out of my hand and pulls them on. He doesn't even bother to button them before he heads over to get his shoes.

I'm still groggy and having a hard time focusing on what I should be doing. Yeah, shoes would be a good idea. Axl is waiting for me by the time I'm done. He already has his backpack on and he holds mine out for me to take. I grab it as we head toward the door, yanking out my knife and throwing the pack over my shoulder without missing a step.

We start pulling chairs away from the door. We've gotten down to the final two when an explosion just like the one from the day before shatters the silence on the roof.

Axl's eyes get big, and we turn to see a huge cloud of

smoke float into the air. It's close. Maybe only one street over. It looks pitch black against the clear blue sky

"Angus?" I ask.

Axl flashes me a grin. There's an admiration in his eyes that Angus in no way deserves. He gives his brother too much credit. "Bastard never does anythin' half-assed."

I have a difficult time maintaining my smile.

I pull the last chair away and motion toward the door. "Well, between the car alarm and the explosion, we should be in the clear."

"Let's hope so," Axl says as yanks the door open.

We rush into the stairwell without pausing, and I pray it's as clear as it was the day before. It smells okay, which is a pretty good indication the dead aren't around, so I try to control my pounding heart as we run through the darkness. An impossible task, really.

When we reach the first floor, Axl shoves the door open and we stumble into the casino. The building is stuffy, and the air reeks of rotten flesh. My heart goes into triple time. If I'm not careful, I'm going to have a heart attack one of these days.

We pause just outside the door and look around. The moans of the dead float back to us from somewhere inside the building, but at the moment, no bodies are in sight. We might be okay. What are the odds that we can make it to the Strip without running into any of the dead? Pretty slim, but then again, crazier things have happened. Like a zombie apocalypse.

"Stay close," Axl says. He grabs my hand and pulls me forward.

My calves burn as we rush through the hotel, and my heart beats a million miles a minute. I grip my knife so tight I can practically feel callouses forming on my palm. The moans get louder, but we still haven't seen a single body. The rooms are so empty that it makes my legs shake. Where the hell are they? It's nerve-wracking, waiting for them to show up. We pass the casino, just as dark as yesterday, and head toward the front. The floors and walls are marble and ornate, but dirty from neglect. Splatters of blood add a foreboding feeling to the room.

I glance into the bar as we pass it, and my legs stop moving. There's a lone woman in the room, and she's surrounded by bodies. Seven or eight of them moan and howl as they try to get at her. They can't quite reach her, though. She's behind a grand piano, wedged between it and the wall holding an aluminum baseball bat. She swings it at them, warding them off. Her face is red and streaked with dirt, and her bleached blonde hair is a tangled mess. Her brown eyes are huge and wild with fear. My heart pounds, and I blink a few times. My eyes are playing tricks on me. They have to be.

But they aren't. She's ten years older than the last time I saw her and looks every day of it, but I'd recognize that face anywhere. My dad never got rid of her pictures when she ran off. I looked at her face every day of my young life. Missing her at first and cursing her later.

My hand tightens around Axl's.

"We gonna help her?" he asks. It makes me jump.

He's breathing heavily, and when his eyes focus on me, he frowns. He isn't thrilled about the idea of running to her rescue. I pull my pack up higher on my shoulder. It's weighed down from the water bottles we took and getting heavier by the second. Plus, Angus is outside waiting for us and we have a very short window of opportunity. It'd be a tough decision to make, even if it wasn't the mother who abandoned me.

She makes a face as she swings the bat. Her mouth scrunches up and her eyes grow hard. It transports me back in time and almost knocks me on my ass. That's exactly how she looked when she'd tell me to get lost. My heart turns to stone. Just like it did when she ran out on me.

Bitterness fills my mouth, so intense I have to fight the

urge to spit. I shake my head and turn away from her. "There are too many. It's a lost cause."

Axl nods and pulls me toward the exit. Away from my mother and my past.

CHAPTER TWELVE

I've only taken two steps when she screams. The sound goes straight through me, breaking through the bitterness and piercing my already shattered insides. It stops me in my tracks. My legs won't move another step no matter how much I want them to.

I look back just as she slams the bat into the side of a dead man's skull. The black ooze sprays everywhere, spattering her and the dead surrounding her. She lets out a scream that reminds me of a battle cry.

"Shit!" I yank my hand out of Axl's and turn back toward the bar, tossing my pack on the ground as I take off. What the hell am I doing? She never gave a damn about me, and here I'm ready to risk my life to save her. I'm an idiot!

Axl is right on my heels when I reach the bodies. I slam my knife into the skull of the nearest one before they even notice us. When it falls to the ground, I move on to the next. Black splatters against my face and arms, but I keep going.

Taking out one after the other as fast as I can. Axl does the same.

I'm gasping for breath when the last one hits the ground, but even then I can't look her in the eye. There's no way she recognizes me. I was ten when she left. But I'm still too terrified to meet her gaze. I focus on her mouth. It looks exactly like mine.

She's panting, and her lips turns up into tense smile. "Thanks."

The sound of her voice after all these years makes my insides twist painfully. I hate that she still has the power to make me feel so small.

"No time for that," Axl says. "We're leavin' now. You come with us or not. Your choice."

He grabs my hand and pulls me toward the door. I barely have time to grab my pack off the ground as I run by it. He's pulling me so hard. The alarm is still blaring outside, but it isn't loud enough to drown out the sound of the footsteps behind me. She's coming with us. It fills me with dread and doubt and fear and too many other emotions to process in the middle of all this shit.

We rush out the front door and head to the street. I have to squint against the sun after the darkness of the casino. The area is pretty clear thanks to the alarm and the explosion, and when we get to the sidewalk, I have the urge to jump with joy. The Nissan is parked about twenty feet away, not too far from our abandoned Explorer.

The back door flies open before we're even halfway there, and the driver's window rolls down. Angus sticks his head out. "Where the hell you been?"

I laugh. I'm so happy to see his ugly face I could kiss him. "Waiting for you!"

His eyes go past us, probably to the woman trailing behind. He grins.

Axl pauses at the car and tosses his pack in. "The road's pretty clear. Gotta get somethin' outta the Explorer before we take off."

Angus purses his lips. "Leave it! We gotta git!"

Axl shakes his head and takes off toward the Explorer. My mom stands next to the Nissan awkwardly, looking back and forth between Axl and Angus. I can't even think about getting in the car with her, so I toss my bag in and run after Axl.

He has the back door open and I get there just as he pulls out a body and tosses it on the sidewalk. It lands at my feet, and the milky eyes stare up at me. Flies circle the open areas, and the stench is so strong I gag.

I cover my nose. "You need help."

"Probably."

He throws out another body, and I step over it so I can help him. I don't want to. Touching the rotting corpses we killed yesterday makes me want to puke. But I know Axl is going for the guns, and he's right. We need them.

He climbs in and stands on top of the mass of dead so he can pull them aside. He has to move three before I catch sight of the bag. I grab the strap and tug, but it barely moves. Axl grunts when he yanks one more corpse out of the way. This time when I pull, the bag comes free.

I stumble back, almost tripping over my feet. The bag flies out at me, and it's so heavy that I'm one hundred percent sure it will knock me down. I brace myself to land on my still sore ass when hands wrap around my forearms, stopping me from falling. I let out a sigh of relief a split second before my eyes focus on the fingers. They're female. The nails are neon pink and pointy.

"Whoa there, honey. You almost ate it."

I cringe and shake her hands off. "Thanks."

I push my matted hair out of my face as Axl jumps out. He lugs the bag up and jerks his head toward the car. "Let's get a move on."

I turn around and come face to face with a corpse so rotten his skin is practically dripping. He chomps his teeth and reaches for me, but I'm ready. When I swing my knife around, it sinks into his eye socket. His mouth drops open, and his body slumps to the floor, taking my knife with him.

"Let's go," Axl says, grabbing my arm and attempting to pull me toward the car.

I shrug him off. "My knife!"

I pull on it, but the head comes up too. So I put my foot on his forehead and press his skull to the ground while I yank harder. The blade slides out, and what looks like brain matter is stuck to the knife. I wipe it on the zombie's clothes before turning to follow Axl.

More bodies stumble our way. My mom swings her bat, and it connects with the nearest head. Black goo sprays out like a sprinkler, dotting us all in the foul-smelling liquid. Axl steps in front of me when a woman in a lace nightie lurches for us. He stabs her in the head, then grunts when he pulls the knife back out.

"Let's go!" he yells, shoving me toward the car.

I jog toward the Nissan with sweat dripping down my back. Angus's face is bright red, and the vein on his forehead is visible through the windshield. The door is still open, and Axl pushes me in the backseat of the car before climbing in after me. He tosses the bag of guns in the back and scoots over to make room for our new addition. My mom gets in behind him and pulls the door shut just as Angus puts the car in gear.

"That was dumb as shit," he growls. "What was so important that you had to run back there after all that? You barely make it out one night and you think you gotta throw your life away?"

Axl rolls his eyes. "Guns, Angus. Just drop it."

He exhales, then a big smile curls up his lips. "Damn, it's good to see you! I knew you'd come." Axl leans forward and slaps his brother on the shoulder.

Angus grunts and presses down on the accelerator. Guess he's still pissed.

Nathan, showered and clean shaven, is in the passenger seat. I expected Winston or Trey. But not him. It's a wonder Moira let him out of her sight.

He turns and gives us a tense smile. "I'm glad you're alright. What you did for us yesterday—" He shakes his head and looks away when his eyes fill with tears.

Angus makes a sound that resembles the word pussy, masked inside a cough.

I roll my eyes at Angus, then pat Nathan on the arm. "We just wanted to make sure those kids had a chance to get out of here."

Nathan nods and he looks like he wants to say more, but he's clearly too choked up to talk about it. The thought of losing your wife and child will do that to a person. Especially when you're one of the few people left in the world who still has something to hold onto.

"You guys cause that explosion yesterday?" Axl asks.

Nathan clears his throat and nods. "Winston pulled over as soon as we were on a less crowded street. Trey, Jhett, and I held them off while he got a fire going at a gas station. It took out the station and a couple of cars parked by the pumps."

"It saved our asses, that's what it did," Axl says. "Couple seconds later and we woulda been nothin' more than blood splatters on the inside of that car."

"You pick up a straggler?" Angus asks, looking over his shoulder.

His jaw is tight, and that little vein on his forehead pulsates. Guess he doesn't like talking about how close his little brother came to death. It's moments like these when I find myself almost liking the guy. Almost.

"Grabbed her on the way out," Axl says. He twists in his seat so he's facing my mom. "Didn't even catch your name."

Angus's head practically turns all the way around so he can get a better view. His gaze zeroes in on her chest, and I fight the urge to hurl. He's actually checking out my mom. I guess it's understandable. He doesn't know it's my mom, and she still has a decent body. Plus, she's wearing tight, revealing clothes. Sure she's splattered in zombie blood, but she still looks good. Well, she looks like an aging showgirl, which is probably exactly what she is. She and Angus are even close to the same age. She's only thirty-seven, and he can't be much younger than that...

I shudder. The thought is just too disturbing to entertain.

"Darla," she says. "And thanks for helping me out. I thought that there was the end for sure."

"Couldn't just leave you," Axl says, glancing my way.

He introduces himself and Angus and gives her a brief rundown of where they came from. Fear prickles up my spine after he's introduced Nathan. My turn is next. Will she make the connection? It's not really something I want to deal with right now. Or ever, really. I wish she'd stayed behind. No way I could have walked away and let the zombies get her, but I don't want her here. Not in the shelter, trapped underground with me where I can't get away. Where I'll never be able to escape her stupid face and her smug smile and all the memories of how awful my childhood was and how lost I felt when she walked out.

I blink when Axl starts asking her questions about where she's been and what she's seen. Skipping me altogether. He glances toward me, but his expression is blank. He knows something is up, but he's giving me space. How does he always know when there's more to the story?

I lace my fingers through his while my mom—Darla—tells us all about her career as a topless dancer at Bally's. Axl stares down at our hands, then up at my face. His stormy eyes search mine for a few seconds before he looks away. He squeezes my hand, and something I've never felt before pinches my insides. Trust, maybe?

"Well, 'bout three years ago I kinda hit that point where things weren't quite as perky as they used to be, so I had to switch jobs." She grabs her boobs and I cringe. Angus is watching in the rearview mirror, and I swear he drools. "The hotel's real good 'bout keeping us girls on though, and I was able to get a job as a waitress in the casino. Serving drinks to the people playing poker and blackjack. That kinda thing. The tips are real good. Were real good. Guess it's all gone now." She sighs and shakes her head like it's the saddest thing in the world.

My face heats up, and I have to clench my jaw to keep from screaming at her. The forlorn look on her face when she talks about losing her precious career in Vegas is insulting. Maybe I should have left her ass to get eaten.

"You and Blondie back there'll have a lot in common. She danced around in the nude too." Angus's eyes lock with mine in the rearview mirror and he wiggles his eyebrows.

I give him the finger, which only seems to make him more excited. Sicko. I wonder if he'll stop making suggestive comments after he finds out Axl and I are together. Doubt it. He knows about the sauna, so I'd be willing to bet he assumes we screwed in Vegas.

Darla leans forward and looks me up and down. She has a big grin on her face. Shit. I look exactly like her. How can she not see it?

"You work at a casino, sweetie?"

"No." It's all I can get out, and even that sounds strained.

Angus looks back, and his eyes zero in on Darla's cleavage. "She was a stripper in Kentucky. Not nearly so glamorous."

"Shut up, Angus," Axl barks.

Darla frowns and shakes her head, wrinkling her nose at me. "Oh, no. That's not the same at all."

She's actually looking down on me? Like she's better than I am! A woman who left her ten-year-old daughter alone with an abusive man thinks she's better than me. I glare at her and squeeze Axl's hand tighter, digging my nails into his skin. He winces and yanks his hand back. He's staring at me, but I can't focus on anything except Darla and her stupid face. I want to punch her so hard all her teeth fall

127

out. Maybe she'll swallow a few. Choke on them.

I can only hope.

I try to block out her constant chatter, but it's impossible. She talks the whole freaking drive. Even when Angus is trying to get details from us about where we stayed and how we got out of the car, she's blathering on. She asks us nonstop questions about the shelter and tells every little detail of her life. Well, almost every detail. Her childhood, her marriage at a young age to an abusive man, how she ran off and left him. Every moment of her life in Vegas since then. The only part she leaves out is how she abandoned her only child. She glosses over it like it's nothing. Like *I'm* nothing.

By the time we get back to the shelter, I have a headache from listening to her, and I'm so angry I'm about to explode.

CHAPTER THIRTEEN

The sight of the shelter looming in the distance should thrill me, especially with Darla's constant chatter and my overwhelming desire to punch her stupid face. But it doesn't, for two main reasons. One, it's still surrounded by a mob of undead. Two, the Sam's Club truck is parked outside the fence. It's clearly too big to fit inside. Something that never even occurred to me when we were loading it up at the store.

Darla is still talking, I don't even know about what, but like me, Axl is focused on the truck. "How much did you get inside?" Axl asks, totally cutting Darla off.

"Not much," Nathan says. "Trey and I managed to unload a little while Winston held them off, but things were just too crazy. Between the zombies, you two missing, and people coming out of the shelter to see what was going on, it was…tough." His face is tense, and he avoids looking at Angus.

Angus, of course, was the one causing the problems. I'm sure his reaction to them showing up without us was colorful. Well, without Axl. I doubt he cared much about me.

"We'll take care of it. Wasn't a priority before," Angus says.

"So what's the plan?" I ask. "How are we getting all that stuff in?"

Nathan shakes his head and glances toward Angus like he's afraid to say anything. He's nothing like the confident, in-control man who made me strip in Sam's Club. He looks like he's intimidated by Angus.

"Let's just get inside then we can figure it out. 'Kay, Blondie?"

When I roll my eyes, Axl gives my hand a squeeze. I could prove myself to be the most useful person in our group, maybe even save Angus's ass or something, and I'd still just be the blonde, trailer trash stripper to him.

I give Axl's hand a quick squeeze in return, then reach for the door. "I'll get the gate."

"Here," Angus says as he tosses a key to Axl. "Found us a lock inside so we don't hafta use them ties no more."

Guess Axl is coming to back me up.

Angus pulls up to the fence, and I jump out before we've even come to a complete stop. The back of the truck is to my left, and most of the dead are hanging around the front of it. We have a little time before they make it to us. Axl hands me the key, and I head over to unlatch the gate while he stands guard.

The dead come at us within seconds. They don't run, but they're not exactly slow either. It's more like they stagger toward us. The movements aren't fluid, and there's nothing about the way they walk that could be mistaken for human. Their arms hang loosely at their sides, as if they have a mind of their own. They occasionally reach out mindlessly, their hands clasping at the air while they walk. They claw their fingers and chomp their mouths, letting out moans and shrieks. Sounds I'm sure no human has ever made.

My heart pounds and beads of sweat break out on my forehead, but I do my best not to pay attention to them. I focus solely on the fence and getting that lock open. My hands shake just a little, not making it easy in the least. But the fear isn't for me. With my eyes focused on the lock, I have no idea what Axl's doing, but I can hear and smell the dead getting closer. Their presence invades my senses, and my entire body tingles and screams at me to turn around and help Axl. I don't like having my back to him, not knowing if he's okay. Everything is different now that I've admitted to myself that I'm in love with him.

After what feels like an eternity, the lock comes undone, and I shove the gate open so Angus can drive through. He looks pissed. The vein is even bigger than before. He was probably cursing my slowness the entire time I was trying to get the gate open.

Axl and I jog in behind the Nissan. He helps me push the gate shut, then takes out a body that gets too close for comfort. With the last bullet in his gun. The one he had saved for himself. The realization hits me so hard I have a difficult time filling my lungs. My legs shake, and if it wasn't so damn hot and smelly out here, I'd lay down on the ground. But at least we're safe. Both of us.

Without thinking, I throw my arms around Axl and kiss him.

"Guess you two had more fun up on that roof than you're lettin' on," Angus says when he climbs out of the car. "Hope you didn't knock 'er up. We don't need no more apocalypse babies."

Axl leaves his arm around my waist and pulls me close as we walk toward the shelter. I bury my face in his chest. I don't want to give Angus the satisfaction of replying. It doesn't matter to me what he says or what he thinks. I'm just happy Axl and I are alive.

"You're an ass, Angus," Axl says.

There's something light in his tone that makes me look up. The corner of his mouth is pulled up just a bit, and his face is softer than usual. I glance toward Angus. His expression is almost exactly the same. God, it's crazy how alike they look sometimes. I guess that was just playful banter between brothers? It's hard to tell with these two sometimes.

Nathan has already disappeared inside the shelter. Probably in a hurry to get back to Moira. Darla stands by the door awkwardly. She looks suddenly scared, like it just occurred to her she got in the car with four people she doesn't know and let them take her out in the middle of nowhere. Her uncertainty doesn't help lessen the bitterness eating away at my insides, that's for sure.

"Come on," Angus says, waving her over. "I'd call ya Blondie, but we already got us one. Gonna have to think of something better to call you..." He stares right at her tits. I'd be willing to bet he has a few dozen things going through his head that he'd like to call her. All of which would make me vomit.

We head down, and the second we reach the first level we're surrounded by people. Everyone must have been waiting in the control room for us to get back.

Hadley swoops in before anyone else has a chance, giving me a big hug. I pat her back awkwardly. I'm not much of a hugger and we don't know one another *that* well, and this is our second hug since we met. She steps back and swipes her hand across her face. She isn't crying, but her expression is pinched. Like she's trying to hold back the tears. She must have been really worried about us.

"Thank God you got back! Angus swore that Axl would get you guys to a safe place, but when Winston and Trey were talking about how crazy it was and how many zombies were on the Strip I just—" She swallows and shakes her head.

"Sorry we couldn't get back to you," Winston says. His left eye is slightly swollen, and there's a long, dark bruise going from the corner of his eye to midway down his cheek. Angus must have really lost it.

"We did what needed to be done, an' so did you," Axl says, shaking his hand and patting him on the arm. "Nobody needs to be sorry. You saved our asses by startin' that fire."

Angus stares at the ground. His face is bright red, and the vein on his forehead is even more prominent than before. What the hell went on when they got back without us?

I'm filthy and too exhausted to focus on Angus, though. We'll have to deal with it later. Right now, all I want is a shower. Too bad we have all that shit to unload from the truck.

"So, what's the plan for unloading the supplies?" I have to raise my voice over the talking—a lot of it being Darla's since she's busy recounting her days as a topless dancer to Hadley.

"We're going to have to get as many people out there as we can and get rid of the zombies," Winston says.

He's stating the obvious, so it shouldn't feel like he's reading a death sentence. But it does. And why wouldn't it? He very well could be for a few of us.

"We got an idea how many of them bastards is out there?" Axl asks.

James sits at the desk in the control room, and just like the first time we came into the room, he pushes his chair out and spins it around. He crosses his arms over his chest as we all stare at him. Guess he likes being important. It's probably a new thing for him.

"I've been watching them. There's about thirty out there right now, give or take. The numbers keep growing. For every one we kill on our way in or out of the fence, two replace it. They're stumbling in from somewhere off in the desert. My guess is they're drawn here. Maybe the building is giving off some sort of electrical hum or something that we can't hear and they can."

"So you're tellin' me they got super-hearin' now?" Angus

asks, pursing his lips and narrowing his eyes like he doesn't believe James.

Winston rubs his eyes and shakes his head. He looks exhausted. "Like a dog or something?"

James just shrugs. He doesn't talk, and neither does anyone else. The room is so quiet we would be able to hear a mouse fart. I'm not sure if the silence is from disbelief or fear. Hell, there are a thousand emotions going through me right now, and everyone else is probably feeling the same thing. But mainly the news just makes me tired. Deep down in my bones.

"I hate to say it," Winston says. He's looking right at Axl. "But it makes sense. Think of how many were roaming up and down the Strip. Of all the buildings and places in Vegas, those hotels are most likely to have generators in them. Maybe just small ones, but still. Could be people hiding out in some of the hotels, trying to take them back and using the generators."

My brain somehow surfaces from the fog of exhaustion surrounding it. What he says explains a lot and makes perfect sense. It's what we did when we got to the hotel in San Francisco, so why wouldn't another group get the same idea? A hotel's a good place to hide if you can clear out the bodies and get the power going. It'd have everything you'd need to live on.

"We didn't see no lights on the Strip after dark," Axl says. He shakes his head and purses his lips, but he thinks Winston's right. I can tell.

"The generators would probably be programmed for minimum electrical use. Just the inside of the hotel, not the lights outside. It would save electricity and keep things within the city's fire code in the event of an emergency."

"You know, now that you mention it, I did notice some activity down by the Monte Carlo. There wasn't no lights or nothing, but I saw men go in and out a few times," Darla says. "I thought 'bout going over to see who it was, but you just can't trust people these days. They'll leave you high and dry first chance they get."

I let out a bitter laugh and then quickly cover my mouth. A few people stare at me, but most are too busy thinking or asking questions. Axl narrows his eyes on my face, but I just shake my head. I'll talk to him about it later.

"Let's just get this over with," I say, once again interrupting everyone. I want a shower.

Winston nods and glances around. We've got a good-sized group: me, Axl, Angus, Winston, James, Trey, Nathan, and Hadley. Maybe even Darla, although I have a feeling she's a pretty useless person despite the fight she was putting up in the bar when we found her. But we can always use more.

"Let's round up as many people as we can and get armed. We need guns and knives. I want to try and save as much of the ammo as we can, so I'd like for people to go in with knives first." Winston pauses, then turns to Angus. "That good with you?"

Angus nods and puffs out his chest like he's trying to make himself taller. Winston has never deferred to that racist bastard's opinion before. It reminds me of how timid Nathan was in the car.

Angus is standing off to the side by himself. No one but Winston, Axl, and I will even look at him. And Darla, but she doesn't count. What the hell happened while we were gone?

CHAPTER FOURTEEN

We manage to get twelve people together, which means we each only have to take out three of the undead. It should be pretty quick and painless. At least that's what I've been telling myself. Standing in the heat with the zombies just a few feet away, shaking the fence as they desperately try to get at us, I'm not so sure. The desert sun feels like a volcano, and the air reeks of decay. I just want to get this thing done so I can get inside, shower, and rest.

"This is going to suck," Hadley says.

Al bounces around like he can't keep still. He passes his knife back and forth between his hands. He looks excited. Like he's been waiting for this day for years. Maybe he has. He was a huge zombie nut before all this. Even though he claims reality isn't as exciting, the huge smile on his face seems to say otherwise.

"We shouldn't open it," he says.

Angus grunts and spits on the ground. "How we gonna get 'em?"

"Through the holes. I saw it on TV." Al steps forward and jams his knife through the fence. He catches one in the side of the head, and it falls to the ground. "See? Minimal effort and less risk."

"Shoulda watched more zombie shit, I guess," Axl says.

It seems like a better idea than letting the zombies in, but there's still room for error. The holes in the fence are big enough for the dead to get most of their hands through, and from what Nathan has said, it's possible to turn just from a scratch. We still need to be careful.

We follow Al's lead and jab our knives through the holes. It works like a charm, and I'm pretty sure the kid's a genius. The bodies are falling faster than panties at a frat party.

Human grunts mix with the moans of the dead as the sun pounds down on us from above. Hair sticks to my neck, and my shirt is so wet with sweat that I'm pretty sure it's transparent. Angus stops stabbing the dead and looks my way, and the way his eyes bulge out pretty much confirms my suspicion. He's practically drooling at my double D's.

I shove strings of blonde hair out of my face and take a deep breath while I push all thoughts of Angus out of my head. I don't need to be distracted right now. As it is, my heart is going so fast that it's hard to control my breathing. I'm exhausted, and my energy level is on empty.

But we're almost done. I can hold out just a little bit longer.

I stab my blade through the fence, and it sinks into a monster's eye socket. The dead man starts to fall, almost taking my knife with him. I grip the handle tighter while I try to yank it back. When half my hand gets pulled through the fence, another body sees his opportunity for dinner and goes in for the kill. His fingers wrap around my hand. I scream and pull back. The bastard moans as he jerks me forward. My heart pounds so fast it vibrates inside my skull. I twist my hand, but it doesn't work. The dead man's teeth are inches from my hand when Axl's knife sinks into the decaying head.

"Shit!" I yank my hand back and cover it with the other.

"Did he get you? Let me see." Axl pulls my hand toward him and examines my fingers. Every muscle in his body is pulled tight.

"I'm okay. He didn't get me."

Axl doesn't seem to be able to hear me, and he won't let go of my hand. He flips it over and even checks out the other one to make sure it's okay as well.

"Axl, I'm okay." I take his face between my hands and force him to look at me. "He didn't get me."

He nods, but his jaw is tight as he hands me his extra knife.

My heart is still pounding like a jackhammer when I turn back to the fence. *Get it together and be careful, you moron!*

The air is full of moans and grunts. The smell of death and the clang of metal on metal as knives make contact with the fence is so overwhelming I have a hard time focusing. Hadley is on the other side of me, wielding her knife like a pro. Maybe that zombie movie she was in helped prepare her for this a little.

We're making good progress, but there are a handful of bodies outside the fence that aren't interested in getting close. They stagger back and forth, a safe distance from our blades, stopping every now and then to moan and claw in our direction. It's unsettling, and a little knot of dread forms in my stomach. There's something about the way they shuffle around, stopping to stare at us, that worries me. Almost like they know not to get too close. Like they're planning their attack.

By the time we've taken down the last one we can reach from behind the fence, I'm breathing heavily. My shirt is so wet it clings to my chest no matter what I do. I wish I was wearing a bra. Angus is just loving it.

I'm not the only one panting, though. Everyone is standing back now, trying to catch their breath before the next part. The part that requires opening the gate for an extended amount of time.

"What do you think 'bout that?" Axl says, tilting his head toward the stragglers.

Winston's dark skin glistens with sweat. He shakes his head and wipes his brow with the back of his arm. "Not sure. You don't suppose they understand what's going on?"

Axl shrugs, but Angus makes a grunting sound that's both rude and disgusting. "They don't understand shit. They're just hanging back 'cause they're stupid."

Angus is underestimating the situation. That's my opinion, anyway, but I keep it to myself. No sense freaking people out unnecessarily by throwing around theories about the evolution of the undead. Even if it seems pretty likely by the way those things stare at us.

"Let's just go on out there an' get 'em," Axl says.

He nods to Angus, who holds the key to the gate, something Axl and I are going to have to discuss. I'm not sure exactly what happened while we were gone—although I have a pretty good idea—but from the way Angus is guarding that key, I get the impression he's taken control of things. People shouldn't feel like they're prisoners. Being underground is hard enough without thinking there's no way to escape.

"Everybody ready?" Angus calls, turning the key without waiting for a response.

The second he opens the door, the bodies move toward us, solidifying the theory in my mind. There are only five of them, though. Angus pulls out his gun and takes three down in a matter of seconds, completely disregarding what Winston said. No one bats an eye, not even Winston himself, who takes a fourth one out with a knife to the back of the skull. The fifth one hits the ground when Axl brings his hunting knife down on the top of its head, driving the blade right into its brain.

Trey has the back of the truck open before the last body has fallen, and we start unloading. It's hot and exhausting work. Not to mention stressful, since we have to keep looking over our shoulders to make sure no other bodies have wandered over. Our goal is to just get the supplies into the building for now. That way, they're out of the sun and inside the fence. We can worry about getting stuff down the stairs and into the actual shelter later. After the sun goes down and it's a bit cooler.

Even though the truck's full, we make quick progress. With twelve of us working, it doesn't take long to get to the back of the truck. A hell of a lot less time than I thought it would, actually. I let out a sigh of relief when I go back for more and see there's hardly anything left.

"Incoming!" James yells behind me.

I spin around and find three bodies lumbering toward him. He's shaking in his Nikes, and based on the terrified expression on his face, I'm worried he's about to shit his pants. Anne, Hadley, and I run over to help him.

I wave off Axl when he tries to come too. "You big, strong men get the rest of that stuff inside," I yell, winking at him as I head off.

James swings his knife at the first one just as we run up, but his aim is too low and he ends up hitting the thing in the cheek instead of the head. It reels away from him, taking the knife with it. The monster has his hands around James's neck before I can react. I take my own knife and stab it into his skull. The hands go slack, and the body sinks to the ground, releasing James.

I turn to help Anne and Hadley, not even bothering to check on James. He's a grown ass man, after all, and the thing's mouth didn't get anywhere near him. Anne's knife gets stuck in the head of a dead woman wearing desert camo, less than an inch shy of its mark. She whips her gun out as the decaying woman—who smells really ripe in the hot sun—lunges at her. The bullet pierces the woman right between the eyes. Hadley, on the other hand, has no problems taking out another former soldier. He's dead on the ground before I even have a chance to see if she needs help.

James is sitting on the ground when I turn back around, clutching his neck. He's as white as a sheet. I roll my eyes and open my mouth to tell him to pull himself together. That's when I notice the blood on his chin.

"Shit," I say, dropping to my knees in front of him. "Did it scratch you?"

He's shaking so hard it's difficult for me to tell whether or not he's nodding. Judging by the look of terror in his eyes, I'd guess he is.

"Let me see it," I say, pulling his hand away.

There are three long scratches across his throat. Shit. If only I could go back in time and act more concerned for him.

CHAPTER FIFTEEN

"He can't come back in the shelter," Nathan says.

We're gathered around a shaky James just inside the fence but not the building. The Nathan who was ready to kill me if I had even the tiniest scratch on my body is back. He's standing over James, holding a gun in his hand. The self-appointed judge, jury, and executioner.

"We can't just leave him out here, and we can't just kill him!" Hadley says.

Her eyes are huge and frantic, and she's crying. I've never seen a person cry so hard. Her shoulders shake, and she has snot and tears smeared all over her face. She doesn't look anything like the Hadley Lucas who graced the cover of *People* magazine just a few months ago. It's doubtful it has all that much to do with James, though. They aren't that close. Probably has more to do with the terror of realizing all this is actually happening. That we aren't completely safe in our little shelter underground.

"He'll turn." Nathan's eyes are cold and impassive. So different from the man who almost cried in the car at the thought of losing his family. But if I had to guess, I'd say that's why he's doing this. So he doesn't lose his family.

"You don't know for sure," Anne says. "Maybe he's immune. It's possible! We were all immune to the virus that started this thing."

Anne and Hadley are the only two arguing for his life. They're the only two who haven't seen a person turn yet. Everyone from our group is silent. We haven't had to kill a human to stop them from turning, so the thought of doing it now is difficult to process. But the people from Nathan's group are adamant.

"He'll turn. They always do," Jhett says. Physically, he looks so young. Thin and lanky, and the hair on his face grows in sparse patches. But he has the eyes of someone who's been around and seen it all. Who has watched people close to him die. Maybe even had to kill a few.

"He's a risk to us all," Brad says. The selfish bastard was mysteriously absent when we needed help killing the undead, but as soon as an important decision needed to be made, he popped up. It reminds me of when we were in Vegas and he wouldn't give up his seat for Jhett.

Hadley looks at me with pleading in her eyes. "You can't just let them kill him!"

I look away. She doesn't know about Emily, and bringing it up now is just too painful. The wound is still too raw. Just thinking about it makes my chest tighten like it's going to collapse in on itself. Talking about it would surely bring the walls of my world crashing down around me.

"We've seen it happen," Nathan says.

"Please," James sobs. "Please!" He can't seem to get anything else out. It's all he's said since we dragged his trembling body inside the fence.

Nathan presses his lips together and shakes his head. He steps closer to James and raises the gun. The barrel presses into the terrified man's forehead. James flinches and quivers harder.

Before Nathan can pull the trigger, Hadley steps between them, pushing the gun aside. "There's a holding cell! They have a holding cell up by the control room. We can put him in there and keep an eye on him. That way if he turns, he's contained."

"We can never be sure," Nathan says, trying to step around her.

He's right, but we can't let him just kill a man. Not when we have another option.

I turn to Axl and grab his arm. "Do something. We can't let one person make a decision for the entire group like this!"

Axl sighs, and his gray eyes are pained. I know he's thinking of Emily. Just like Nathan, he thinks James is a lost cause, but he steps forward anyway. "We gotta vote."

Nathan shakes his head, and both Brad and Jhett start arguing. Yelling at us that it won't do any good.

Winston steps forward and plants himself next to Axl. "He's right. If there wasn't a holding cell, I wouldn't even bat an eye. Taking him in would be too dangerous. But there is, so we need to think this through before we just rush off and kill a man."

"We aren't taking him in," Nathan says. He won't take his eyes off James.

"You ain't in charge," Angus growls.

Nathan's eyes flicker up, briefly meeting Angus's gaze before he looks away. He wavers just a little.

"We go in and give everyone a chance to vote," Hadley says. "How can it hurt you if he's in a cell? If he's locked up!"

Nathan's face relaxes, and he finally nods. He seems to know he can't win. Not with Angus against him. "He's not going inside, though. I'll stay out and guard him. If the group decides he gets a chance, I'll abide by it. If not, I'll take care of it."

"I'm not leaving you alone with him." Hadley's

expression is conflicted. She wants to go inside and plead his case, but she's worried what will happen if she leaves.

"I'll stay and make sure Nathan doesn't kill him." I pull my gun out and give Nathan a hard stare.

Hadley relaxes and flashes me a tense smile before running to the shelter.

"Let's get this over with," Axl mutters.

He gives me a quick look. Like he hates to leave me or thinks this is pointless. I'm not sure which one. Then follows Hadley into the building.

In a matter of seconds, Nathan, James, and I are alone under the hot desert sun. My body is sticky with sweat. Every time the wind blows, it brings with it a sprinkling of sand that clings to my skin. The dead have really started to pile up, and the heat has made them even ranker than they were in their short, undead existence. A few giant black birds fly above us, and their shadows dance in circles on the desert floor. Teasing us.

"You know this is pointless. I can see it on your face," Nathan says. He hasn't lowered the gun since he raised it. His hand is steady despite how long he's been holding it in the same position.

"Doesn't mean we don't give him a chance. Hadley's right. If he's in a holding cell, he can't hurt us."

Nathan shrugs. "Still pointless."

James doesn't talk. He's lapsed into what seems to be a slightly catatonic state. Staring at the sandy ground silently. No expression on his face. If I hadn't seen this before, I'd think he was in shock. But this is too similar to how Emily acted after she was bitten.

"He'll go fast," Nathan says. "The closer it is to the brain, the faster they go." His expression is still blank, but his voice is strained. Like he's trying to control his emotions.

"How many? How many people did you lose before we found you?"

He swallows, and the gun wavers a tiny bit. "Ten. Would

have been less if we had been smarter, taken care of the problem right away. But we were stupid. The first person in our group to get bitten was an older lady. We didn't know for sure how it worked, if it was like the movies or not. She wasn't sick, didn't have a fever or anything, but she was really quiet. Didn't do anything but lay around. We thought she was in shock. Then she just snapped out of it and seemed better. It gave us hope that maybe this thing wouldn't spread. But out of nowhere she collapsed and died. One minute she was talking and the next she was laying on the ground dead. At least we were prepared when she turned. She came back less than ten minutes later, and we took care of her before she hurt anyone. The second time it happen we weren't so lucky.

"Alex and I were out looking for food when we got overrun. We lost two guys, and he got bit. We made it back to the house, but he wasn't in good shape. We talked about killing him right away. Alex was even okay with it. But we thought the same thing Anne does. Maybe some people are immune. Like the virus. He turned faster than Mrs. Johnson did. We didn't know at the time that where you're bitten determines how long it takes. She was bitten in the ankle, but Alex's bite was in the shoulder."

Nathan pauses and glances at James, leaning over just a bit so he can get a better look at his face. He's worried. It's there in his eyes. Can a person really change this fast? He's acting like it can happen at any second.

"He turned when we were sleeping and attacked a few others. By the time I got a bullet in his head he'd bitten three more people. Two kids..." He swallows and looks away. "I didn't want to kill them, it was just too hard. So we waited it out again, hoping they might be immune. They weren't, but at least they didn't get anyone else.

"We had five more people get bitten or scratched at random times. The scratches were a surprise. We treated them but never dreamed they would turn from something so small. We recognized the signs by that point though, and as soon as the people lapsed into a lethargic state we put a bullet in their brains. Ended it before they could do any damage."

He looks up, taking his eyes off James for the first time. "You've seen it. I can tell."

My throat tightens, and I turn away. My insides are so torn up that I ache from the inside out. There's no way the damage is contained to my insides. It has to have seeped out. I look down and blink. I can't believe I'm still in one piece. Not shattered and broken like I expected. Why hasn't the pain destroyed my exterior as thoroughly as my interior?

"Once." It's all I can get out before the pain rises to my throat and threatens to choke me.

He doesn't say anything, and I try to pull myself together. If he makes a move for James now, I'm useless. I can't even bring myself to move my head, let alone save a man from getting shot.

He doesn't shoot, though. When I look up, he's just staring at James. Nathan's face is still hard and his eyes are just as cold. Was he always this tough, or is it a result of everything he's seen? It seems so at odds with the emotional man from the car that I'm inclined to think it's the latter. I shudder. Just a few weeks ago, our lives were normal. It seems like a long way to fall in such a short time. If he can change from a family man to a hardened mercy killer in just a matter of weeks, what can we expect the world to be like a year from now?

I don't want to think about it.

We don't talk. I'm too emotionally exhausted to hear more, and I'm afraid if I open the floodgates, he'll never shut up. That he'll keep talking and talking until my brain explodes from overload. Luckily, he's too busy keeping an eye on James. Nathan probably doesn't even remember I'm here.

When Hadley, Axl, and Winston come back, I can tell

right away by the look on Hadley's face what they've decided. She's not smiling—that would be too much to expect at a time like this—but she does look satisfied.

"We're taking him down to the holding cell," Winston says.

Nathan shakes his head but doesn't argue. He even helps Winston pull James to his feet and lead him toward the shelter. James doesn't act like he has a clue what's going on, and Nathan holds him at arm's length as he walks.

"Keep a safe distance," he tells Winston.

Winston frowns and steps back. He shakes his head a little. I get the impression he didn't vote to give James a chance.

Hadley follows them inside, and Axl puts his arm around me wordlessly, leading me toward the door. All I want to do right now is get to my condo and shower so we can crawl in bed. I'm so tired that instead of following the others to the holding cell, I steer Axl toward the stairs.

When we walk into the common area, I stop dead in my tracks. In the wake of James's attack, I completely forgot about the other complication. Now it all comes screaming back as her shrill laugh pierces the air. My insides twist, and I clench my fist. Angus is flirting with Darla by the bar.

She has a drink in her hand, of course, and she gives Axl and me a big smile. "Come on over an' have a drink with me! For saving my life."

"I'm tired," I say, turning away from her.

"I don't think I ever caught your name," Darla calls after me.

I duck into the elevator as soon as the door opens and pull Axl in behind me. My heart is in my throat as I pound my thumb against the button that closes the door. It's so slow! Why won't the damn thing shut?

The door starts to slide shut, and I slump against the wall. Thank God.

"It's Vivian." Angus's voice floats in just before the door

shuts.

Damn.

I push the button for three and lean my head against Axl. He doesn't ask, not that I expected him to in the elevator. He'll wait until the time is right. Hopefully, after I'm clean and rested.

When we stop on three I pull Axl out with me. "I don't want to be left alone."

"Wouldn't dream of leavin' you," he says, allowing me to lead him into the condo and back toward the bedroom.

Warmth floods my insides, filling in some of the cracks left in the wake of Emily's death. Soothing the pain just a bit. I stop in the middle of the living room so I can kiss him. Hopefully, it will make the pain ease a little more. It helps when his lips touch mine and his arms wrap around my body, pulling me close. It makes me feel more whole. Like I may one day be able to put some of the pieces back together.

"You're dirty," I whisper.

He chuckles softly and kisses my neck. "More than you know."

"Let's get dirtier in the shower."

CHAPTER SIXTEEN

When I wake, I'm curled up in my bed all snuggled up against Axl. He's wide awake, staring up into the darkness. He seems to sleep so little.

According to the clock on the bedside table, it's almost midnight. It was late afternoon by the time I drifted off. After a shower and sex—safe sex, thanks to the condoms Axl swiped from his brother—I was more than ready for some real sleep. A lounge chair on the roof of a casino is not good rest.

My stomach growls so loudly Axl can hear it. He raises his eyebrows, and the corner of his mouth twitches, making the scar on his chin dance. "Hungry?"

I roll onto my back and stretch my legs, flexing my tired muscles. They're sore from all the physical exertion. "Of course. We've barely eaten a thing in the last twenty-four hours." The words are muffled by a yawn, but he gets the point. "I'm actually surprised it didn't occur to me earlier how hungry I was."

He smiles again, softer. There's a teasing glint in his eyes. It makes him look younger. "I think you had other things on your mind."

I try to smile because I know he's referring to the sex, but it isn't easy. Yes, that was on my mind, and it was good. It wasn't what had distracted me from my hunger, though. The appearance of my mother, unloading the supplies and killing the undead, the situation with James…

"I need some food."

I climb out of the bed and rummage around in the dresser for some clothes. This friend of Hadley's brought such impractical stuff that it takes me a while to find anything. She must have had something against clothes. I need to do some laundry today so I don't have to keep walking around in skimpy dresses. "Do you know where they put the food they brought down?" I ask once I'm wearing a very short cotton dress.

"Probably up by the control room." He's still lying in bed.

"Well, come on! You have to be hungry too."

He gives me a half-smile. "I got no clean clothes here." He motions toward his naked body. Seeing him lying in my bed with nothing on is surreal. In a very good way.

But I'm hungry and I need to eat and he's just lying there…Why doesn't he have anything to wear in this condo?

"You didn't grab some clothes when you went to get condoms last night?"

"Wasn't really high on my list of priorities at the time."

I snort. "You mean you didn't have enough blood left in your brain to think about grabbing them."

He chuckles and shakes his head. "Somethin' like that." He starts to sit up, and I'm momentarily distracted from my hunger by his muscled chest. There's something so mesmerizing about him. "I can just put my dirty clothes back on."

I put my hand on his shoulders to stop him from

standing. "Those are covered in sweat, dirt, and black goo. You're not putting those back on. I'll go get some for you."

"You gonna brave Angus after I swiped his condoms?"

There's a smirk on his face, but the worry in his eyes is unmistakable. How is Angus going to react to us sleeping together? When we first met, he would have thrown a fit. He was so determined to make sure a woman didn't come between him and his little brother. But we've almost become friends since then. It didn't really occur to me that it would be a huge deal at this point. Judging by the look on Axl's face, I'm not sure now.

"I can handle Angus," I say with more certainty than I actually feel. How chummy he and Darla were earlier flashes through my mind. The last time we saw them, they were drinking together. I cringe and say, "Darla's probably there with him, anyway. I bet those two jumped right in bed together."

Axl's gray eyes search mine, and he raises an eyebrow slightly. "You gonna tell me 'bout it?"

I don't want to say it out loud. Don't want to admit to anyone who she is. But he's looking at me so intently that the words come out before I can stop them. "Darla's my mom."

There's no shock or disbelief in his eyes. He already knew. Of course he did. Axl can read me like a book. Even if he couldn't, he's smart enough to see the resemblance. I hate that we look so much alike, but we do.

His expression may not change, but he does pull me down next to him and wrap his arms around me. "I'm sorry."

"You knew." He doesn't argue, so I take it as a yes. "When did you figure it out?"

"Didn't take long. I knew right off that somethin' wasn't right. How you almost ran off an' left her. Wasn't like you. Then when she started talkin' in the car, you were so tense. Wasn't 'til I looked at her real close that I knew why. You got her smile."

I cringe, hating myself when tears try to force their way

to the surface. A part of me wishes we had just left her so I didn't have to deal with all this. I never wanted to see her again. Never thought I would once the world collapsed. To have her here now is so unbelievable.

"Did you know she was in Vegas?"

"There were rumors. She ran off about the same time as a man in the trailer park. He left behind a wife and three kids. About a year later he came crawling back to his wife, saying that he'd left my mom in Vegas. My dad swore up and down she'd never run off with that 'piece of shit.' Of course, he and I both knew it wasn't about who she was running off with, but who she was running from." I have to pause before I say the next word because it hurts too much. "Me."

"She didn't run from you. She ran from your dad."

"She ran from me a little bit, otherwise she would have taken me with her. Would have at least checked on me. But she didn't. She ran off and never looked back." A tear forces its way from my eye and trickles down my cheek, leaving a hot trail behind.

"You gonna tell her?"

I shake my head and stand up, wiping my face with the back of my hand. "No. I'm not telling anyone. I don't want people thinking that trash is in any way a part of me."

Axl flinches just a bit. "You think she's trash? What 'bout me? She and I, we ain't that different."

I step closer and tilt his face up so he's looking me in the eye. "You are nothing like her. You are nothing like Angus or my father or your mother. Axl, you are so much more than you give yourself credit for."

He doesn't look convinced, but when I kiss him, he kisses me back. It's half-hearted, though. I want to say more, but he acts uncomfortable, so I let it go and step back. I know Axl has a tough time believing he's more than what he used to be, but I want him to. Angus has kept him down, intentionally or not, I have no idea. But that needs to change. Axl is better than any man I've ever known. It doesn't matter where he lived before all this. What matters is who he is on the inside.

He stands up and looks away from me like it hurts to see the admiration in my eyes. "I gotta pee."

He walks toward the door, but he's not wearing a stitch of clothing.

"You're naked. What if you run into Hadley?"

He doesn't turn to look at me, but the corner of his mouth twitches. "Then I guess she'll get a good show."

I laugh. "You're mean. Here she is at the end of the world, stuck underground. Who knows when she'll get laid next?"

He turns around to face me and leans up against the wall. Completely naked and so sexy. A little smile lights up his face and turns my insides into Jell-O.

"She thinks you're hot."

He purses his lips. "No, she don't."

I climb to my feet and walk over, stopping in front of him. My hands run up his stomach and over his chest to his shoulders. "She told me. Before she knew I liked you." God, I feel like I'm twelve saying it that way.

He lifts an eyebrow and puts his hands on my hips. He pulls me close and presses his lips against mine. I wrap my arms around him then run my fingers through his dirty blond hair. My heart pounds when his mouth moves faster, and for a moment I consider forgetting my growling stomach and going back to bed.

He pulls back, and his gray eyes study me. All teasing gone. "I'll try not to let her see me," he whispers.

He opens the bedroom door and heads to the bathroom. My eyes follow his every move. Why did I have to wait until the world ended and everything had gone to shit to find the one person who might actually make me happy? It seems unfair.

As if life for me has ever been fair.

My stomach growls again. Right. There was a reason I

got up at midnight. I need to get clothes for Axl, then food.

There's no sign of Hadley in the condo when I head out, but the door to her room is shut, and it's late. She's probably asleep, but I can't help laughing as I wait for the elevator. She's going to lose her shit if she bumps into Axl naked. Or maybe she'll be sorry she missed it.

The elevator door opens, and I almost jump out of my skin. I didn't expect anyone to be standing there, and Joshua is so tall and gangly he had my mind playing all kinds of terrifying tricks on me. A shudder runs down my spine when I step in next to him.

"You okay?" he asks.

I nod and put my hand to my heart, trying to calm the pounding in my chest. "You surprised me. Why are you up so late?"

He sighs and rubs the back of his neck. "Sophia wasn't feeling well, so we went up to the clinic to make sure everything was okay. Then I checked on James."

Guilt and worry twist inside me. I need to be more involved. To worry less about getting laid and focus more on making sure everyone else is doing alright. "Is everything okay with the baby?"

"Yeah. Thankfully, they didn't sell off the ultrasound equipment, so I was able to get a good look at things. I think she just needs to eat more, to be honest. We'll have to work on getting that food down here tomorrow so everyone has some in their condos." He looks tired. His eyes are red and bloodshot, and there are bags under them.

"Are you okay? You look like you could use a week's worth of sleep."

He nods, but his mouth tenses and his eyes flit away. "Haven't been sleeping really well. Dreams and stuff like that. Plus, I'm worried about the medical supplies."

The doors open on the ninth floor and I step out with Joshua so we can finish our conversation. I can walk down the two flights of stairs to get to Axl's condo.

"What are you worried about? We have all that stuff we took from Walmart. What more do we need?"

He leans against the wall, but even then I have to look up. He's so tall. "We have the meds we took, but they won't last forever. And we have nothing for emergencies. No suture kits, no way to transfuse blood, nothing that will help me out if I need to do surgery. We're going to need to get to a hospital so we can collect supplies."

"Shit," I mutter.

I was never a huge fan of zombie movies, but even I know a hospital is the last place you want to go in a time like this. It will be overrun.

"Yeah," he says. It's almost a whisper, and it's full of dread. Like he knows sending people there will be a death sentence. "I'll really need to go too. So I can get the right stuff."

"No," I say firmly. "We need a doctor here. We can't risk something like that."

"There's another doctor," he argues.

"Really? Have you seen him? Because I haven't. Not even once."

Joshua runs his hand through his hair and nods. "I've seen him a few times when he came out for food. He looked severely depressed. Hadley said he lost his wife."

"Who hasn't lost someone," I mutter. I don't have a lot of sympathy for people who can't get their shit together. Everyone's hurting, everyone had their lives destroyed.

"Whatever." Joshua stands up. "I need to get some sleep. We'll talk about it later."

"Wait!" I say, stopping him as he opens the door to the condo he's sharing with Jhett. "How's James?"

Joshua shrugs. "Dying. Getting ready to turn." He pushes the door open and steps in, calling over his shoulder, "No different than we expected."

My body jerks when he shuts the door in my face, but I shake it off and head for the stairs. My legs are heavy again, and even the two floors I have to go down are suddenly daunting. We have to go back to Vegas. It's not a surprise—even if we didn't need medical supplies, we'd still have to get fuel—but it sends a jolt through my body that makes every inch of me tingle with fear and dread. And going to a hospital? There's got to be another way to get medical supplies.

The condo Angus and Axl are sharing is unlocked. I crack the door and peek inside before entering. The living room is empty, and I have a clear view of the kitchen. Also empty. Taking a deep breath, I race through the living room and back to the bedroom, letting out a sigh of relief when I make it without running into Angus.

Or Darla…

When the door's shut, I flip on the light. Axl's stuff is thrown around the room, but most of it is on the floor around his duffel bag. Not folded and most likely not clean. I sigh and start shoving it into the bag. Might as well do his laundry while I'm doing mine.

I've just about gotten it all when a purple backpack catches my eye. I freeze, and my heart constricts. It's Emily's. I didn't know he took it with him when we left the gun store. That's where she died. Where we went after she was bitten and where she turned. I woke up in the middle of night and saw that she wasn't in her sleeping bag. Axl and I searched the dark store for her. I thought she'd just gotten up to use the bathroom and gotten lost. I never dreamed she'd turned into one of them.

When we found her, Axl held me while I cried and Angus took care of putting her down. But I was there. I saw the bullet go into my baby's brain. Saw her crumple to the floor. That was the moment when my world shattered into a million pieces.

My hands shake as I pick up the backpack. Tears fill my eyes and I try to make myself unzip it, to look inside. But I can't. I just can't face it right now. If I open it, the floodgates will come down, and I'll never be able to put everything back in place again. Never be whole.

I toss the bag aside and wipe the tears from my face as I climb to my feet. I want to get out of here so I can focus on something else. Anything else. I grab Axl's duffel and stumble from the room. Not caring if Angus hears me as long as I don't have to be in that room anymore

CHAPTER SEVENTEEN

I don't mention Emily's backpack to Axl when I get back. Maybe we'll talk about it one day, when things have settled down. But not now. It's too hard for me, and I know it would be for him too. He loved that girl, which makes me love him just a little bit more.

Axl raises an eyebrow when I toss his duffel bag on the floor in front of him. "You askin' me to move in?"

My smile doesn't quite feel genuine. "Your clothes need to be washed. I was going to do laundry later anyway. Figured I do yours too."

He nods and starts digging through the duffel for clothes. His body is stiff and he won't meet my eyes. He's uncomfortable too. Why?

"What's wrong?"

"Nothin'. Let's just get some food."

He gets dressed without looking at me. He has something on his mind, but I let it go. Axl typically says what's he's thinking. He'll tell me when he's ready. I have no doubt about that.

The common area isn't empty like I expected it to be. Winston, Nathan, and Hadley sit on one side of the room, talking quietly. Angus and Darla are on the other side, still at the bar.

Axl stops when we walk in, and his eyes go back and forth between the two groups. Angus looks up. He purses his lips, and his eyes grow hard. His face is flushed and his eyes are bloodshot. He's drunk. No way I'm going near him when he's like that. Especially not when I have no idea how he's going to react to Axl and me.

"Go on over an' sit with Hadley," Axl says. "I'll get us some food."

I don't argue. He obviously doesn't want me near Angus right now either.

I join the group on the other side of the room, but it isn't any more relaxing than being with Angus would be. They're all worried, Hadley especially.

"What's going on?" I ask when I sit next to her on the couch.

"Just keeping an eye on James." Her voice is tense, and she glares at Nathan. She really doesn't believe James is going to turn.

If only I could muster up even a shred of hope that he'll pull through this. But I can't. There probably isn't going to be much to hope for in this life from here on out. Not being eaten alive by the undead, that's about as much as a person can wish for these days.

I glance toward Axl, standing on the other side of the room talking to Angus.

Love. That's another thing to hope for. Just a little bit of love, if you're lucky.

"Hadley doesn't think he's going to change," Nathan says.

I tear my eyes away from Axl. It isn't easy. He and

Angus seem to be having a very heated discussion about something.

"I just think we shouldn't make any decisions until we know for sure," Hadley says defensively. "You yourself said you've never seen it take this long for someone to turn. Not when the infected area is so close to the brain. Maybe some of us are immune! It's possible."

Nathan shakes his head. He's still holding his gun, and his hand flexes around it. "But we killed the last several people in our group before it got this far. It could have taken this long for them to turn, but we didn't wait to see."

"And they could have been immune." Hadley's voice is firm and stubborn.

Does she really believe it, or does she just need it to be true so she can hold onto her sanity? Either way, she's wrong. I don't understand this virus any more than the others, but I do know James is going to end up just like Emily. We were all immune when this thing killed most of the population. But whatever it is in our bodies that fought off the infection when it was only airborne can't protect us from the virus once it enters our bloodstream. We're just as susceptible now as all those other people were before.

"When's the last time you checked on him?" I ask Hadley.

"About thirty minutes ago. He didn't have a fever at all and he didn't even seem that sick anymore. He actually talked to me!"

Nathan exhales and runs his hand through his blond hair. "I keep telling her that means the end is closer. She won't listen." His words are clipped like he's getting impatient with her.

"Because it could also mean he's getting better," she snaps, and her green eyes flash. She looks like she's ready to jump up and punch Nathan in the throat.

They glare at each other for a few seconds, then Hadley gets to her feet in a huff. "I'm going to get something to eat."

She stomps off just as Axl comes over with a box of food. He glances at her briefly as she walks by, and his cheeks turn a little pink. He must be thinking about Hadley saying he was cute. It makes me smile and helps ease the tension inside me.

He sets the box on the coffee table. It has some canned food and coffee, a big box of granola bars along with some other snack food. My stomach growls, and I grab a granola bar greedily. I rip open the package and wolf the thing down in two bites. Like I haven't seen food in a week. It barely makes a dent in my hollow stomach. Damn. I'm hungrier than I originally thought.

Axl leans back and opens a bag of chips. "So what's up the actress's ass?" he says between bites.

A few crumbs fly from his mouth and land on his shirt. I snort out a little laugh and wipe them away. Axl's lips pull up into a smile. It's amazing how such a small gesture can turn me into a pile of goo.

Winston scratches at his beard like it's bugging him. It's growing out of control. "She's still in denial about James."

It's the first word he's said since I sat down. He barely batted an eye when Nathan and Hadley were arguing a few minutes ago. But he's thinking things through, I can tell. He must have something else on his mind entirely.

"You gonna tell me what you're thinkin'?" Axl asks.

Winston rubs his eyes. "The food is good. That solves one big problem for the time being. But we've got quite a few other issues going on still."

I take a handful of chips from Axl and lean back next to him as I wait for the bad news I know is coming. I want to snuggle up against him and get comfortable—I always feel stronger when I'm near him—but I don't know how Angus would react, and right now he's on the other side of the room glaring at us.

In between flirting with Darla, that is. I do my best not to look that way, but it isn't easy. It's been ten years since I saw her face and I was pretty sure I never wanted to see her again, but now that she's here, I can't stop myself from staring at her.

"Let's have it, then," Axl says.

"We've got the obvious issue, which is fuel. We're going to have to make another run soon so we can get some. It isn't going as far as we thought it would. Then this James thing is a problem. He knows all about the control room and the security, but no one else really has a clue. Al's telling me he can figure it out, so we're going to get him on that right away. Hopefully, that will work. Then there are the gardens. I don't know the first thing about the aquaculture thing and neither does anyone else. What I do know is those plants are a mess, and even if we can get them back in shape, it's going to be a while." He stops talking and sits back a little, but I get the feeling he isn't done.

Axl must too, because he leans forward just as Winston sits back. His eyes narrow, but he doesn't look pissed. At least not at Winston. "What else?"

Winston glances toward the bar where Angus and Darla are still at it. Why the hell don't they just grab a few bottles and go to his condo? Angus throws back the last of his drink, then looks our way. He presses his lips into a little sneer. Shit. He's sticking around so he can keep an eye on everybody. Like he's in charge or something.

"We have a problem with your brother." Winston tears his eyes away from Angus and looks down at his hands. "I hate to bring it up like this, I know you two are close, but it has to be said."

"What'd he do?"

"He was real mad when we came back without you."

Axl purses his lips and tilts his head toward Winston. "He give you that shiner?"

"He was out of control. Screaming at everyone, trying to leave right away so he could go find you. Wouldn't listen to reason. I took the brunt of his anger." Winston glances up,

165

and I can tell he hates putting Axl in the middle of all this. "He wants to be the one calling the shots from here on out. He took the keys to all the cars."

I knew Angus was a hothead, but I didn't think he'd risk our safety like this. He's a racist prick, but even he has to know if we don't work together, we're done for. Locking people underground isn't exactly going to help us bond as a group. We need to pull together so we can get through this.

Axl purses his lips and shakes his head. He looks like he just tasted something bitter. "I'll take care of it."

"Axl, you're a real good man and an asset to have around. We need people like you if we're going to make a go of this thing and survive. But we can't have someone down here who's a danger to others."

"I said I'll take care of it," Axl says again, but this time his voice is hard. Angry.

Winston doesn't look hurt or even surprised. He just nods, then he relaxes a bit like he trusts Axl and he knows it's going to work out now.

"What we gonna do about the fuel then?" Axl says, changing the subject.

Winston shakes his head, but anything he was going to say is cut off by a scream. It's coming from the upper level where the control room and holding area are. It's slightly muffled, but I'd know that scream anywhere. I've heard it in dozens of movies.

"Hadley," I say, jumping to my feet and dashing toward the stairs.

The others follow, even Angus and Darla. Hadley must have gone in to check on James. It's the only logical explanation. If she didn't take proper precautions, he could be attacking her at this very second.

I'm halfway there when it hits me that I'm unarmed. Even if I get to the holding cell, I can't do anything to help her. I glance over my shoulder and see Angus right on my heels. He has a gun. Probably had it to intimidate the others. I don't care right now because it will help Hadley.

The door to the holding cell is ajar, just like I knew it would be, and Hadley is nowhere in sight. My heart jumps to my throat, and I have the sudden urge to scream. She has to be inside. Why wouldn't she listen?

I reach the door first and jerk it open the rest of the way so we can see what we're dealing with. It's a small room, only about six feet by six feet, with nothing but a toilet, a sink, and a bed inside. Hadley and James are both in the room. Hadley stands on the bed with a pillow in her hands, pressing it against James while he tries to get at her. It's her only defense as he does his best to bite and claw at her through the pillow.

Being weaponless doesn't stop me from running in. I grab James by the hair and jerk him away from Hadley. Then shove him to the other side of the room. He's strong, but I caught him off guard. He stumbles back and slams against the toilet.

Angus is in the doorway, and I know I don't even have to look to make sure he takes care of James. Angus won't hesitate. He steps forward with his gun raised as James charges again, putting a bullet in his brain before he can even take two steps. The gunshot echoes through the room, making my ears ring, but I can still hear Hadley's sobs.

I grab Hadley's face between my hands and look her over. She looks okay. Shaken. Scared. But not hurt. "Did he get you? Are you bit or scratched?"

Her entire body trembles, but she manages to get out a few words. "No. I'm okay."

Tears stream down her face as she looks at James's body crumpled on the floor. I'm not a real touchy-feely person, but I hug her anyway. She needs comfort.

"I needed him to be okay," she says, sobbing into my shoulder. Her voice and body shake from the devastation.

I was right. This wasn't about James really at all. Not because Hadley is selfish or callous, but because she needed to believe he could be saved. That all this wasn't hopeless. Now her hope is shattered.

"I know," I whisper. "It's alright."

She won't stop shaking, so I lead her out of the room, ignoring the others as they show up and begin talking about what to do with the body. Trying to block out the pungent odor seeping from the bullet wound in James's head. The smell isn't as intense as it is from the ones that have been dead for a while, but it still makes my stomach lurch.

I lead her back to our condo and sit with her on the couch while she cries. She doesn't talk, and I don't either. Sometimes a person just needs to cry it out. Before long, she's fallen asleep.

There's a blanket on the back of the couch, so I cover her up. The gesture feels oddly maternal, which just makes me think of Emily again. My throat tightens, but I try to force the pain back down. I'm so tired of feeling tired and lost. With the way things are now though, I guess I should get used to it.

The door to the condo opens, and Axl walks in with the box of food. Angus is with him. Great. He's alone though, so I can be glad of that. At least he didn't drag my mom in here with him so I'd have to sit through the two of them drooling all over each other.

"She okay?" Axl asks.

"Are any of us? She just needed to believe there was some hope for the future."

Angus grunts and throws himself in a chair. I don't want him here. He's still drunk, and the images of him and Darla flirting in the common area are still strong in my mind. Not to mention the bruise on Winston's face. He's a tyrant and a prick, and I don't want him near me right now. But I keep my mouth shut. He's still Axl's brother, and loving him means loving all of him. Even Angus.

"Thought you might want some soup," Axl says as he carries the box into the kitchen. "I'll heat it up for ya."

My heart aches with gratitude, and once again tears sting at the back of my eyes. I've never cried this much in my life. But I'm starving still and soup sounds perfect, and the fact that Axl thought of me with everything else going on makes me feel like someone. Like something important. Even if I am only important to him.

Hadley's limp body weighs me down, and my left butt cheek has started to tingle. Like it's on its way to a nap. No way I'll be able to sit like this for long. Slowly, I ease her head off me and onto a pillow. She groans and shifts in her sleep, but doesn't open her eyes. I move to the loveseat across from the chair Angus sits in. His gray eyes are hard and he doesn't look happy.

We eat chicken noodle soup. It's warm and takes me back to my childhood, which for some reason isn't totally depressing. I guess there are some good memories buried deep inside.

When my stomach is full, exhaustion takes over again. It's late—well after three—and I'm having a difficult time keeping my eyes open. Axl is next to me. I could put my head in his lap, but I don't want to cause problems with Angus. So I move the other way and lay my head against the arm of the loveseat, closing my eyes and drifting off while Angus and Axl discuss finding fuel in Vegas.

The brothers' voices wake me. I have no idea how long I've been asleep, but judging by the fogginess in my brain, I'd say it wasn't long. I hear my name and freeze, keeping my eyes shut. I don't want them to know I'm awake.

"You gonna choose her now, when it comes time for us to split?" Angus sounds angry. Angrier than I've heard him for a while now.

"Why would we split?" Axl asks.

Angus lets out a little grunt that I take as disbelief. "You wanna stay here with these folks for the rest of our lives? Live underground with these pansies who'll use you to get supplies and never take no risks themselves? Takin' orders from niggers?"

I cringe at the word. It reminds me so much of my father and his friends. I heard so much of that as a child, and even then I knew it was wrong. I could never understand where my father's hate came from, or why he was so angry. There had to be a story behind his rage. Just like there has to be with Angus. I'll never be able to figure out Roger, he's long gone, but maybe Angus won't be a mystery forever.

Axl lets out a frustrated sigh, but when he talks his voice is calm. "You gotta stop this, Angus, it's dumb as shit. Things are different now. It ain't like it used to be. There's no black or white no more, no Oriental or Mexican. All that's left now is humans and fuckin' zombies. Stayin' in a group like this is safe. It don't make no sense to run off on our own. Where we gonna go? What're we gonna do? You want it to be just the two of us for the rest of our lives? The James brothers against the world! That was all well an' good when there was a world to go up against, but now there's nothin' but zombies out there." He pauses, and even though I can't see his face, I can picture the look on it perfectly. The hard line of his jaw, the storm that rages in his eyes. I know every one of his facial expressions inside and out. "We got a good thing goin' on here. I don't want to screw that up."

My heart swells just a little. Those are my words. I said the exact same thing to him once. After Emily died, when we stopped to save Anne and little Jake from a horde. He asked me how I was able to pull myself out of it and think of others first. I did my best to explain how I felt, why I didn't want to go through life valuing my own ass over everyone else's. I wasn't sure if he got it, but I guess he did.

"She's changed you, lil' brother. Gotten in your head and screwed up the way you see things. You woulda never said shit like that before her." Angus lets out a growl. "You got a weak mind. That's the problem. It was the same back with that bitch when you was in high school. You started datin' her and got all these ideas in your head 'bout going to college

170

and stupid shit like that. You let these women talk you into believin' you're somethin' that you ain't."

There's a sharp stab of pain in my chest, and I have the urge to sit up and slap Angus across the face. No wonder Axl's never thought much of himself. No wonder he always puts himself down. Angus was his only role model as a child. His father ran away when he was young, and his mother was a drunk who slapped him around and neglected him. Angus looked out for him, in his own twisted way.

"I love 'er," Axl says. There's no joy in his voice, and his sad tone delays my own happiness. He sounds pained when he admits it, and I'm not sure why.

"Weak," Angus replies. "You an' I both know it ain't gonna last. Happily ever after ain't real. A fuckin' zombie apocalypse don't change that. Well, I can't guarantee I'll be stickin' 'round to watch you two lovebirds tear each other to shreds."

He doesn't say anything else after that. A few minutes later, I hear him get to his feet. The front door opens, then closes, and Axl swears.

Why does loving me hurt him so much?

CHAPTER EIGHTEEN

Slowly, I surface from my dream world of death. A chill runs down my spine, and I curl into myself. It's partly from the dream and partly because the bed is like ice. But that makes no sense. Why the hell is the bed so cold? I scoot back, trying to warm my cool skin against Axl. His side of the bed is even icier than mine, though. I flop onto my back and force my eyes open, but reality isn't any different now that I can see. Axl is gone.

I roll out of bed, barely landing on my feet, then stumble out to the kitchen. Groggy and desperately in need of a cup of coffee. I expect to find Axl, but Hadley sits at the table by herself. She gets up when I fall into the chair next to her and silently pours a fresh cup of coffee for me. Her face is red and puffy from crying. She isn't dressed, and she's not wearing any makeup. She looks like shit.

"Thanks," I say when she sets the cup in front of me.

She sits back down and gives me a tense smile. "Thanks for last night. I'm not usually a very emotional person. I don't know what came over me."

"Zombies." It's the first time I've said the word out loud since this whole thing started. It stings a little, and I can't stop the tightening of my throat or the burning behind my eyes. I was right. Saying it makes this all feel so much more real. More than seeing it with your own eyes or almost having to blow your own brains out to escape a horrible death. Zombies. Damn zombies. Who would have ever thought such a thing could really happen?

Hadley nods and takes a drink, glancing away from me when her eyes fill with tears again. "I feel like such a bitch. I didn't care about James dying, not really. I just wanted to convince myself there was a chance. That if I go out on a run and get bitten I have a shot of coming through it okay." She lets out a bitter laugh and shakes her head. "It's stupid."

"You don't have to go, you know. No one would blame you."

She cocks one eyebrow. "Because I'm a woman, right? Everyone is sure pissed at Mitchell and how selfish he's being. Not that I blame them, but still. It would be okay if I sat here and let everyone else risk their lives for me just because I'm not a man?"

"You can contribute in other ways, and you would. That's why people are angry at Mitchell. He wants all the benefits, but refuses to take any of the risk or do any of the work."

She shrugs but doesn't look convinced. "Maybe. But it doesn't matter. I don't have any skills that are useful. But I'm tough, and I can do this."

I don't argue with her because I know how she feels. I can't see myself sitting around here, helping out with the kids or passing out food. Growing up, I had it rough, and I learned how to work for things. When I ran out on my asshole dad, I had nothing. I took his money and split, then drove until I ran out. That left me with twenty bucks and a nice body, so I did what I had to. I didn't love it, but stripping was a good way to make fast cash. Hadley and I are the same. We're both willing to do what needs to be done, regardless of how hard or scary or shitty it is. And I respect her for that.

"Axl snuck out of here pretty early," she says out of nowhere.

I chew on my bottom lip and think about what I overheard last night between him and Angus. He said he loved me, but he didn't sound particularly thrilled by the idea. I'm not sure why, but it scares me. Axl is still a big mystery to me despite how much alike we are.

"Did you talk to him?"

She gives me a half smile and nods. "Just for a minute. He wasn't dressed when he came out. God, he's hot. He was a little embarrassed, I think."

I can't help laughing. I wish I'd been there to see his reaction. "He was naked?"

"He had boxers on, but he may as well have been." She sighs and looks up at the ceiling. "Man, I'm pathetic. All the shit I've lost and all the crap going on, and all I could think about when I saw him was how much I'm going to miss sex. All these people down here, and my only options to get laid are Angus or Mitchell. Neither one is appealing."

I laugh, but quickly put my hand over my mouth. "I'm sorry, it's not funny." I can't even think about the possibility of Hadley sleeping with Angus. It gives me the creeps.

Hadley's nose wrinkles. "No, it's not! It's disgusting!"

"There's always Joshua." I shrug, and she presses her lips together like she's thinking it through. "He's a doctor."

"He's a nice guy, but I just can't see it happening. I mean, he isn't really my type." She looks down like she's afraid to admit the truth. Joshua is too tall, too thin, and kind of different looking. Like a giant, awkward kid. I understand her hesitation.

"Well, if you get desperate…"

"Yeah." She takes a sip and won't look up.

"So what did Axl say?"

She waves her hand in the air dismissively. "He said something about going to talk to Winston. How they needed to plan or something like that. Then he grabbed some coffee and went back to your room to get dressed. Honestly, I was too busy staring at his abs." She fans her face. "He was in a hurry. I think all my drooling made him uncomfortable."

I grin into my coffee. Yes, seeing his reaction would have been nice.

I don't really understand what's going through his head. But there's nothing to worry about, right? He has other things on his mind, so he got up early. He doesn't sleep much anyway.

It doesn't ease the knot in my stomach.

"I'm going to get dressed and go find him. See if they have a plan yet. I know Winston is concerned about the amount of fuel we have," I say, getting to my feet.

Hadley stands too, gulping down the rest of her coffee. "Good idea. I'll come with you."

WE DON'T HAVE TO LOOK VERY HARD FOR AXL AND the others. They're in the common room just like they were last night. With the power shut off in most of the shared spaces, there aren't a lot of places to go.

This morning, though, the place is crawling with people. The kids are in the theater watching a movie despite Winston's earlier decree that we needed to conserve energy. They probably needed something to do, and between that and the pool, it was the lesser of the two electrical evils. Jessica, Sophia, Moira, and Parvarti are busy dividing up the food. It looks like most of the stuff we got from Sam's has been brought down. There are piles of it lining the walls in the common room that weren't here last night.

Axl sits on the couch. Winston, Angus, Nathan, Anne, and Trey are also gathered around the sitting area. Hadley and I walk over, and Axl smiles when he sees me, relieving some of the tension in my body. There aren't any seats left, so I sit on the arm of his chair. He puts his hand on my lower back, and my skin tingles from his touch.

"We have to send people out tomorrow," Winston says. "There are a couple of possibilities for fuel, but it's a long shot at best."

There's an open phone book in his lap and a map spread out on the table. I lean forward a little so I can get a better view. It's a map of Vegas. There are a few areas circled in red.

"So who's going?" Anne asks.

Her hands are clasped tightly in her lap. She keeps glancing toward the theater area where Jake plays with the other kids. She volunteered to go and I know she'd do it if she had to, but I get the impression she'd rather not. I don't blame her either. Jake already lost his parents. It would be awful for him to lose her as well.

"I think we need to send more than four people out this time," Winston says. "The way we were overrun on the Strip... It was too close. I'd like to send out six people."

"Angus an' me are in," Axl says.

Winston nods, and his shoulders relax. Getting Angus away will help out everyone. "Sounds good."

"I'll go again," I say.

Axl tenses, but I don't look at him. I'm not letting him go without me. I think I'd die if he didn't come back and I had to spend the rest of my life wondering what happened to him.

"I'm going too," Hadley says from behind me. "Angus spent a lot of time teaching me to shoot, and I'm getting pretty good."

Winston nods, but before he can talk Angus speaks up. "We gotta get you outside later. Get you to practice on movin' targets."

Hadley nods, and Winston looks around at everyone

else. Waiting.

"I can go," Nathan says quietly. He glances over his shoulder, back toward Moira. She's too busy with the food to pay attention to our conversation. "Just don't anyone mention it to Moira until I get a chance to talk to her about it."

"I'll go," Anne says quietly. She doesn't look up when she says it, though.

No. Her leaving Jake behind isn't good for either of them.

My eyes meet Trey's. I know he's hanging back because of Parvarti, but he's no coward and he's a good guy. He was raised in a nice family and he knows the importance of a child having parents. He'll offer to take Anne's place.

Trey nods, then clears his throat. "I don't want to sound sexist, but I think Anne should stay. She has Jake to look after, and it just doesn't seem fair to put her at risk. I'll go instead."

Anne gives him a grateful smile, and Angus swears under his breath at the same time. He was probably thankful for how white the group was going to be. Racist asshole. I guess Axl's little talk went in one ear and out the other.

Joshua walks into the room with a man I've never seen before right behind him. They pause in the doorway and Joshua looks around, then they head our way. "Sorry it took me so long. I was down talking to Dr. Gates."

"Victor, please," the man says.

He looks to be in his late forties, and he's tall and thin, although not nearly as thin or tall as Joshua. His chin-length blond hair looks greasy, and his skin is white and pasty. He looks ill. There are bags under his eyes, and his complexion has an unhealthy color to it. Plus, it looks like he hasn't showered in a couple of weeks. And he smells.

"What's going on?" Winston asks.

Joshua sighs and runs a hand through his hair. "We need medical supplies. Badly. I know going to a hospital to get things isn't the best idea, but I'm afraid we're going to be in trouble real soon if we don't do it. I'd like to go on the run."

A cry of opposition comes from the group sitting on the couches. Apparently, I'm not the only one who thinks Joshua is needed here.

"We need a doctor," Winston says. "Putting you at risk is a bad idea."

"You'll have one," Joshua argues. "That's why I went to talk to Dr. Gates — Victor. I knew you'd react this way, and I wanted you to know there's nothing to worry about. Victor is here, and he is more than capable of taking care of patients if something happens to me."

"I think you're wrong," Hadley says. "He was here before I got here and we've barely seen him. He's severely depressed — which no one blames him for — and I just don't think we can trust him to be capable of responding in an emergency. No offense, Dr. Gates."

Joshua starts to argue, but Victor stops him. "They're right. I wouldn't be any good to them. I should go out on the run instead. I can get everything you need. That way if anything happens to me, they'll still have a good doctor."

Joshua doesn't look thrilled, but he does relax a little. He must know there's no way he's going to win this argument. "Okay, fine," he says, shaking his head. "Now we just have to figure out where to go. I spent some time looking through the phone book and found a medical supply warehouse here." He picks up a marker off the table, then circles an area on the map. "I'd go there first because it would be less of a risk. Your second bet would be an urgent care. There's one here, right down the street from the hospital. If all else fails, you're already in a good place to get into the hospital."

Winston nods and scratches at his beard. "Okay, but I need to tell you, as important as the medical supplies are, the fuel will be the priority. If we don't get it, we're in real trouble down here. We can always go back for medical supplies, but we have to get that fuel. And soon."

Joshua nods. "That's fine."

"Do we need Trey now that Victor's going?" I ask. I know he doesn't want to go. It would be nice if he could stay behind.

"No, that should be good. He went last time, so it's only fair we take turns," Winston says.

No one bothers to mention that Axl and I went last time, not that it would matter to either one of us. Axl will probably volunteer to go every time, and there's no way I'm letting him out of my sight. I have nothing to lose but him now.

"So these places you got us goin' to look for fuel? What exactly are they?" Axl asks.

"You folks looking for diesel?" I turn at the sound of the voice and find Brad standing behind us. He must have just walked into the room, because I didn't notice him before. He has that same damn ratty hat on, and his beady eyes are barely visible. There's something about this guy that gives me a bad vibe. Ever since the Sam's Club incident, I haven't felt good about him.

"Yeah," Winston says. "For the generator."

Brad nods and pulls off the hat. The lights shine on his scalp through his thinning hair. No wonder he wears it. "I was a truck driver based in Boulder City before all this." He puts his hat back on and walks toward us.

A trucker? Gross. The lowest of the low in my experience. Never met a truck driver who wasn't an asshole. Never met a Brad who wasn't an asshole either, if I'm being honest. I even dated a Brad, back when I first got to Kentucky. It didn't last long, though. Commitment and fidelity weren't exactly his cup of tea.

Brad stops in front of us and straightens his shoulders. Trying to look important, probably. I know his type. "We had a trucking yard in Boulder City, and usually had a tanker or two sitting around. I was there the day before everybody started getting sick. There were two trucks parked in the yard, if I recall correctly."

Everyone leans forward in anticipation.

180

"Full?" I ask, my heart pounding a million miles a minute.

Brad nods. "Sure."

"Where's Boulder City?" Angus asks.

"It's about thirty miles south of Vegas."

We're about an hour north of Vegas.

Winston studies Brad carefully before responding. "Okay, then," he says slowly, like he's choosing his words carefully. "You can go in Nathan's place. You can show the group how to get to the trucking yard and drive the tanker back."

Brad's eyes grow wide and his mouth drops open. He wasn't volunteering to go, and right now he looks like he's about ready to pee his pants. The look on his face reminds me of how he wouldn't give his seat up for Jhett and how he popped up out of nowhere, all ready to decide James's fate. He doesn't want to risk his own neck, and Winston knows it.

"Sounds good," Axl says, standing to his feet.

When I look up, he and Winston are staring at each other. They both know Brad will try to weasel his way out of this if he can, and they're not giving him the chance.

"What time are we headin' out?" Angus asks.

"Let's shoot for five. That'll give everybody time to get some rest before we go," Axl replies.

Angus nods and turns to Hadley. "Let's go out and use them bastards outside the fence for shootin' practice. You ever shot a gun, doc?" He turns and looks around, but Victor is already gone.

Axl purses his lips. "I'll go down and talk to him. I wanna make sure we can trust that guy before we head out." He turns to Joshua. "You make a list of the shit we need so we got it in case. And where to find it."

"Axl." Winston jerks his head to the right, and Axl follows him to the side of the room.

I stay where I am. I'm not sure if they want me to overhear whatever they're cooking up, but I want to wait for

Axl.

Someone giggles, but it sounds too old to be one of the kids. I turn to find Lila on the other side of the room, leaning against the bar. Al sits in a chair less than a foot away from her. She's all dolled up like she's getting ready to hit a club. Perfect makeup and a short, little black dress that probably cost a couple grand. Her heels are candy apple red. I don't know where she thought she was going when she packed those clothes, but with the way she's batting her eyes at Al, I know where she's hoping they'll take her.

Unlike the way he acted at the pool, he seems to be playing it cool. He has a drink in front of him — I'm not sure if I should put a stop to that or not — and he barely looks at her. I'm sure it isn't easy for him to ignore her. Not with those teenage hormones swirling around in his body. Plus, Lila's gorgeous. I'm actually proud of the kid. Hadley's little talk must have hit the mark.

Axl comes back over and looks toward them, then back at me. "What?"

"Nothing." I turn away from the teens and grin at Axl. "Just people watching."

He blinks like he has no clue what I'm talking about, then heads toward the elevator. I hurry after him, jumping in the second the door opens. It slides shut, leaving us alone.

He looks at me out of the corner of his eye, but he doesn't turn. The smile melts off my lips when the uncertainty from earlier returns full force. I want to pull him against me and ask what he's thinking. I want him to tell me he loves me and reassure me we'll come out of this okay. But Axl is such a hard person. I need to wait until he's ready. I can't push him.

"You didn't get much sleep last night," I finally say.

He shrugs like sleep is nothing. "Don't sleep much."

"I've noticed. Why?" Is he going to share? I want him to. I want to know everything about him.

He purses his lips and leans against the wall. "No reason."

He doesn't want to talk to me about it. It stings, but I let it go. He'll tell me in his own time. I know he will. This is just Axl. Trust isn't an easy thing, and it's something I get because it's the same for me.

"I was sad when I woke up alone," I say instead. I can't stay away from him any longer, so I grab his hips and pull him against me.

He bites his bottom lip, and one corner of his mouth turns up. "You miss me?"

I lean forward and press my lips against his. He kisses me back and wraps his arms around me. Being near him is like standing in a furnace.

But he turns it off like a switch the second the door opens. He steps out of the elevator and nods toward the apartment in front of him. "We got stuff to do."

He's right. I exhale slowly as I follow him to Victor's door, trying my best not to feel disappointed. It would be dumb to feel that way. We have more important things going on.

CHAPTER NINETEEN

Axl knocks on the doctor's door and steps back. Then we stand awkwardly in the hall as we wait for him to answer. I shove my hands in my pockets while Axl pulls out his gun and double checks that it's loaded. A few minutes pass and the doctor still doesn't come to the door, so Axl knocks again.

"Maybe he didn't come back down here?"

Axl shakes his head. "Where else would he go?"

There's no way for me to answer that, so I shrug. I can't think of a single place the doctor would have gone off to. I haven't seen him once before today, so I doubt he's been out wandering the shelter or anything. Axl knocks a third time, and I hold my breath. Nothing.

"Shit," he mutters.

Something that feels similar to a bowling ball lodges itself in my throat. There's something about this whole thing that doesn't seem right. Why isn't he answering?

"Try the door?" I say uncertainly.

Axl nods and turns the handle. The latch clicks and the door cracks just a bit, so he pushes it open a little more. The smell hits us before we even step inside.

I cover my nose with my arm and try not to breathe it in. "Oh my God, what is that?"

"One guess." Axl doesn't cover his nose, but he breathes very deliberately through his mouth.

I look at him with wide eyes and shake my head. "How is there a zombie in here?" I whisper.

"It's just a guess, but I'm assumin' it's his wife."

As soon as the words are out of Axl's mouth, I know he's right. My stomach twists painfully. It's classic horror movie shit but completely believable. There always has to be one person who just can't stand to let their loved one go, and with the way the doctor's been acting, he seems like the obvious suspect. We should have guessed. He's been holed up in his place since we got here, and he smelled so bad in the common area. Like death. It makes perfect sense. His zombie wife is here.

We haven't set foot inside the condo yet, and I'm not in a hurry to rush in. I know what we're going to find and how we're going to deal with it, but I have no idea how the good doctor is going to react. I'm not sure if he'll let us take care of her or try to kill us to protect her. He's obviously unstable, so we need to be prepared for anything.

Axl pulls out his gun. His lips are pursed and his weapon is up, but he still hasn't moved.

"What should we do?" I whisper.

"I think we just go 'head an' take care of it ourselves. If we bring more people in, things could get outta hand. We don't gotta worry people for no reason."

I nod and pull out my own gun. I almost left the condo without it, but I'm trying hard to remember to carry it everywhere I go. I want to be prepared from now on.

It's a good thing, too.

"Ready?" he asks, taking a small step forward with his

gun held up.

I follow him wordlessly. Tensing up more and more with each step I take. The condo reeks so much I have to stop to catch my breath. The quick breakfast of prepackaged muffins I ate this morning threatens to make a reappearance.

"You alright?" Axl asks.

I nod and take a deep breath through my mouth, trying to ease the nausea. It only works a little, though. I can't smell the rot this way, but every time I inhale a mouthful of air, the coating on the inside of my mouth thickens. My tongue feels heavy like it's covered in layers of decay. And I can taste it. Like rotten meat.

My stomach spasms, but I fight it. I can't get sick. Not now.

We head through the condo to the bedrooms. Both doors are closed, but now that we're closer, I can hear movement behind the first one. That must be where he's holding her. We stop outside the door, and a couple of erratic thumps come from behind it. My stomach tenses even more.

"You think he has her tied up?"

Axl shakes his head as he reaches for the doorknob. "Be ready for anything. She probably is tied up, but just in case..."

I swallow around the lump in my throat as he slowly turns the knob. He manages to get it turned and pushes the door open without making a sound. The first thing to hit me is how bad the room smells. It's the sickening mixture of death, along with the stench of the black ooze that fills the zombies. I gag and turn away, swallowing against the bile rising in my throat.

Movement catches my eye and distracts me from the queasiness. I turn to see what used to be a woman tied to a chair on the other side of the room. Her mouth is covered by a gag that's coated with thick black goo. The same goo seeps from her eyes and ears, out of her nostrils. Her skin is a sickly gray color and hangs loosely on her body. Her dark hair has fallen out in clumps that lie in piles on the floor. She struggles against the ropes when she sees us, moaning against the gag in her mouth. Victor isn't in the room.

"Shit." Axl lowers his gun and shakes his head. He looks away like he can't stomach seeing the woman.

"What are you doing?" I ask. "Shoot her!" I can't figure out why the hell his gun is down. She's right there, and the sooner we take care of her the sooner we can get this mess sorted out.

"Not 'til we talk to the doc. He deserves to tell her goodbye."

I turn to face him and blink probably ten times. I can't believe what I'm hearing. "He's had a lot of time to say goodbye and he hasn't been able to. You need to take care of it."

Axl shakes his head again, but before he can say anything there are footsteps in the hall behind us. We spin around and come face to face with Dr. Gates. His face is red and angry. He's holding a gun in his shaky hands. It's pointed at me.

"What are you doing here?" he yells.

Axl steps in front of me, putting himself between me and the gun. "We came to talk 'bout the run. Didn't know 'bout all this 'til we opened the door. Looks like we got some other things to talk 'bout."

"There's nothing to say!" he growls. "She's my wife and I want you to leave. Now!"

"Can't," Axl says, taking a step closer.

He's only about a foot away from Victor, and my heart pounds when I see the barrel of the gun so close to him. I grab Axl's arm, trying to pull him back. But he won't budge.

"You want me to kill her. Just like you killed James. But I won't do it," Victor says. Tears stream down his cheeks, and he shakes even more.

"We gotta do it," Axl says.

His voice is soft and kind, understanding. I don't get it

because I don't understand. No matter how much I loved a person, I couldn't keep them like this. It would be torture to see them every day, to think they might be stuck inside the head of zombie for all of eternity. Suffering and trying to get out. I couldn't do it.

"I can't," Victor says. "I can't let her go."

"She's sufferin'. Just look at her," Axl says.

Victor looks at his wife, and his whole body seems to crumple. He releases the gun, and it drops to the floor as his shoulders go slack and his body slumps. He's still standing, but he seems to have shrunk a foot in that instant.

Axl picks up the gun even though he has his own. "I can do it for you, if you want."

Victor doesn't look at Axl, but he does look at his wife. The despair in his eyes is overwhelming. I can't understand his actions, but I can understand his pain. I think of Emily and the hole in my heart expands, making an ache shoot through my entire body. I press my hand to my chest, trying to hold myself together. To keep myself from shattering into a million pieces. I don't think it works, because I still feel broken.

"I can't kill her," Victor whispers. His body is wracked with sobs, and he shakes his head. "Please, do it for me."

Axl nods and turns toward the zombie woman. He tosses Victor's gun on the bed as he walks forward, and every muscle in his body gets tighter as he goes. The thing that used to be Dr. Gate's wife thrashes in the chair, growing more and more frantic the closer Axl gets. She screams behind her gag, and more of the black ooze seeps out of her nose, coating the cloth even more. By the time Axl is standing right in front of her, she's so frenzied that the gag has ripped into her skin. It tears the decomposing flesh from her mouth, revealing her rotting teeth and black gums.

Axl stops in front of her and raises his gun. He glances back toward the doctor. "You have anythin' to say before I put her out of her misery?" The doctor shakes his head, and

Axl turns back. "I'm gonna do it on three. If you don't wanna watch, you have 'til then to leave."

I turn away from the pitiful creature and face Victor. He shakes and sobs, wringing his hands.

"One."

Victor whimpers and takes a small step back, toward the door.

"Two."

Victor shakes his head and shuffles forward before backing away even further.

"Three."

Victor turns and rushes from the room just as the gunshot fills the air.

Axl walks over to stand next to me, holding both his and Victor's guns in his hands.

"What are we going to do? Can we trust him to come with us?"

Axl shakes his head and walks into the hall. "Let's go talk to him and find out."

I follow him, shutting the door behind me. I don't think it will really help contain the smell, but it's worth a shot. It's going to take a long time for this condo to air out. Maybe never. It's not like we can open a window or anything.

Victor's in the living room, sitting on the couch. His elbows are on his knees, and his face is in his hands. He's sobbing. I can't imagine the kind of pain he's going through. The hurt from Emily is so intense it almost cripples me at times, and I only had her for a few days. But this man, he and his wife were together, side by side for years. It must feel like a mountain is crushing him.

"I'm sorry," Axl says, sitting down in one of the chairs. "But we gotta talk 'bout this."

Victor nods and looks up. He doesn't bother to wipe his nose or his eyes, and his face is covered in tears and snot. Streaked with dirt. He looks awful.

"We gotta ask if you're gonna be able to handle this trip,"

Axl says.

Victor sniffs. "I can do it," he says in a shaky voice. "I know it's important. That people need the medicine. You can trust me."

I don't know if we can, but Axl seems convinced. He stands up and pats Victor on the back. "Get cleaned up and we'll see you in the mornin'."

He turns toward the door, grabbing my hand as he goes.

"Do you trust him?" I ask once the door's shut and we're alone in the hall.

"We got no other choice. I think he really wants to try, but we won't know for sure 'til we're out there."

"What are we going to do about the body?"

Axl purses his lips and glances back toward the door. "I'll go talk to Winston and we'll get it worked out. Why don't you go pack your shit so you're ready to go?"

I don't want to leave him, but I need to do laundry anyway, so I nod in agreement. "Okay. You going to come to my place when you're done?"

He nods and gives me a half smile. "'Course."

I GET STARTED ON THE LAUNDRY SO I'LL HAVE CLEAN clothes to wear. And get disgustingly filthy all over again.

What a waste of time.

Hadley isn't back from target practice yet, so I find myself alone. I don't like it. It's much too quiet. I pace the room for a few minutes, waiting for Axl or Hadley to show up. When neither one does, I decide to take a shower. I feel dirty after my encounter with Victor's wife. Like I'm covered once again in the black goo that flows through their lifeless bodies.

I turn the water up as hot as I can stand it and hop in, letting the scalding heat of the shower flow over my body. I try desperately to keep the memories from coming, to stop myself from thinking about Victor's wife and his misery. To keep Emily's innocent face from my mind.

I can't.

Before long, it's all I can think about. How would I have reacted if no one else had been there to take care of Emily when she turned? Could I have shot her in the head to put her out of misery? Could I do it for Axl if the time comes? Thinking about it makes my body shake. What will I do if something happens to Axl? How will I be able to stand it?

My eyes sting, but I don't even try to hold back the tears. I lean against the wall as they fall from my eyes, mixing with the hot water. Getting lost on the way down my cheeks. This new reality of zombies and the constant threat of death is so scary and overwhelming it makes all those years I suffered with my father seem insignificant in comparison. Who would have ever imagined that I'd be able to look back on those days and think of them as being anything but miserable?

After a few minutes of sobbing, I sink to the bottom of the shower and pull my legs up against my chest, wrapping my arms around them. I tuck my face down so the water hits the back of my head, then try to pretend everything is normal. It's impossible. The pain in my chest won't let me forget.

"Vivian?" Axl's voice is suddenly there. A rush of cool air hits me as he opens the glass door and steps in. He's still dressed when he helps me to my feet. "You okay?"

I shake my head and start to cry again. Axl pulls me out of the shower and wraps me in a towel before lifting me off the ground. He carries me to the bedroom like I'm a small child, pulls the covers down and lays me in the bed. Then he strips out of his wet clothes and climbs in with me.

"What's wrong?" he whispers, kissing my face gently. Like every other time he's gentle with me, it makes me think of when I was sick and he took care of me. It makes me feel loved.

"I just couldn't stop thinking about Victor's wife. How

devastated he was. How I would feel if it was you…" The words get lost on their way out. Talking about it is too difficult.

Axl doesn't respond. He pulls me close and covers my mouth with his, draping his damp body over mine. Slowly, he eases away my pain, moving down my body with his touch and kisses. Caressing every inch of my skin until all the hurt has faded to the far reaches of my mind and all I can think about is Axl and this moment. And how much I love him.

I want to tell him, but I'm so afraid of how he'll react. I've never had another human being tell me they loved me. Never felt with any certainty that I loved someone else until I had Emily. But this is different. So explosively and amazingly different than anything I've ever felt before.

"Vivian," he whispers as his lips trail up my jaw and to my ear. "Would you do somethin' for me, if I asked?"

"What?" I gasp. I can't promise him until I know what it is, because I have a sneaking suspicion it has to do with me going on this run to Vegas.

"Stay here," he says, confirming what I already thought. "Don't go on the run."

He kisses his way down my body, between my breasts and to my stomach, then to my inner thigh. I tremble. He's taking advantage of me, asking me when I'm weak.

I let out a moan as his tongue teases me. "You know I can't do that." It takes every ounce of willpower I have to get those words out.

He looks up at me, his eyes pleading. "I don't wanna see you in danger."

"And I don't want you to be in danger. But this world is dangerous now, and that's just the way it is." He frowns, and I reach down, putting my hand on his cheek. "We'll be okay. Just like before."

His eyes grow dark. He crawls back up the bed, lying down beside me. His hand caresses my cheek, and I lean into it. "I ain't sure if I could do that—" He swallows, and it takes him a few seconds to get the words out. "I understood. When I realized Victor kept his wife because he loved 'er too much to let 'er go. I understood."

My heart leaps. He's telling me he loves me without telling me. It's a big step for him. I know it is because he and I are the same. My eyes fill with tears, and the words bubble up inside me, just dying to come out. But I can't force them. No matter how hard I want to say it, no matter how true I know they are, I can't make the words come out. It's too scary.

Instead, I pull him to me and kiss him again. He presses himself closer to me, and his body feels hot and muscular against my skin. I wrap my legs around his waist and cry out when he pushes inside.

"We'll be okay," I whisper.

He buries his face between my breasts, and his lips are warm against my skin. "Stay."

His body moves faster, and I squeeze my eyes shut. I dig my nails into his back and cry out. I can't speak. I can't do anything but gasp.

"Please," he says.

"I can't," I finally manage to get out. "I can't let you go without me."

Axl grunts and his mouth covers mine. He moves faster and faster until everything fades away and all that's left in this whole world is just the two of us

CHAPTER TWENTY

In the morning an odd sense of déjà vu comes over me. We're all congregated in the common area, some of us getting ready to head to Vegas while others come to see us off. It feels like we were just here, and the ball of dread in my stomach isn't any less intense this time around. How can we be doing this again already?

When Victor shows up, he's showered and dressed in clean clothes. He looks and smells a million times better, and his expression is serene, like he's a little more at peace than he was when we left him yesterday. Maybe that means he'll pull through for us. That taking him on this run won't be a total mistake.

One can only hope.

Axl told me that Winston and Nathan dragged his wife's body out of the shelter last night after everyone else had gone to sleep. They buried her on the surface. Somewhere behind the building, probably close to wherever they buried James and the pilot. Axl said they all agreed to keep the incident quiet. It's for the best.

I can't disagree.

To my annoyance, Darla is here to say goodbye as well. As if any of us want to see her stupid face before we head off. Okay, maybe Angus does. Well, not her face exactly. Darla is draped all over him, and he can't keep his hands off her. It's obscene. They obviously had a fun night together. It doesn't surprise me, but it still makes my already uneasy stomach lurch.

My eyes meet hers and everything inside me twists painfully. No matter how hard I try to keep my emotions off my face, I can't. My mouth scrunches up into an expression that I'm sure has to resemble the brothers' whenever they purse their lips.

She must take my expression of disgust to mean something else, because she pulls away from Angus and actually comes over to me. "You scared, Vivian?"

It's the first time she's said my name since she got here. I flinch at the sound of it rolling off her tongue. It takes me back, but the feeling isn't pleasant. I can't make myself answer her. It doesn't seem to matter, though. She's one of those people who loves to hear the sound of her own voice.

"I wanted to go, but Angus told me to stay here where it's safe. He's such a sweetie. I've dated a lot of assholes in my life, so believe me, I know the difference. It's just so strange how I had to wait until the whole world ended to finally find a nice one." She rolls her eyes so far back that all I can see are the whites.

I cringe again. I had an almost identical thought about Axl just a couple of days ago. Why do she and I have to be so similar? Why can't I look at her and pretend that I don't have the same dimple or that her eyes aren't the same color as mine? It makes my stomach churn like the waters of a rocky river.

She blabbers on, talking about falling in love and how often she's done it and how wrong it always was. The more she talks, the sicker I feel. It's torture, listening to her talk about love so casually when it's clear she has no idea what love really is.

"Okay, everybody. We gotta head out," Axl calls out.

Darla abruptly stops talking. An emotion I don't quite recognize goes through her eyes, and she looks away from me, down toward the floor. "You be careful out there, you hear?"

She won't look me in the eye, and her cheeks turn red. It hits me hard in the gut. Like a freight train. She knows.

"Were you ever going to tell me?" I ask before I can stop myself.

She looks up, but she doesn't seem ashamed. "Didn't need to. Was clear you knew."

"But you didn't have the decency to at least talk to me about it after what you did? After everything you put me through?"

She rolls her eyes and looks away. "So dramatic, just like your father."

Tears sting at the back of my eyes, and this time I'm the one who looks away. If I have to look at her a second longer, I'm pretty sure I'll throw up. "You're a bitch."

A sob shakes my body, but I manage to keep it down. When I look up, my eyes meet Hadley's. Of course she saw and heard it all. I was stupid to think I could keep it quiet.

"What did I do to you that was so bad? I left you with your dad. It ain't like I ran off and left you alone."

I turn toward Darla with eyes as big as golf balls, and before I can stop them, tears fall down my cheeks. I hate her. I've hated her for so long, but right here, right now, I hate her even more. It has nothing to do with her leaving me or my father beating me, or the fact that she doesn't love me. I hate her because she's the reason I couldn't tell Axl I loved him last night. I wanted to, so badly. But I was too afraid to say the words.

"I have to go," I say, turning away from her.

I wipe the tears from my cheeks and do my best to pull myself together as I head up the stairs with everyone else. Hadley puts her arm around my shoulder and gives me a half hug. I have no doubt she heard the conversation, but she doesn't ask any questions. And I don't tell her. I can't. Not now, maybe not ever. Darla was supposed to be a part of my past. If only I could have kept her that way.

Axl stops outside the control room and catches my eye. He gives me a concerned look, but I shake my head. We don't need to focus on my drama right now. If it were up to me, we'd just ignore it forever. We need to concentrate on the undead walking around. To make sure we don't get ourselves killed.

Al sits at the desk in the control room since there is no more James. Jhett is with him, and Al stops in the middle of explaining how things work so he can turn our way. I guess he's showing Jhett the ropes.

"Looks like there's about ten of them up there," Al says, swiveling around in his chair to greet us. He has a big smile on his face. He must be happy to be back in his element around electrical equipment. Even if it is just monitoring the undead outside our shelter.

Angus is going with us, so Winston will throw the flare today. Trey and Anne will back him up.

"Let's head out," Winston says tensely.

He leads the way to the surface with the rest of us following behind. For some reason, the tension in my stomach lessens the higher we go. We aren't headed to Vegas straight off, so that definitely helps me breathe a little easier. Boulder City will be crawling with them too, but it will be nothing like the numbers we saw in Vegas. Even going into Vegas doesn't concern me as much this time. We know enough to avoid the Strip, and I'm confident we'll be able to find everything we need at the medical supply warehouse or the urgent care clinic. Axl and I came within a second of death on the last trip and managed to make it out alive. What could go wrong this time?

The six of us going on the run head toward the Nissan. Angus climbs in the driver's seat, and Hadley gets in the front next to him. Axl and I take the middle, leaving the back row for Victor and Brad.

Brad hasn't spoken a word since he arrived in the common area this morning. He's pretty pissed about going. He's definitely the "sit back and let others take the risks" type of person, so I know he never would have volunteered for this if we'd left it up to him.

"Everybody buckle up," Angus growls as he pulls the car around and gets ready to head through the gate.

Winston tosses the flare over the fence before jogging to the gate. Unlike last time, most of the undead don't take the bait. Three stumble after the flare, but the rest follow Winston. Anne and Trey are at his side, and they jab as many of the undead through the holes in the fence as they can. They have their guns as backup, but since we're trying to conserve our ammo, they aren't using them right off.

"Bastards are gettin' smarter," Axl hisses.

My shoulders tense, and I shake my head. Even though I know he's right, I can't believe it's possible. They're dead. They don't have the ability to think or feel. How can they be getting smarter?

"This is gonna be rough," Angus says through clenched teeth. "Hang on."

Winston swings the gate open. The second it's wide enough to drive through, Angus hits the gas. He speeds past Winston, taking out two of the undead in the process. The tires thump over the rotting bodies, and we bounce in our seats.

I twist around and watch the shelter fade in the distance just like before. It's hard to tell because Angus is driving so fast, but it looks like one or two got inside the fence. I tense up and grab Axl's arm.

"Can you see? Did they get them?"

He looks through the back window as well. "Looks like they got 'em all."

"I hope everyone is okay," I say as we both turn around to face the front.

"Should be more worried about our asses than theirs," Brad mutters from the back.

I'm already irritated, so I have the overwhelming urge to tell him to shut up.

Axl beats me to it, though. "Shut the hell up." He turns away from the prick in the back and puts his arm around me. "You okay?"

I nod and try not to let the tears build behind my eyes. It's impossible, though. I've never cried this much in my life. Something about the world as we know it ending and the dead coming back has turned me into a blubbering idiot.

"She knew," I whisper. "This whole time she knew who I was and didn't say anything. She doesn't care. Just like I thought."

He squeezes my shoulder and kisses me on the temple.

"Hey now, we don't need none of that," Angus says. There's teasing in his voice, but when my eyes meet his in the rearview mirror, they're hard. "Ain't fair to the rest of us."

"Seems like you had a pretty good time last night," I say bitterly. I shouldn't be angry at him. He doesn't know Darla is my mom. But I am. I feel like he's betrayed me in some way. Maybe it has more to do with the things he said to Axl than him sleeping with my mother.

He chuckles and shakes his head. "That woman's wild, let me tell ya. I was pretty pissed off when I found out you two swiped all my condoms. Lucky for you, she can't have no kids, otherwise I woulda been bangin' on your door in the middle of the night to get me some."

I sit up straight. No way she lied to him, right? "You mean she had her tubes tied?" Makes sense after me. It would be the only way to be sure she'd never have another obligation to look after.

He shakes his head. "Nope. She said she couldn't ever have no kids, that she was born sterile."

I roll my eyes and look at Axl. Should I tell Angus the truth? It's just like her to make up a lie that's so easily refutable. Axl shrugs and shakes his head. He's leaving it up to me. Great.

"Don't trust her," I tell Angus. But that's all I can get out. I just can't go into the whole thing. Not here. Not like this.

Hadley looks back at me, and her green eyes quietly study mine. She keeps her mouth shut, though. I don't know what she's thinking or if she knows about Darla being my mom, but she obviously knows now that we have some kind of history between us. I can tell by the way she's looking at me that she thinks I need to be honest with Angus. But I just can't, so I look away.

Angus scoffs. "Why would she lie 'bout somethin' like that?"

"Some people just lie."

He shakes his head, but doesn't say anything else. My gaze meets his in the rearview mirror again. His lips purse and he narrows his eyes. Angus isn't as smart as Axl, but he isn't a total moron. I'm not sure if he'll be able to figure it out, though.

THE DRIVE TO BOULDER CITY IS AS SILENT AS THE outside world.

In the back, Victor stares through the window wordlessly. On the surface, he looks better. He's clean and his hair is combed. But a shower can't wash away the depression. He's struggling. Anyone can see that. Maybe he can pick himself up some antidepressants while we're out.

Brad sleeps. Or he pretends to sleep, anyway. His head rests against the window with his ratty hat pulled down low, but I don't think he's really out. He just doesn't want to talk to any of us.

We aren't able to avoid Vegas completely. The interstate we take to Boulder City gives us a great view of the hordes of zombies—the word is getting easier to think—that have taken over Vegas. It's unreal, and the sight of it makes everything inside me feel heavy like my organs are filled with lead. If only there was some way to avoid going there. But there isn't. We need to get medical supplies.

Then again... "Maybe we can check out a hospital or something in Boulder City," I say as we stare out over the masses. "See if it's any less overrun."

"It has to be better than that," Hadley says.

Her eyes are huge and full of terror. I feel for her. She was terrified to come. Maybe I should have encouraged her more to stay behind. There's no reason for her to risk herself like this when other people could have done it. She's determined, though. I doubt it would have worked.

"We'll check it out," Angus says. "But we got no idea where any of that shit is. Don't wanna be drivin' all over the city lookin' for it."

I sit back. He's right. We have everything mapped out in Vegas already. To drive around aimlessly in Boulder City doesn't make sense, not when we already have to drive back through Vegas anyway.

"Maybe Brad knows where one is," Hadley says.

I glance over my shoulder at Brad. His eyes are still shut, but his mouth twitches slightly like he's listening. Asshole. I turn back around.

"I don't think he's going to be much help. He seems more like the look-out-for-yourself type of person," I say, not caring whether or not he can hear me. Actually, I hope he *does* hear me.

"It could help him one day." Axl looks over his shoulder too, and I know he's saying it in hopes Brad will come to his senses. "If he gets sick or hurt, he'll need them supplies, same as everybody else."

Axl's right. I just hope Brad realizes it and can think of an easier way to get them. From the way he's curled up ignoring the world, I doubt it.

When we reach the outskirts of Boulder City, Angus looks back at us. "Wake that son of a bitch up so he can tell us how to get there."

Axl turns around and yells at Brad, who makes a good show of pretending to be groggy when he sits up. Rubbing his eyes like a little kid and stretching out. It doesn't look real. If we all didn't already know he was faking it, we would now.

He gives Angus directions, leading us through the city easily. The undead wander the streets just like in Vegas. They are just as rotten and just as covered in the black ooze. They go for the car like a wild animal trying to attack its prey. Throwing themselves in front of us and banging on the side of the car when Angus slows to turn corners. But there aren't nearly as many of them here as there were in Vegas.

"You know where the hospital is in Boulder City?" Hadley asks.

Brad pulls that ugly hat off and scratches his scalp through his thinning hair. "Can't say I do." He stares out the window and refuses to meet Hadley's eyes. I think he's lying, but it's tough to tell.

When we reach the truck yard, my heart leaps. The area is fenced off, and dozens of semis are parked inside. Two tankers are just visible parked near the back. I only hope they're full of diesel, which is what we need for the generator.

Zombies lumber around outside the fence. About a dozen of them are within a twenty foot radius of the gate, meaning we're going to have to fight our way in. Great.

Angus does a quick drive-by of the truck yard so we can check things out and decide on the best approach. "It's chained up."

Axl nods and leans closer to the window. "We got them bolt cutters and a new lock. We'll have to cut it open and lock it up once we're inside."

Angus nods and glances over his shoulder, frowning. "Wish we had some more useful people with us." He shakes his head and looks everyone over. "I guess Blondie and Hollywood are gonna hafta cover you while you cut through that chain. It's thick, you're gonna need to put some muscle into it."

"You good with that, Hadley?" Axl asks.

She nods while she chews on her lip like she's trying to gnaw through it. Her eyes are wild, but she holds her gun determinedly in unshaking hands. "Guns or knives?"

"Knives if you can." Angus jerks the wheel to the right and does a U-turn in the middle of the street so he can head back to the truck yard. "Get ready to hop out as soon as I stop."

The three of us grab the door handles and wait. As soon as Angus stops the car in front of the gate I hop out, not even waiting for the others. I'm immediately greeted by a mostly bald, rotting woman who once had long, red hair. She only has a few patches of it left on her head now, though. The rest of her scalp is gray and wrinkled, torn in places and smeared with black goo. She stumbles toward me with her arms raised and her mouth open. As I swing my knife toward her head, I notice a few of her teeth have fallen out and her gums are dark gray.

She goes down, and I move toward the fence. Hadley's in front of me. She easily takes out a man who's about a foot taller than her by ducking around him and driving the knife up through the back of his skull and into the brain. More of the undead head toward us, but Axl has the lock cut before they get too close. He works fast at unraveling the chain and pushing the gate open, and Angus speeds through. Hadley and I run in after him and help Axl get the gate shut. He's just secured the lock when the next wave of the undead reaches the fence. But it's too late for them to gain access, and I let out a sigh of relief as I step back out of reach.

CHAPTER TWENTY-ONE

We're safe inside the fence, and we're all armed. Even Victor and Brad have their guns out. Brad is so jumpy he can hardly stand still, and his eyes dart back and forth between the rows of trucks constantly. None of us are foolish enough to think it's going to be clear. There's bound to be one or two zombies hanging around the yard or inside the building.

"Let's do a sweep of the outside first," Axl says. "Then we'll go inside an' check it out."

We all nod—except Brad, who gives more of a shake—and head out. The truck yard is huge, but the farther we walk away from the fence, the quieter it gets. If there are any zombies trapped in here, there can't be many. The only moans we hear at the moment come from the area we just left behind.

We walk down the rows, looking between the trucks as we head to the back where the tankers sit. I spot a couple trucks with their doors hanging open. I'm not sure if someone died inside and crawled out after they came back or if the owners were just in too much of a hurry to worry about shutting the doors. It puts me on alert, though.

We're almost to the back when we spot one lone zombie shuffling between the trucks. His back is to us when we round the corner, and he's about ten feet away. He stops and spins around as soon as the sound of our feet comes to his attention. Angus walks forward with a machete in his hand and lops the guy across the top of the head. The knife sticks in the guy's skull and goes down with the body. I watch with a sick feeling in my stomach as Angus puts his foot on the man's head to keep him still so he can dislodge his weapon. I comes out covered in goo. Angus swings it toward a truck, and thick splatters of black blood spray everywhere.

"Gross," Hadley whispers.

I nod as Angus wipes the remaining blood on the dead guy's pants, then heads our way. He grins, like he's proud of himself or having fun. Weirdo.

By the time we reach the tankers, I'm afraid Brad is in serious danger of peeing his pants. He jumps at every little sound we hear, even if it's obviously a bird. He's making me nervous and pissing Angus off. Every time Brad freaks out, Angus grunts and squeezes the handle of his machete harder. I get the feeling he'd like nothing more than to take Brad out the same way he just took out that poor zombie bastard.

Brad hops up and opens the tanker's door without even being told to. Probably has more to do with wanting to hurry up and get the hell out of here than actually being helpful. I cross my fingers and wait for him to tell us what's in the truck.

"It's got a full tank," he calls down. He picks up a piece of paper and reads it. I can only assume it's the truck's manifest or work orders or something like that. "And it's diesel."

I let out a sigh of relief, and Hadley flashes me a giant grin. We'll have electricity after all. I don't know how long this will run the shelter, but it's got to last a while.

"What about the other one?" I ask.

Angus climbs into the cab, and I turn to watch him, almost bumping into Victor. I'd forgotten he was even here. He's been so quiet this entire time. I try to catch his eye, but he seems to be lost, staring off into space. He's barely present, which is dangerous for all of us. We shouldn't have brought him.

"Tank isn't full, but this one's got diesel too," Angus says when he climbs out.

"Well, we can't take 'em both." Axl scratches his head and looks back toward the truck Brad still sits in. "You can drive that one today. We'll come back later for the other one."

"Sounds like a plan," Angus says. "You wanna head on in and find the keys or try to hotwire the mother?"

"Don't know if it would work the same on one of these. It'd be better to have a key." He turns to Brad, who has finally climbed out of the truck. "You know where they keep 'em?"

Brad eyes dart around nervously. "Yeah. I know." His voice shakes.

"Let's get this done, then," Angus says.

Hadley sticks close to me as we make our way to the building. It's small, no bigger than a McDonald's restaurant. There aren't many windows, which means it's going to be pitch black. Good thing we all have flashlights.

Axl tries the knob when we reach the side of the building. It turns easily, and he pushes the door open. The stench of death is so strong it makes my eyes water.

"Stay alert," Axl whispers as he flips on his flashlight. "Keep your eyes and ears open."

More flashlights flick on as we step in, and I press the button on my own. I pan it around, illuminating every corner as we head down the dark hall. Axl's in front. He's pulled Brad up next to him, probably so he can show us where to go. It's easy to tell which beam is Brad's because it's erratic and shaky.

"This sucks," Hadley says, almost making me jump out of my skin.

"You scared the shit out of me," I whisper.

"Sorry."

I glance back at Victor, who is trailing behind us. He moves like a robot, following us around but not really registering anything he sees or does. I'm worried he's going to be a risk.

"There's an office at the end of the hall." Brad's voice travels back to us. There's an edge to it.

No one responds. We keep moving down the hall silently, passing closed doors and dark, empty rooms. The smell grows stronger as we walk, and I have to cover my nose. The hair on the back of my neck stands up. I keep waiting for something to jump out at us. This is the perfect scenario for it, straight out of every horror movie I've ever seen.

Right before we reach the end of the hall, we pass a large open doorway that leads to the lobby. There's movement in the shadows and my heart jumps. I pan my flashlight over to illuminate the room, and a figure rushes forward. The zombie's rotten and distorted facial features are intensified by the beam, and the smell that floats with him turns my stomach.

Hadley screams. We all scatter in different directions. The zombie howls somewhere in the darkness. Everyone's flashlights move around so erratically that it's impossible to tell for sure where the zombie is headed or who's in its path.

I take two steps back and freeze, forcing myself to remain still. My hand shakes when I pan the flashlight around, and it only gets worse when I find the body. I have to fight to keep my hand steady. To keep him in the beam so he's visible.

Axl steps into the light and swings his knife. His aim is low, and he ends up getting the bastard in the ear. Too low to pierce the brain. He curses and pulls the knife out before giving it a second try. This time, he hits the mark. The body falls to the ground just as Brad reaches the office door at the end of the hall. He jerks it open and lets out a terrified howl as another zombie blasts out of the room, landing right on top of him.

"Dammit!" Angus growls as he hurries forward.

Axl and Hadley sprint toward Brad and the zombie. Every muscle in my body screams to run forward too, to help them. But I stay where I am. They need my flashlight or they'll never be able to see what they're doing. Victor stands next to me, but the beam of his flashlight is pointed down. He doesn't have a clue what's going on.

Brad and the zombie struggle on the floor in front of the open office door. The dead thing howls and grabs at Brad, who's giving everything he has to hold him off. Angus claws the zombie by the shirt and jerks him up. He shoves the body across the room before raising his gun. When he pulls the trigger, the bullet pierces the zombie between the eyes. The gunshot echoes through the building and leaves behind a ringing sound in my ears.

"Get up," Angus growls at Brad. "Did he get ya?"

Brad can't seem to talk, but he stumbles to his feet and shakes his head. It takes him a few tries before he finally manages to force out the words. "No. He didn't."

Angus yanks his flashlight out of his back pocket and puts it on Brad. "Turn 'round. Let me see."

Brad complies, raising his arms and turning in slow circles so everyone can get a good look at him. He looks clean, but I walk closer to get a better view. He's shaky and his face is bright red after his brush with death, but I can't feel too bad for him. I remember how adamant he was about killing James and how he wouldn't give up his seat for Jhett. Since we met, he hasn't done a single thing that hasn't pissed me off. The longer I'm around this guy, the more I dislike him. Asshole is too nice of a word to describe Brad.

"He looks clean," Axl says. "Next time, wait for us. You run off, you get killed."

Brad's head bobs up and down a few times, reminding me of a bobblehead. He puts his arms down and takes a few deep breaths but continues to shake.

"Keys are in there?" Angus asks, tilting his head toward the door.

"Yeah," Brad replies shakily.

"Come on then." Angus grabs him and hauls him toward the door as the rest of us stay where we are.

I head over toward Axl, stopping briefly to check on Hadley, who looks pretty shaken up. "You okay?"

She nods, but even in the beam of my flashlight I can see how pale her face is. I don't think she's a strong as she wants to believe she is. Maybe she was before she had to face the undead, but I'm not sure if she's cut out for this.

I pat her on the arm, then go stand next to Axl. I lace my fingers through his.

He leans down and kisses the side of my head while keeping an eye on the lobby and the hall behind us. "You doin' alright?"

"Yeah. I'm a little worried about Victor though. He doesn't seem to be all there."

Axl purses his lips. In the darkness, his expression looks creepy and evil. "Yeah. That guy's messed up."

I nod, but I'm not sure if messed up is the right word for it.

"Got it. Let's get the hell outta here," Angus says as he and Brad come back out of the office.

BRAD CLIMBS INTO THE TANKER'S CAB AND TURNS THE key. The engine roars to life, and a huge smile breaks out across my face. Hadley grabs my hand and squeals like a cheerleader at Homecoming. The tanker's engine is the most beautiful sound I've ever heard.

Brad looks down at us from the driver's seat, and his expression is like stone. All the fear has been wiped away, and all that's left now is coldness. It reminds me of how Mitchell looked when he refused to let us in the shelter. Pure selfishness.

"Now, if you'll go on ahead and open up that gate, I'll be on my way. I ain't going to the hospital with y'all. I didn't volunteer for this shit, and one brush with death is enough for me."

"Son of a bitch!" Hadley says.

"Like hell you are." Angus reaches up and grabs Brad by the shirt, ripping him from the cab.

Angus shoves him aside and pushes him to the ground. Brad hits the gravel parking lot on his hands and knees, wincing when the sharp rocks dig into his palms. He doesn't make a move to get up. Angus looms over him, but Brad's expression remains calm. Like he holds all the cards, which he kind of does at this point.

"You're goin' with us to Vegas, and you're gonna help us get them supplies," Angus says through clenched teeth.

Brad shakes his head and stares back at Angus unblinkingly. "No, I ain't. The fuel's more important anyways. Since none of you knows how to drive a truck, you don't want to risk my life. I'll take it back, and you can come to the shelter when you're done."

Damn. He's right, as much as I hate to admit that anything this selfish prick says has any merit to it. We need that fuel. My only concern is him running off with the truck instead of going back to the shelter.

"I'll drive that truck myself." Angus pulls out his gun and presses the barrel against Brad's forehead.

Axl steps in. He pulls Angus's arm back so the gun is no longer pointing at Brad. "Cut it out. The bastard's got a point." He shakes his head and runs his hand through his hair. "You swear you're gonna take it back? You ain't gonna run off with the fuel?"

"And go where?" Brad asks. "I just want to be safe, that's all. I'll take the fuel back, and my good deed is done. You can't force me to go out again. If you want that other truck, you can send Winston. He knows how to drive them too."

A taste so bitter fills my mouth that I have the urge to spit. Right on Brad. What an ass. But he's just coward enough to be telling the truth. I can't see him running off with the fuel. He wants someone to take care of him while he hides underground.

"Get up," Axl says gruffly.

Angus curses and turns away. He kicks a few rocks across the parking lot. They fly through the air and hit the sides of some of the trucks, making a pinging sound that echoes through the silence.

Brad climbs to his feet. He brushes the dirt and rocks from his hands and clothes. "I'll want to be on my way as soon as possible."

"Get in and shut the hell up." Axl turns away from Brad and heads after Angus, walking toward the front of the parking lot.

He grabs my hand as he goes by me, and Hadley trots along after us. I look back to make sure Victor is coming as well. He is, but he looks just as much like a zombie as the things banging on the gate in front of us.

"You trust him?" Hadley asks.

"He's too much of a pussy to run off on his own. He wants a place where he can hide out an' let everybody else do the dirty work." Axl shakes his head and spits on the ground. "He'll go back, alright."

Angus is waiting for us by the car. He's so pissed that the vein on his forehead looks like it's going to pop at any second. "Let's get this shit over with." Angus walks toward the fence. "You drive, I'll get the gate."

Axl nods and climbs in the driver's seat.

"I'll cover you," I call after Angus, who waves over his shoulder like he can't be bothered with even looking at me.

Hadley watches Angus for a second, then looks at me. Her eyes look like balls of terror in her pale face. "I can do it, if you want."

Her hands are so shaky that I doubt she'd be much help. I have to give her points for volunteering, though. It takes a big person to offer to do something that scares the shit out of you. That's real bravery.

"Go ahead and get in the car. I'm good."

Hadley nods and turns toward the Nissan, almost bumping into Victor in the process. He blinks like he doesn't know what's going on. Hadley sighs and grabs his arm. She has to drag him to the car.

Shit. We are in real trouble with this guy.

I head after Angus just as the rumbling engine of the tanker comes up behind me, and I know without having to look that Brad has arrived. The urge to give him the finger is overwhelming. That or shoot him, which might be even more enjoyable.

Angus doesn't even look back. He unlocks the gate and shoves it open. The dead immediately go for the opening, but Brad moves forward. He plows them down before they have a chance to get through the gate. Axl drives through once Brad is clear, and Angus and I run out into the street. I hold off the undead while he gets the padlock back in place. This time, I use my gun. We're on our way out, so who gives a crap if we draw attention our way? I want to keep my distance. Luckily, I only need to take two down before Angus is ready to go.

"Let's hit the road," he says as he jogs to the car.

He shoots a couple just for the hell of it as I climb in the passenger seat, and when he gets in the back next to Hadley, he has a big smile on his face. I think he actually enjoys killing them.

CHAPTER TWENTY-TWO

"Hey Victor, what do you think the chances are we'll find the stuff we need at the medical supply place?" I ask as we head to Vegas.

He's sitting in the back by himself, and he looks startled by the sound of his name. He stares at me with blank eyes, blinking a few times before he says, "Maybe everything but the meds?"

Why does it sound like a question? This guy needs to snap out of it or we're screwed.

Hadley twists around so she's facing him. "But the urgent care should have those things. Right?"

He clears his throat and shifts around in his seat a little. "No. But if we pass a pharmacy, that would be better than the hospital. Assuming it hasn't already been ransacked."

He seems to snap out of it a little more with each word. Some of the light comes back into his eyes, and he swallows between sentences like he's really trying to concentrate. I want to keep him talking so he's more alert. Keep him from getting us killed.

"Okay, so we should hit a pharmacy first and then check out the medical supply warehouse. Between the two you think we'll be able to make it work?"

Victor nods his head slowly. "Most likely."

Hadley glances at me and raises an eyebrow. She's as worried about him as I am. Only she doesn't know all the stuff about his zombie wife, so she doesn't know how deep his depression—or insanity—really goes.

"You doing okay, Victor?" she asks.

He glances at her and narrows his eyes like he just noticed she exists. "I miss my wife."

"Shit," Angus mutters. He shakes his head and leans forward. "Is this for real? They sent this bastard to help us out?"

"He'll be fine," Axl says. But when his eyes meet mine, I can see that he's just as worried as the rest of us.

When we reach the outskirts of Vegas, Angus directs Axl through the city from the back seat. After our last attempt, I don't even try to look at the atlas. I guess map-reading isn't my thing.

We're a couple of blocks from our destination when Axl slams on the brakes.

"Pharmacy," he and I say at the same time.

He pulls into the CVS parking lot and parks right in front. Too bad the windows on the door have already been smashed in. Obviously we're not the first ones to come here. Hopefully, the pharmacy is intact and people just came for the food.

"We all going in?" I ask, glancing back at Hadley. She's shaking so hard she looks like a Chihuahua.

"Better that way," Axl says. "We gotta stick together."

I know he's right, but I hate to drag her in. Of course, leaving her in the car by herself might be worse. She's pretty jumpy.

"Knives first." Axl shoves the door open and hops out of the car.

We all climb down, and I help Victor out of the third row while Angus and Axl head up to the door to stake out the store. Hadley stands next to me with a knife in one hand and her flashlight in the other. She's chewing on her lips so hard that they're bright red.

Once Victor's down, we head over to where the brothers stand. They both wear the same tense expression on their faces. It's times like this that I wish Axl didn't look so much like his brother. It's too creepy.

"You okay?" I whisper to Hadley as we walk.

She nods, but she doesn't look it. Her skin is pale, and she has beads of sweat on her upper lip. This is Vegas and the sun is pretty hot, but we were just in an air conditioned car. There's no real reason for her to be sweating. Other than fear.

"The place smells clear," Axl says when we join them by the doors. "Stay alert anyways. Angus, you and Hadley head over to the first aid shit and load up. Vivian, the doc, an' me'll hit the pharmacy."

Angus nods and jerks his head forward as he steps through the broken doorway. Hadley follows, and I go next, being careful to avoid the broken glass that juts out from the metal frame of the door. Victor comes in behind me, and Axl takes up the rear.

Victor appears a lot more alert than he was at the trucking yard. More determined. He even holds his flashlight up as he walks, shining it on the merchandise as we go through the store. I don't know what snapped him out of it, but I'm glad.

The floor is littered with bottles and trash that we have to be careful to step over as we head back, but Axl was right. It smells clear. There's a faint scent in the air that's sickeningly sweet, but I have the feeling it has more to do with the rotting food on the other side of the store than anything dead.

I pass a display of reusable shopping bags and grab a handful. They'll come in handy not only here, but at the warehouse and hospital. It'll be a lot easier to carry the bags than a heavy box full of supplies.

Axl and I are tense and silent as Victor leads us toward the pharmacy. Hadley and Angus must not be talking either, because the entire store is as silent as a tomb. I can't see them, but I can follow their progress by the beam of their flashlights. They bounce across the walls as Angus and Hadley make their way through.

When we reach the pharmacy, Axl hops over the counter. He doesn't open the door right away, though. He heads back through the shelves, sweeping the area for anything dangerous while I stand tensely next to Victor. My skin is moist with sweat. The store is stuffy, and I'm nervous as hell. I just want to get this over with. I can't wait to get back to the shelter.

When Axl comes back, his knife is in its sheath, and his face is a little more relaxed. "It's clear."

Axl swings the door open, and Victor heads off. He moves through the rows of pills like a man on a mission. So different from how lethargic he was at the truck yard. I follow behind him and hold open the bag so he has somewhere to put the drugs he finds. It's clear we aren't the first people to come here looking for meds. There are bottles of pills knocked over on the shelves and scattered around on the floor. Shit.

My eyes land on a familiar label. Birth control pills. I picked the same ones up when we stopped at Walmart, after we first got Emily. They only had a few packets, and even though I haven't really started taking them consistently, it wouldn't hurt to have a few more.

There are four on the shelf. I grab them and toss them in the bag, then hurry after Victor who's already on to the next aisle.

"There isn't a lot left," Victor says.

Even though I already knew it, my heart still sinks. I was hoping we'd be able to find everything we needed between here and the medical supply store. But it's clear from the frown on Victor's face and how little he's put in the bag I'm holding that we won't be able to.

"So we're gonna hafta go to the hospital?" Axl asks.

Victor nods, and Axl swears. I squeeze the canvas bag tighter when my hands start to shake. A feeling of dread squeezes my insides. Everything these days feels like it's going to be the end of the line for us.

"Well, this isn't good at all."

I turn at the sound of Victor's voice and find him staring at a tall cart on wheels. It has rows of drawers with locks on them. Most of the drawers are open and now empty.

He shakes his head, and the more he does it, the more my stomach hardens. "What's that?"

"This is where they keep the controlled drugs. The stronger stuff. Pain killers and things like that. Whoever came here cleaned them out." Victor shakes his head even harder and looks up at us. "We're done here. Unless we want to drive around and find another pharmacy, the hospital is our only option."

"Shit," Axl says. "We could look for a pharmacy, but odds are it's cleaned out too." He spits and looks at me like he's waiting for advice.

"Hospital?" I say meekly.

Axl nods and runs his hand down his face. He looks exhausted. "Well, let's get the hell outta here, then."

We find Hadley and Angus strolling through the aisles. They have a few bags, which are overflowing with first aid supplies. There are also several boxes of condoms in Angus's bag, as well as more chewing tobacco and a few cartons of cigarettes. He looks like he's preparing for one hell of a party.

I'm glad Angus took my advice and got the condoms, though. Last thing I need is a little brother or sister running around. What would that make me if Axl and I end up getting married? Sister or aunt?

The thought of Axl and I getting married creeps into my head and catches me completely by surprise. It's a strange thought, since I never intended to get married to begin with. Now that things are so screwed up, it seems even crazier. Will people even bother getting married anymore? What would be the point?

"You got everything?" Angus asks.

His hard, gray eyes meet mine, and I try to picture what it would be like to have a half-sibling fathered by him. To be honest, he'd probably do a better job than my own father did. Angus was actually pretty good with Emily. For the short amount of time she was with us, that is.

"Nope, but there ain't a whole lot left," Axl says.

Angus adjusts the bag on his arm and stares at the tobacco like he's just dying to rip into it. Probably is. "We ready to go, then?"

"Yup," Axl says.

I stare at the bag in Angus's hands, but I don't focus on the tobacco. It's the condoms I'm thinking about. It wouldn't be a bad idea for me to grab some while we're here. Who knows when we'll get the chance again, and I doubt Angus intends to share. I have the birth control pills, but they won't last forever. It doesn't hurt to be prepared.

"Just a second, I need to grab something."

I dash across the store with my reusable bag slung over my arm, panning my flashlight around. Axl doesn't come after me or yell for me to be careful, but I can feel his eyes following my every move. It takes me two seconds to find the right aisle, and when I do I grab a handful of boxes. Enough condoms for everyone. Axl and I aren't the only ones sleeping together, and we've got enough to worry about without a pregnancy epidemic.

When I make it back to the group, we head out. Axl only glances down at my bag once. He doesn't talk and he doesn't ask questions, but he grins. Guess he's looking forward to getting some use out of them when we get back.

THE PARKING LOT OF THE MEDICAL SUPPLY STORE IS crawling with the undead. Dozens of them stagger around the empty parking lot, walking back and forth aimlessly. Seeing it still makes my skin crawl.

"Why are there so many?" Hadley asks anxiously

"Who the hell knows," Angus says.

He's armed once again with an empty Coke can. He spits into it, and I cringe. Every time he runs out, I hope he'll just decide to get off the stuff. Eventually he's going to run out for good. Why not get it over with now?

A zombie lurches toward the car as Axl slows in front of the medical supply store. He slams his entire body against the passenger side, right outside my window. The thump echoes through the car, and Hadley screams. I almost jump out of my skin.

Axl speeds up. "I'm gonna drive 'round back, see if it'll be easier to get in that way."

The bodies come alive when we pull into the parking lot. They go from strolling aimlessly to charging the car within seconds. Axl rolls over them without slowing. I grip the door handle and bounce in my seat as the tires thump over the bodies. He takes the turn so fast I slam against the window.

"Sorry," Axl mutters.

I rub my head. "Forget it."

He's driving too fast for them to catch up. The tires squeal when he slams on the brakes at the back of the building. There's a door, and it's wide open. Someone's been here too.

"Looks like we weren't he first people to have this idea," Victor says. He's now sitting in the second row with Hadley and me. He's even more clear-headed now than he was at CVS.

"The hospital is going to end up being our only option," I

say. Shit. The thought of going there makes me sick.

"Should we just call this a loss and head to the hospital anyway or risk it?" Hadley asks. Her eyes are wide and scared-looking, and she's once again chewing on her damn lip. She glances out the window. The bodies haven't made it back here yet, but it won't take long.

"We're here," Axl says as he grabs his pack. "And the less we gotta get at the hospital, the better off we are. I don't wanna be there any longer than we hafta be."

I agree, as much as it sucks to have to make an extra trip. "Okay," I say, grabbing my stuff. The first couple zombies round the corner only ten or so feet away. We have to move fast. "So what's the plan?"

Axl looks out the window and purses his lips. "Gotta make a run for it."

"That's your brilliant plan?" Angus grumbles.

"Can't kill 'em all now. We're gonna hafta fight 'em off when we come out. Might as well make it easy on ourselves on the way in," Axl snaps as he opens his door. "Let's fuckin' go already."

Hadley and I look at each other, and I roll my eyes. Brothers. I hop down and run after Axl. Angus grumbles but follows his brother anyway. We sprint toward the already open door. Axl is inside by the time the rest of us get there, and we manage to make it in without having to kill a single zombie. Of course, Axl is right. We're going to have to fight them to get out.

We find ourselves in a back room where the walls are lined with shelves. The whole place reeks of death. Axl is already checking things out. He shines his flashlight in every corner in search of the stench. My heart pounds faster and faster the farther away he gets. I don't like the idea of him being off by himself and possibly getting attacked without any backup, so I hurry after him.

His flashlight lands on the source of the smell just as I jog up, but it isn't a zombie. It's the leftovers from a zombie's meal. The remains of what was once a living, breathing human lie in a rotting, bloody mess on the floor of the back room. There are flies everywhere. They fly in circles and land on the mess, crawling around before taking off again.

My stomach churns, and bile rises in my throat, making me gag. I turn away, coughing. "I think I'm going to be sick."

"Go ahead if you gotta," Axl says.

I bend over and breathe slowly through my mouth, trying to fight off the nausea. I can hear him shuffling around behind me. What's he doing back there? I want to help him, but my face is still hot and my head's swimming.

Angus walks up and shines the flashlight on the remains. I try not to look, but I can't help glancing over. What is it about the blood and gore that's so impossible to resist? Like passing an accident on the highway.

"Bastards ate his face off," Angus says.

That does it for me. My stomach lurches and my throat spasms, and there's no holding it back. I heave, and everything I've eaten today comes up in a foul-tasting pile of vomit. Axl comes over and pulls my hair out of my face. He pats my back as I retch and heave.

When I'm finally done, I stand up and wipe my mouth. Now the back room smells even more wonderful. Death with a hint of vomit.

"You okay?" Axl asks.

I nod and try to avoid looking at the body. Or at Axl. I feel stupid. All the crap we've seen and all the zombies I've killed, and this is what gets me. A bloody mess that doesn't even resemble a human anymore. But that's probably what it was more than anything. The knowledge that it was once human and the torture it must have gone through when it died.

"You check out the rest of the place?" Axl asks Angus. He's still rubbing my back. It's so nice and gentle that even in this smelly store, which is suffocatingly hot—on top of stinking—the gesture turns my insides to Jell-O.

"It's clear." Angus looks down at the carnage on the floor. "Looks like they got this bastard and wandered out."

"Let's go rest for a bit then," Axl says as he pulls me toward the front of the store. "Get somethin' to eat. It's gotta be close to lunchtime by now."

I can't imagine eating. Not after throwing up all over the floor and not with the image of that body in my head. But as soon as Axl forces me to sit—in a wheelchair, of all things—and hands me a granola bar, my stomach growls. I scarf it down and move onto a second one, downing a bottle of water after that. My mouth tastes a hell of a lot better now, and my stomach isn't quite as uneasy. Of course, it doesn't smell as bad in the store as it did in the back room, which could be a good reason for it.

Victor refuses to eat and instead walks around the room, gathering anything he thinks might be useful. He has a pile of stuff on the floor, and it's getting bigger by the second. It doesn't look like there's much of the essential stuff, though.

"Someone's been in here too," Hadley says.

She plops down on the floor at my feet and digs some food out of her pack. I feel dumb, watching her sit on the floor from my wheelchair. I climb out and sit next to her. The floor is hard but better than the chair.

"Is he actually finding anything useful?"

"Some, but not the most important things. Chances are the hospital has been cleaned out too." She seems a lot more relaxed now, but I don't know if it's because we're in a building that's clear of zombies or because she's somehow adjusted to the idea that we may die. Probably the first one. I don't know if it's possible to ever adjust to the realization that you could at any time face a horrible death by being eaten alive.

Axl sits next to me and I lean my head against his shoulder. The memory of being in bed with him last night sends a shiver down my spine. He pulls me closer as if he knows what I'm thinking. He very well could. He seems to always be able to read my mind.

"You feelin' better?" he asks.

His lips are close to my ear. They brush against my skin, making me tingle inside and out, and all I can do is nod. I should have told him I loved him before we left. Now doesn't seem like the right time or place. Hadley is next to us, and Angus stands just a few feet away, looking out the front window at the zombies walking around outside. A little privacy would be better.

I get to my feet and grab Axl's hand, pulling him up behind me. He raises his eyebrows questioningly but doesn't resist when I lead him through the store. Away from the others.

Once we're alone, I can't get the words out. A lump the size of a baseball forms in my throat, and my stomach does a flip-flop every time I try to open my mouth. Maybe waiting is better. Like it will give me an incentive to get back to the shelter alive. Now, here in the middle of the medical supply warehouse with zombies surrounding us, it just feels wrong.

Axl tilts his head, and he narrows his eyes. "You alright?"

I shake my head and swallow. Yeah. Waiting is the right thing to do. "I'm okay."

He nods and pulls me against him. Tears come to my eyes and my throat tightens, and I hate how it all feels because it's so ominous. Like the end is just around the corner. And I don't want that. Not now that I've found someone to love and something to live for.

Axl's mouth finds mine, and I savor every second of his kiss. The end for us could very well be near, but right now we're together.

CHAPTER TWENTY-THREE

"You two done screwin' so we can head out?" Angus calls from across the room.

I break away from the kiss and give him the finger, but he just chuckles. Angus's moods are all over the place when it comes to Axl and me. Almost gives me whiplash. At least at the moment he seems less concerned about it. Probably because he's getting some himself. It would be nice if it stays that way, although Darla's track record doesn't give me a whole lot of hope.

We head back to the group, and Axl looks down at the supplies. "We get much?"

"It was pretty cleaned out before we got here." Victor gives Axl an apologetic look.

He already has everything packed up in a box and ready. He seems almost excited at the prospect of going to the hospital. Not scared like Hadley or dreading it like the rest of us. Doesn't seem right.

We head to the back, and I gag as soon as we step into the storage room. The smell is even more repulsive than I remember. I follow Axl to the door and do my best not to think about the body back there or the mess I left behind. It's impossible, though.

"Guns or knives?" Hadley shakes so hard I doubt she'll be very accurate with a gun, but it may make her feel better if she doesn't have to get close to them.

"Whatever you need," Axl says. His expression is tense, and he glances over at me.

"It'll be okay." I do my best to sound reassuring. The last thing I want is to have him distracted out there because he's worried about me.

"Let's stop talking 'bout it and just get it done," Angus growls. He walks to the door and only gives us one quick look before shoving it open.

The bright light almost blinds me, and I have to squint so I can see. There are zombies everywhere. Angus fires off two shots before he's even taken a step out. He motions for Axl to go out ahead of him, and I go next, followed by Hadley. She's almost on top of me, and her body is so stiff I'm afraid for a moment she's frozen from terror. But she finally shoots her gun. It takes her three shots to hit one in the head, her aim is so bad. Better than nothing, though.

Victor comes out behind us. He carries the box of supplies, so he doesn't have a free hand for the weapons. He seems unconcerned about it, though. I'm not sure if it's because he's suicidal, or because he's wedged in between Angus and me. It's hard to say, but he's in good shape. Angus is a good shot and so am I, and we won't let the zombies get him. Whether he wants them to or not.

The car's only six feet from the door, but the zombies are on top of us every step of the way. I take out four before I've even gone a foot, and more come up behind them. Every nerve in my body is screaming at me to check on Axl. He's leading us toward the car and is the most vulnerable, and with the horde closing in on us, I can't get a good look at him. But I can't afford to get distracted. One false move and I'm zombie chow. Something that looks even less pleasant than it sounds.

A rank, saggy man in nothing but a filthy pair of tighty whities charges me. I sink my blade into his skull, and I'm just puling it out when a scuffling sound comes from the front of the group. Axl curses, and I glance his way just in time to see his head disappear. Less than a second later Angus shoots off a stream of vulgarity more colorful than a rainbow. My heart goes into overdrive. I can't see Axl!

Angus rushes forward, leaving Victor vulnerable. More zombies charge, and I slam my blade into the head of a decaying woman so hard that it vibrates down my arm. Angus disappears into the mass of bodies like he's been swallowed up by a wave. He's going after Axl, and my insides scream to help him. But Victor stands in front of me like a sacrificial lamb, ready for the slaughter. We need that crazy man, and I can't think of myself first. No matter how much my body aches inside.

I shove Victor toward Hadley with one hand while swiping at a body with the other. My blade slices open the neck of a nearby zombie, and black goo sprays everywhere.

"Get Victor to the car!" I scream.

The zombie I nicked moves closer. I keep him in my line of sight while searching for Angus. There's a scuffle up there, but I can barely see the top of his head.

Hadley grabs Victor and pulls him forward. I put my foot in the center of the zombie's chest and kick him backward as hard as I can. He falls, taking a few others with him, and I dash forward. Searching for Axl.

My heart almost explodes at the sight of him lying on the ground. I don't even have enough time to figure out what's happening. All I know is he's down and there are zombies everywhere. Angus is fighting them off, but he's running out of time. He needs my help.

I look up in time to see Hadley pull Victor into the car. Good, that's one worry off my mind.

Axl kicks at a zombie in front of him while grabbing for his gun. He must have dropped it when he fell, and it's just out of reach. Why doesn't he use his knife? I frantically look around, but his hands are empty. Then I spot the knife lodged in the head of a zombie at his feet.

Angus is fighting them back, but a zombie is almost on top of Axl when I raise my gun and shoot it in the head. The bastard goes down, and it gives Axl enough time to grab his own gun and pull his knife free. He scrambles to his feet, and Angus attacks the zombies around his brother with his machete. He chops through their skulls like a pro.

Once Axl's up, I grab his hand and pull him toward the Nissan. I can hear the heavy breathing of Angus behind me. We're at the driver's side, but I climb in first anyway and crawl over the center console to get to my seat. Axl and Angus shut the car doors before I've even had a chance to catch my breath.

The zombies outside converge on the car, attacking us from all sides, and I have a sudden flashback to Axl and me trapped in the Explore outside the Paris casino. It makes me want to cover my ears and scream. This was too close.

I'm panting when I look Axl over. He's dirty and sweaty and covered in black gunk. But he looks alright. "Are you okay? Tell me you're okay!"

Axl nods and wipes his forehead with the back of his hand. All he manages to do is smear the dirt and black spots across his face.

"What happened?" Angus asks from the back seat.

"Bastard was on the ground. Didn't see him. Grabbed my leg and pulled me down." Axl starts the car and gives me a tense smile as he puts it in gear.

"No scratches? No bites?" I ask with a shaky voice. The pounding on the windows is making me crazy but not as much as not knowing if he's been bitten.

He puts the car in gear and hits the gas, plowing through the dead piled around us. "Nothing."

WE'RE THREE BLOCKS AWAY WHEN THE HOSPITAL comes into view. We knew it would be overrun, but knowing and seeing are two different things. The knowledge in no way prepares me for the sight. Hundreds of zombies surround the hospital. So many that it reminds me of the crowds at a fair or carnival. Not nearly as festive, though. It isn't quite as overwhelming as the Strip was, but it's close.

The zombies start to follow the car when we're still a block away, banging on the sides and throwing themselves in front of us. I bounce up and down in my seat as we roll over body after body, their bones crunching under the wheels as we go.

"This is going to be impossible," I say.

"Where do I go?" Axl asks.

Victor sits forward, suddenly more animated than I've ever seen him. "Go to the opposite side of the ER. It's the first place to get overrun when an emergency hits. I would look for a smaller entrance, maybe a place where the employees go in after regular business hours."

Axl nods and heads away from the ER, and I study Victor. He looks almost happy. Maybe this is what he needed to pull himself out of his depression. To feel useful and have something to distract him. Sitting in that condo thinking about his dead wife couldn't have been good.

Except he had his wife tied to a chair in the other room. No, that can't be it. A stable person doesn't do something like that. I need to keep my eye on him.

"'Employee Parking,'" I say, reading the sign out loud as we drive by.

"I see it," Axl says through clenched teeth.

He's driving slowly, plowing over the undead. I look behind us at the carnage we've left in our wake. Some of the bodies are trying to get back up on broken legs, pulling themselves after us with their arms. Dragging their damaged bodies behind them. It makes me shudder, and I have to turn away.

"I'm gonna go 'round once and check it out," Axl says.

He slows as we drive through the parking lot designated for employee parking. There are fewer zombies back this way, but more trail behind us. There's a door just off the parking lot that's slightly ajar. It seems like the perfect place to enter. Except that we have no idea what it's like inside.

"We're attracting them as we drive," Hadley says. She almost sounds hysterical. "How are we ever going to get in there alive?"

Axl accelerates and takes off toward the other side of the parking lot. The undead run after us. "I'm gonna draw them over this way, then haul ass back. We'll have to make a run for it."

His voice is tense as he pulls the Nissan to a stop and honks the horn over and over again. As tense as I feel. Every muscle in my body is on edge as I grab the reusable bags I took from CVS and double check my weapons. Gun full, extra clip in my back pocket, two knives attached to my belt, and my flashlight. Doesn't seem like enough when I think about what we're about to face.

The zombies rush at us. It's a terrifying sight. The dead lumbering across the parking lot, dressed in hospital gowns that blow in the wind. Wearing scrubs and coats that used to be white but are now covered in dried blood and black goo.

They surround us, and my heart races as panic closes in on me. All I can think about is being trapped in that car with Axl and how close we came to death.

"What if we can't get out?" I yell over the banging and screaming.

"Go!" Hadley shouts. Her eyes are wide, and her face is as white as a ghost.

"We'll be okay," Axl says.

He puts the car in gear and moves forward just a bit. The dead scream, and a few in front of us fall to the ground.

"Hang on," Axl says as he slams his foot down on the gas pedal.

My hands are full, so instead of grabbing the door or the seat, I grip my gun and flashlight. It doesn't keep me from lurching forward as the car takes off. Axl moves through the mass of bodies easily, then accelerates toward our target. We're almost in the clear. They're behind us and they're running, but the area around the employee entrance only has a few milling around.

Axl slams on the brakes, and I fly forward as we come to a screeching halt outside the door. "Run!" he yells before the car is even in park.

I shove the door open and jump out, praying the area inside the door is clear. No zombies are even close to us, so getting inside is a piece of cake. But I'm gasping for air when I stumble through the doorway and am thrust into total darkness. The rank odor of death is overwhelming, and my feet bump into something solid. I lurch forward, almost falling, but manage to regain my footing. My hands shake as I flip my flashlight on. The beam illuminates the rotting face of what used to be a zombie. That must have been what I tripped over. Hopefully, he's the only one.

I'm searching the darkness when the others rush in behind me. The door slams shut, and one by one their flashlights flip on. The only sound is our heavy breathing and the moans from the other side of the door. But they're faint. Muffled by the metal separating us.

I pan my flashlight around so I can reassure myself everyone made it. Angus swears, and Axl lurches back when I shine it in his eyes. Hadley is busy checking every dark corner for the dead, and Victor just stands there. We didn't lose anyone. That's something.

We're in a hall of some kind, and our heavy breathing echoes through the empty corridor. There's a wall to our left and a door about twenty feet away on our right. Other than the body at my feet, the hall is empty.

Now for the deadly part.

"Everybody ready?" I say, trying to sound confident.

No one says no, so I take that as a yes and head toward the door.

"Everybody stay together," Axl whispers. "And remember. Knives. Don't wanna draw attention to ourselves."

I stop in front of the door and take a deep breath, but my hand still shakes when I reach for the doorknob. "Here goes."

Slowly, I turn the knob and ease the door open. The place is oddly silent, and when I shine the flashlight out into the hospital, no zombies are in sight. The stench of human decay is even stronger than it was in the hallway, though. It chokes me.

I don't move while I check out the area. After a few seconds of straining my ears, I make out the sound of moans off in the distance. Dozens and dozens of bodies moaning perfectly in synch. It sends a shudder through me.

After determining the coast is clear, I step into the hospital and the others are right behind me. None of us talk. With the door to our backs, we silently spread out in a semicircle. I pan the flashlight around. We're in a hallway just outside the cafeteria. There's a gift shop to my right and a florist next to it full of dead and wilted flowers. In the distance, I spot an information desk. That must be where the main entrance to the hospital is.

"Which way?" Hadley whispers.

I know she's trying to be quiet, but her voice is so shaky that the words come out louder than she probably intended them too. They echo off the walls. The moans that follow sound almost tortured.

My heart skips a beat. I frantically move my flashlight around, looking for the source. It isn't here though, at least not yet.

"Victor?" I ask, trying to cover up the panic in my voice. It doesn't work.

"Surgery would be a good place to find what we need." His voice sounds perfectly calm. Level.

I glance over my shoulder. He's standing straight. Totally relaxed. He moves his flashlight around, lighting up the walls so he can read the signs. He isn't even holding a weapon. Did he even bring it, or did he leave it in the car?

"This way," he says, walking forward without looking to make sure we're following him.

I trade nervous looks with Axl before heading off after Victor. He seems to be on a suicide mission. It's his choice. I can't stop him if that's what he wants, but I do want to make sure he at least waits until we have all the supplies we need.

"The stairs should be back by the elevators," he calls over his shoulder. He doesn't even bother lowering his voice.

"Talk quieter," Hadley hisses.

He shrugs and keeps walking.

Angus clenches his machete. "Is this bastard insane?"

I pick up the pace, trying to keep up with Victor. "Depressed."

"Fuckin' nuts is what he is."

The moans get louder as we move. Axl keeps level with Victor, and the distance between us feels bigger than the Grand Canyon. As much as I'd like to be closer to him, I stick with Hadley. She seems to be holding up okay right now. Who knows how she'll react if we run into a horde, though.

The hospital air is thick and humid. My whole body feels sticky with perspiration. I ignore the beads of sweat on my upper lip and forehead, but it's impossible not to notice the moisture dripping down my back.

The scent of decay grows stronger with each step we take. I pull my shirt up over my nose and do my best to breathe as little as possible. My palms are sweaty, making it difficult to grip my knife. It's only partly from the heat.

My whole body jerks when a horrifying scream breaks

through the air right in front of us. No human has ever made a sound like that. A zombie screeches down the hall. His horrifying face illuminated by Victor's flashlight. He rushes toward us like a banshee, moving faster than any I've seen. His arms are raised and his mouth is open. He lets out a horrifying shriek that makes every hair on my arms stand up. Even in the erratic light, I can see how decayed he is. His flesh hangs from his face in flaps, and in some places, it's missing entirely. He's fast, but not fast enough. Angus swings the machete and takes him out with one powerful blow to the head.

CHAPTER TWENTY-FOUR

The body slams into the floor, and Angus kicks him with the toe of his boot. "You see that? He ran at us like a goddamn bat outta hell."

I aim my flashlight at the zombie so we can get a closer look. He's nothing but a rotten mess of gray flesh and bones, but he ran like he was alive.

"The stairs are over here," Victor calls.

We don't have any more time to look the zombie over. Victor is already on his way, and we have to jog to keep up. He rips the door to the stairwell open and steps inside without even pausing to make sure it's clear.

"Son of a bitch," Axl says as he hurries to get in front of Victor. "What floor, doc?"

"Three."

Moans come from behind us. I glance back as I hurry up the stairs, only to see that a mass of zombies has entered the stairwell at our backs. They're climbing the stairs, and fast.

"Shit!" Hadley cries, taking the steps two at a time.

We race up, but the zombies keep pace with us. When we get to the third floor, Victor once again jerks the door open without waiting. It's like he's trying to get us all killed. Axl swears and shoves the doctor aside so he can goes first.

"They're right behind us!" I call as I run through the door after him.

The zombies behind us aren't the only problem, though. Axl is surrounded, and there are way too many to be cautious. I shove my knife in its sheath and pull out my gun. Holding it in my right hand, I balance my flashlight next to it with my left hand as I take aim. I squeeze the trigger, firing off three quick shots. The three zombies closest to Axl fall.

Someone behind me shoots. I glance over my shoulder to find Angus and Hadley shooting into the stairwell. The zombies just keep coming. Where the hell did they all come from? It's like the asshole that charged us downstairs rang the dinner bell or something when he screamed.

I leave the ones at our back for Angus and Hadley and focus on helping Axl. Gunshots and screams and cursing echo through the hall. Victor stands off to the side while the rest of us fire at the dead. I try not to focus on how useless — and reckless — he's being.

My gun clicks, and I swear. "Tell me you have a plan!" I yell as I replace my clip.

"Hell no," Axl calls over the gunfire.

Angus is suddenly next to me, firing as the zombies lumber forward. He and Hadley must have cleared out the stairwell. I glance over my shoulder and find Hadley talking to Victor, but I can't hear what they're saying over the gunfire.

"We're going to make a run for it!" Hadley calls.

She points to the hallway to my left. Since most of the zombies are coming from the right, I nod in agreement. That way seems to be clear at the moment, and standing here is only going to get us killed.

Victor takes off with Hadley at his side, and I follow,

grabbing Axl's shirt as I pass him. "Let's go!"

Axl fires one more shot before taking off after me. He yells over his shoulder at his brother as he runs, "Come on, Angus!"

I follow Hadley and Victor as closely as possible while keeping Axl in my field of vision. He keeps slowing down to check on Angus. The moron is coming, but he keeps pausing to shoot the zombies following us. He's grinning. Hopefully he runs out of ammo soon so he'll stop his insane firing and run.

The beams from our flashlights bob around in front of us, illuminating the hall as we go. Victor keeps his aimed at the walls so we can see the signs. I keep mine straight ahead. We can't afford to be taken by surprise.

A zombie rushes out in front of us. Hadley lets out a little shriek and slows. Victor charges ahead, not caring that he doesn't have a weapon and the monster in front of him would like nothing better than to rip him to shreds. I pick up speed, leaving Axl behind as I hurry toward the zombie with my gun raised. It's a woman, or used to be anyway. She's completely nude. Her former breasts are saggy, and they sway as she rushes toward me. She grasps at the air in front of us like she's trying to dig her nails into my face from seven feet away. I squeeze the trigger, and a bullet hits her between the eyes. She goes down right in front of me, and I have to hop over her body so I don't trip.

Victor turns to the left without warning and bursts through a set of closed double doors. Hadley follows him. I skid to a halt and look back and forth between the doors and Axl. What do I do? Check to make sure the room is clear or wait on Axl and Angus? They're still so far back.

"Axl!" I scream.

He waves me forward and yells at Angus. Again. Angus is still firing. How many clips did he bring with him? If I were closer, I'd punch him in his smiling face. How the hell is he enjoying this?

They finally catch up, and we rush through the double doors, slamming them behind us. I can breathe easy once we're inside. Both because we're out of the hall and because the smell of death is faint in here.

"It's clear," Hadley says.

I shine my flashlight her way. Victor is in the background, clearing out a few cabinets. She puts her hands up to shield her eyes from the beam of my flashlight, and I flick it toward the ground.

"Sorry."

"Watch out, Vivian," Axl says.

He and Angus push a metal cabinet across the room and shove it against the door. I'm not worried, though. They'd pretty much taken out all the zombies in the hall. I doubt any will stumble in just to check the place out.

I head over to Hadley and Victor and put my hand on her back. She jumps and spins around, wincing when she sees it's just me. "Sorry. I'm a little on edge, I guess."

"It's okay. How are you holding up?"

She shakes her head and stares at the gun in her hands like it's a snake ready to bite her. "This doesn't feel real. Or maybe it feels too real, and that's the problem. I keep running around expecting someone to yell 'cut.' But it never happens."

I never thought of it that way. Maybe that's why she's having a harder time adjusting than the rest of us. It isn't because she's not tough or brave. She definitely is. I remember how surreal this all felt for me the first time I went out. What if I'd been an actress and scenarios like this were just part of my day-to-day life? Maybe it wouldn't have been so easy to focus.

"It'll be okay," I tell her. "You're just having a harder time adjusting because of your background. That's all."

She nods, but her eyes are full of self-doubt.

"How we doin'?" Axl asks as he walks up behind us.

"I got most of the stuff on the list," Victor says, climbing to his feet.

There's a pile of medical supplies on the floor, but the bags are draped over my shoulder. I drop them and start piling stuff inside. The sooner these are filled, the sooner we can get out of here.

Hadley kneels down to help me and whispers, "Thanks."

She gives me a shaky smile, and like a dozen times before, I have the sensation of being at a movie. I remember going to see one of her films and telling a girl friend of mine how annoying Hadley Lucas was. Now here she is at my side. And what's more, I actually like her. It makes me laugh, and I have to cover my mouth.

Hadley arches her brow, and her green eyes narrow on my face. "What?"

"I feel bad saying this, but I always hated you. Not as an actress, I thought you were good. But I thought you seemed like you'd be such a bitch in real life." She grins. Good thing she has a sense of humor. I bump her with my shoulder and return the smile. "I was wrong."

"I'm glad to disappoint you," she says with a laugh.

"Me too."

Angus stomps over. He grins down at us, then turns his head and spits right on the floor. Hadley cringes. I guess he couldn't carry a Coke can and a gun. "You two gonna make out? 'Cause I ain't gonna lie, I think we could make time for that."

I roll my eyes and stand up to face him, deliberately shining my flashlight in his eyes. "Oh, sorry," I say, giving him a smile as I lower the light.

Angus glares at me.

"Everybody ready?" Axl snaps.

I tear my eyes away from Angus and focus on Axl. He's looking my way, and even in the limited light, his body looks tense.

I sling the bag over my shoulder and walk across the room. "You doing okay?" I whisper, wrapping my arms around him.

He pulls me close and kisses my neck. He doesn't smell like Axl. He smells like sweat and death. When will this nightmare end? Who knows if there will ever be a time when we can just relax and be together? Without having to worry about zombies or starving.

"I'm okay. I just wanna get outta here so you're safe."

Warmth floods my body and I stand on my tiptoes so I can look him in his eyes. "We're almost done." I pull him close, and his lips brush mine. It's brief and not enough. I'll never have enough of Axl.

"Let's get to the pharmacy," he says as he steps away. He gives Victor a hard stare. "You know what floor it's on?"

"First floor. I saw a sign for it on our way up but thought it would be better to save it for on the way out."

Victor is so relaxed. So casual about the whole thing. He walks to the door and stands off to the side as Angus and Axl pull the metal cabinet back. They open the door. Victor stares straight ahead without blinking while they check the hall. The brothers motion for us to move out, and Victor doesn't even hesitate. It's like he's accepted the end is near. And he's ready.

"Keep close to Victor," I tell Hadley as we follow the men down the hall.

"He wants to die," she says flatly.

"Did he tell you that?"

She shakes her head and looks around as we walk. She seems more put together since our talk. I hope it helped to have her feelings validated.

"He just keeps talking about his wife and how much he misses her. How he can't wait to be with her."

Should I tell her what Axl and I found? It could freak her out.

"What?" she asks, raising an eyebrow the way she always does.

"He had her in his condo. Axl and I found her tied to a

chair. She was a zombie."

Hadley glances toward Victor, and when she turns back her eyes are filled with tears. "That's so sad."

Sad isn't exactly the word I'd use for it. More like insane.

We round a corner and come face to face with six zombies. Angus and Axl are already hacking away at them with knives, and I hurry forward to help them. Hadley follows, and in a matter of minutes, the zombies are on the ground at our feet. Victor is already hurrying toward the stairs.

It's the same stairwell we came up just a few minutes ago. When we left there were several zombies staggering around the hall, but it's empty now. Thankfully. We jump over the zombies we killed earlier and rush into the stairwell behind Victor. He hasn't slowed. Axl hurries after the doctor, and I have to run to keep up.

The first floor looks as empty as it did when we left it. Too bad the moaning of the dead is still there. They have to be around, but no matter where I shine my flashlight as I follow Victor down the hall, I don't see them. It's putting me on edge. I keep waiting for them to jump out at us whenever we turn a corner.

But we reach the pharmacy with no problem. Victor rushes forward, and we all hurry in, shutting the door behind us. The doctor gets busy searching for meds while the rest of us stand around, impatient and tense. The zombies are out there. We all know it. The scary part is waiting for them to attack.

Victor works fast, loading his bag with medicine, syringes, and anything else he can find that might be useful. By the time he's done, Axl, Hadley, Angus, and I are all carrying a bag. Victor's hands are oddly empty.

"I think I got everything on Joshua's list and then some. You should be set for a while."

I don't miss the fact that he says *you* rather than *we*. I doubt anyone else does either. He seems almost euphoric now. There's a big smile on his face.

"So we're ready to leave?" Hadley asks.

He nods, and I let out a sigh of relief. We aren't far from the door we came in, and the hall was almost empty. We should be good to go.

CHAPTER TWENTY-FIVE

I'm almost relaxed as we leave the pharmacy. Well, as relaxed as a person can be during a zombie apocalypse. It should be a straight shot to the exit. Then we're off to the parking lot. That could be a little rough, but nothing we haven't faced before. After that we're in the clear, and we'll be headed back to the safety of the shelter.

Victor leads the way, taking long strides that Hadley and I have to jog to keep up with. I don't care, though. I'm just as anxious to get out of the hospital as he is to get wherever he's going. To his wife, I'm assuming.

We turn a corner, and Victor almost bumps into one of the undead. It's a massive man who probably weighed over four hundred pounds in life. In death, he's become gray and saggy. He's shirtless, and folds of decaying fat hang on his body. His skin is torn and oozing. His eyes are milky and lifeless. Several of his teeth are missing. He grabs Victor and leans forward with his mouth open, ready to take a big bite out of the doctor.

Victor just stands there, waiting for it to happen. He closes his eyes, and his mouth turns up into a smile. This is what he wanted. The perfect way to be with his wife. My heart pounds, and everything seems to move in slow motion while I try to decide what to do. Help him or go? There's only one zombie. We can get away if we leave him. It's what he wants, so maybe we should.

Just as I've made up my mind to run, Axl slams his shoulder into the zombie's side. The monster stumbles back and loses his grip on Victor's arm, then lets out a bloodcurdling scream. The doctor cries out and moves after the zombie like a madman rushing toward the edge of a cliff. Hadley grabs him and pulls him back as Angus points his gun at the zombie's head.

He pulls the trigger, and the zombie collapses. Victor lets out a cry of despair that sounds so much like the zombies it makes the hair on the back of my neck stand up. Just then, a chorus of moans fills the hall, followed by a stampede of zombies rounding the corner and rushing toward us. Cutting us off from our escape.

"Shit!" Axl grabs my arm and pulls me away from the charging mass of undead. He doesn't even look at anyone else. Not even his brother.

I can barely keep up with Axl as feet pound down the hall behind us. The strap from the canvas bag slides down my arm. It almost falls. A pill bottle falls out and skitters across the floor. Angus swears behind me. Victor is crying. I glance over my shoulder long enough to see Hadley dragging the doctor forward. Angus is behind them, shooting over his shoulder as he goes. The zombies are hot on their tail.

Dozens of zombies scurry after us. The smell and noise is so intense that it feels like a wave pressing down on us. Axl yanks on my arm, and his fingers dig into my skin, bruising me. He keeps pulling.

We're running back the way we came. Toward the

pharmacy. I'm panting, and the muscles in my legs ache. Axl's fingers dig deeper and he pulls harder. When we reach the pharmacy, he shoves the door open, pushes me inside, then turns back toward the others.

I stumble forward and fall to the floor, slamming against a shelf full of drugs. Bottles fall, pummeling me on the head and shoulders. I can't catch my breath. Axl stands with the door propped open, hanging half in and half out. He fires out into the hallway and yells for Angus to hurry. Seconds later, Hadley rushes in, dragging Victor with her.

I still can't catch my breath, but I can't stay where I am. Not with Axl still standing at the door. I pull myself up and run to the door, grabbing Axl by the shoulders. Trying to pull him in.

He shrugs me off and fires again. "I ain't leavin' Angus."

Where the hell is he?

I stick my head out into the hall. Angus is barely running. He shoots at the zombies and laughs when they fall. He acts like this is some kind of game. Like this isn't a matter of life and death. He's a damn psycho.

Axl and I scream at him to run. Angus looks toward us with his lips pursed, then finally turns and jogs our way. He makes it inside, and we barely have it shut before the zombies slam into it.

Axl's face is red from exertion, and his back is to the door. He's leaning against it, trying to hold it shut while the bodies pound on the other side. "Get a shelf!"

Angus and I work to together to drag a metal shelf across the room. Zombies throw their bodies into the door, trying to get it open. Banging fills the pharmacy, and my heart beats in tune with their pounding.

Axl moves out of the way when Angus and I get the shelf to the door. I collapse on the ground, panting and gasping for breath. Axl sinks down next to me, and I lean against him, burying my head in his chest. He smells like sweat and dirt and death. I probably do too.

His strong arms wrap around me, and that does it. Something in me crumbles. We're trapped again. This time there's no one on the outside to set off an explosion, and no Angus to come to our rescue. No escape. This is truly the end.

"I hate Vegas," I say into his filthy shirt.

"I'm sorry." His lips brush against my head when he talks. "I wanted to get you out. I'm so sorry."

I suck in a deep breath and pull my face away from his chest. "This isn't your fault."

Axl leans down, and my lips find his. I squeeze my eyes shut and try to block out all the nose and banging. Everything awful in this place.

The sound of crying distracts me, and I pull away from Axl. My gaze lands on Victor, who is sobbing into his hands. His whole body shakes.

"I wanted to die," he says between sobs. "If you had just let me die, we wouldn't be here. I did what you wanted. I got you the drugs. Why couldn't you just let me die?"

Angus curses. He paces back and forth, kicking the shelves and hurling anything he can get his hands on across the room. "Shoulda let the bastard die! Now look where we are!"

The undead outside the door scream louder. Banging on the door harder. Every sound Angus makes seems to drive them wild.

"Shut up, Angus," Axl says.

He kisses my forehead and climbs to his feet, then swipes his hand through his filthy hair. His lips are pursed and his body tense. He glances over at Victor occasionally as he paces. He's thinking something through. I just don't know what it is.

Victor is still crying. He shakes his head, and his body slumps to the floor. He curls up in a ball like a child. Closing in on himself. I'm not really sure he's been with it since his wife died. Here in Vegas he came back a little, but only because he thought it would all be over soon. And we took that away from him. We should have let him die. It was his right.

Hadley crawls over to where I'm sitting and scoots up next to me. I'm not sure if it's because she wants to be closer to me or further away from Victor. It doesn't matter to me, though. I put my arm around her and pull her closer.

"I didn't really think we were going to die today," she whispers.

Tears fill my eyes, but I blink them back. I have to fight to keep my voice level. "We aren't going to. Axl will think of something," I say with more confidence than I feel.

Axl is smart. So much smarter than he gives himself credit for. If there's a way out of this, I have no doubt he'll figure it out.

I just don't think there is.

Angus keeps cursing, and eventually Axl goes back to talk to him. I can hear their voices, but I can't make out the words. Axl is trying to talk Angus down, though. I know that much for sure.

After a few minutes, Axl comes back and sits down on the floor next to me. I still have my arm around Hadley, but she scoots away. Guilt squeezes my stomach, but I lean against Axl anyway. I need comfort too.

"Do you think if we're quiet enough they'll eventually leave?"

He squeezes my shoulder. "I hope so."

We sit in tense silence for what feels like hours. The moans and banging on the door goes on. It's constant and overwhelming, and it threatens to drive me crazy. My head throbs, and the longer we sit here the more I feel like throwing up. No one talks. It's like we're dead already.

I curl into Axl, then take a deep breath and look up. "This can't be the end."

His Adam's apple bobs when he swallows, and his gray eyes sweep over my face. My chest tightens. I love him so much that it physically hurts. Like my insides are in a vise.

"If I could get you outta this, I would. I'd die to save you."

"I don't want to live without you anyway."

Axl grabs my face in his hands and pulls me toward him. His mouth crushes against mine. It's so violent it catches me off guard, and I have trouble finding my breath. He parts my lips with his tongue, forcing my mouth open. The kiss gets deeper. More urgent. There's too much space between us, so I pull myself up and move so I'm straddling him. My chest brushes against his, and his hands move down my back. He pulls me closer until it feels like I'm being crushed in his grip.

"This has to stop!" Victor screams.

I pull away just as the doctor jerks open the shutters covering the pharmacy window. I'm still straddling Axl. His hands are still on my back. Angus watches with his mouth hanging open and Hadley scrambles to her feet. But none of us are close enough to stop Victor when he climbs over the desk and throws himself out the window. Right into the mass of zombies outside.

Cries of agony break through the silence and slam into me. Hadley screams, and Axl jumps up so fast I fall on my ass. I scurry to my feet. Axl rushes toward the shelf, but I can't move. I'm paralyzed in shock while Axl struggles to pull the shelf away from the door.

Angus runs forward to help his brother, but the expressions on their faces are very different. Angus is ready to run. He's always easy to understand. Axl, on the other hand, has a different kind of determination on his face. He's tense and frantic. Growing more and more panicked with each passing second. He wants to *save* Victor. A man who was lost before we even left the shelter.

They finally get the shelf away from the door, and Axl runs out into the hall. Rushing to help Victor. Is he insane? I scream for him to stop, and my heart twists in agony. Angus runs after his brother, and my feet move on their own. Axl could be in trouble, and I'll do anything to help him. Including throw myself in the path of any zombie that threatens to hurt him.

Hadley grabs me before I can rush out of the pharmacy. "Angus will get him."

I try to pull away, but her nails dig into my forearm when she holds me back. She's surprisingly strong for someone so thin.

She won't let me go, and my body shakes. Axl needs me, but if I can't get to him, I need to help from here. I shake Hadley off. Her gaze meets mine, and she nods. I pull out my gun and start shooting into the horde. From somewhere deep inside, Hadley manages to find the courage that's been eluding her all day. She pulls her own gun out and shoots into the hall, putting down two of dead.

Angus's face is covered in sweat. He hacks away at the bodies in front of him, trying to extract his brother. Arms reach for him, and he grunts when they pull him down. The hand holding my gun shakes. I can't distinguish my friends from the horde of the dead anymore. Desperately, I search for a good shot, but I'm so afraid I'm going to hit Axl or Angus that I can't make myself pull the trigger.

Victor's agonized screams penetrate the air, and my hand shakes harder. He's lost. I knew it the second he jumped through that window.

But where are Axl and Angus?

"Axl!" I scream again.

I focus on the zombies and pull the trigger. Hadley shoots too, and slowly the mob thins. My heart races, and I search the mass of bodies for Axl. I don't see him. Is he gone? Did Victor take Axl down with him?

Two gunshots ring out, and Angus pushes his way through the bodies. He shoves the zombies aside, then reaches back. When he steps forward, Axl is with him. He's covered in blood and black goo.

He's hurt.

My insides threaten to crumble.

I manage to keep it together. I tuck my gun into my waistband and run forward, grabbing the arm Angus isn't holding and pulling Axl down the hall. Away from the bodies feasting on Victor. Hadley runs behind us with the bags of medical supplies, and a few zombies trail after her. Angus releases Axl and turns around. He fires at the zombies as we go.

Axl pulls me against him, but I have no idea if he's doing it to keep me closer or to steady himself. There's no time to stop and find out. No time to check him over for bites. Just looking at him makes my legs weak. He's covered in blood. Real human blood.

Axl stumbles, and his weight almost pulls me down. Somehow I manage to keep us upright. Hadley struggles under the weight of the bags. Angus is still shooting, and Axl is breathing heavily. He holds his left bicep and blood seeps through his fingers. Now I know that he is in fact bleeding. We need to stop and check him over. I keep my eyes ahead and focus on the hall. Every time I look at Axl, my body shakes.

"We need to stop!" I yell over my shoulder.

I point to an office in front of us, and Angus jogs ahead. He breaks down the door, and the four of us stumble inside. Axl falls to the ground just as Angus shoves a bookcase in front of the door.

Hadley drops the supplies on the floor next to me and wipes her forehead. It's covered in sweat.

I aim my flashlight at Axl. My hands shake, and it takes me a minute to focus on his bloody arm. "Where are you hurt? Did they bite you?" My fingers fumble on the buttons of his shirt so it takes longer than it should to pull it off.

Axl tries to push my hands away. "Vivian, calm down. I'm alright."

I can't. Not until I can see his arm. Not until I know if my world is about to end. "Let me do this."

I strip his shirt off and wipe at the injury, praying he hasn't been infected. All I can focus on is the blood.

"Vivian." His voice is so soft that it finally breaks through my frantic thoughts. "I ain't bit. A stray bullet grazed my arm."

A sob pops out of my mouth. I cover my lips and choke back the tears. "I thought they got you."

"It's gonna take a helluva lot more than that to take me down."

Hadley kneels next to me and digs through the bag of supplies. Luckily, she had the foresight to grab them. We didn't lose anything. I hold Axl's hand while she cleans up the wound. Thank God we have stuff with us to treat the injury.

Angus has been silent this entire time, but when I look at him, I can tell he's just as relieved as I am. Losing Axl would have been just as devastating for him.

"What now?" I ask, looking back and forth between the brothers. I'm still holding Axl's hand. He gently moves his thumb back and forth over mine. "We're completely cut off from the way we came in."

"Gotta find 'nother exit," Angus says.

Axl gives my hand one quick squeeze before letting go and climbing to his feet. "We get the hell outside so we can make our way back to the car." He grabs his shirt and pulls it back on as he talks.

"Great. So we just go out into the zombie-covered parking lot and mosey on back to the car? Sounds wonderful," I say sarcastically. My eyes meet Hadley's as I get to my feet, and she frowns. She looks as thrilled by the plan as I feel.

"We'll be okay." Axl pulls me in for a quick hug and kisses my earlobe.

I gnaw on my bottom lip, fighting back the tears. Why does it feel like he's kissing me goodbye?

Angus clears the door then looks back at us. "Ready?"

CHAPTER TWENTY-SIX

We rush back out into the hospital. Angus and Axl lead the way, putting themselves between us and any danger that may lie ahead. Thankfully, the hall is clear of zombies. But their moans are present with every step we take, making my heart pound and my pulse quicken.

The sound of shuffling feet echoes through the hall, but it's impossible to tell where it's coming from. I pan the flashlight around, but I'm greeted with emptiness. There's nothing in front of me but Axl and Angus. Nothing behind me that I can see at all. Hadley's eyes meet mine, and they are full of terror.

"It will be okay." I try to sound reassuring, but my voice cracks and my eyes sting from the tears that threaten to spill over. I just have to hold it together long enough to get out of here.

We race ahead. Hadley reaches out and grabs my arm with her free hand whenever a sound makes her jump. She squeezes it, and her fingers dig into the area Axl grabbed earlier, making me wince. I'm going to have a bruise there later.

The halls are so dark that the second an exit comes into a view it's like the light at the end of a tunnel. My heart leaps, and I want to cry out in excitement, but I swallow it down. We're almost in the clear.

Hadley isn't able to keep her excitement inside, though. "An exit," she calls out.

I glance her way and give her a smile. It's tense, but it's genuine. She's still shaking a little, but she smiles back. I can see the relief in her eyes clearly now, thanks to the sunlight shining through the small window on the door. We're almost there. Just a few more seconds, and we'll be outside.

Less than twenty feet from the exit, a zombie stumbles out of an open doorway. He comes out of nowhere, appearing right in front of Hadley and me. Cutting us off from the brothers. She screams, and I stumble back, grabbing her arm to pull her with me. The zombie lurches toward us, and my heart pounds in my ears. It's just one zombie. Just one insignificant, rotting corpse standing between us and freedom. I raise my gun without thinking and pull the trigger, shooting it in the skull.

His body hits the ground just as several more lurch from the doorway behind him. Hadley screams and fumbles for her weapon, which for some reason she has put away. More of the undead appear, crowding out of the doorway, moaning and grasping at air.

The zombies push Hadley and me further back. Axl shouts my name, but I can't see him through the horde. Hadley screams as one lurches at her, but before I can come to her rescue, she has him down. Her knife sticks in his head when he falls, and she's forced to pull out her gun.

They keep coming. Hadley and I shoot while we back away, but we aren't making a lot of progress. I'm constantly looking over my shoulder to make sure none are sneaking up behind me. It's throwing off my aim. Sweat drips down my face, running into my eyes. I wipe it away and search the dark hallway for Axl. I can't see him, though. We're completely cut off. There are more than fifteen zombies between us and them.

I can hear the gunfire, so I know the brothers are attacking the bodies on their side. Hadley and I continue to shoot the ones coming toward us, but more pour from the doorway. It's never ending. I squeeze my trigger, but the gun just clicks.

I pull out my knife in frustration. "I'm out of bullets!" I shout.

I don't know if I'm telling Hadley or Axl or just myself. Whatever it is, the realization that I now have only my knife to defend myself with isn't comforting. Especially not when more zombies have followed the sound of our fight and stumbled through the doorway. It's now obvious that we're not going to get out of this alive if we stick around.

"Make a run for it! Find 'nother way out!" Axl yells.

I guess he came to the same conclusion. I still can't see him from where I am, but the tension in his voice is unmistakable.

"We'll see you in the parking lot!" I yell back, grabbing Hadley's arm.

We turn and run back the way we came. We'd passed another hallway just a few feet behind us, so I head that way, praying it's clear. The sound of moans and shuffling footsteps follows us. I look over my shoulder just before I duck into the hall. A large group of the undead is hot on our trail.

Hadley and I run down the hospital corridors. The beam of my flashlight is our only source of light, and it bounces along as I sprint. Hadley must have lost hers somewhere along the way. A zombie appears in front of us, but thankfully Hadley still has a few bullets. She fires with a shaky hand, but misses on the first shot. The second hits the mark though, and the zombie goes down.

We run around the body, and I pray we don't bump into a big group. If we do, it's the end for us. The mass of bodies running after us is closing in. The only way we're going to be able to get out of this alive is if the hallway in front of us remains clear.

I'm breathing heavily as I turn the corner and find myself faced with three options. Option one appears to have two zombies running toward me. Option two looks empty, but the unmistakable sound of moans echoes through the hall. Option three is a closed door that leads to the ER.

I'm not stupid. I remember what Victor said about the ER. But at this moment, with zombies coming at me from three sides and the lure of a door we may be able to close and block off, I feel like whatever might be lurking behind door number four is my best option.

I run toward the ER and press on the handle, then try to push the door open. It doesn't budge, but the handle moves, so it can't locked. I hold the handle down and ram my shoulder against the door, putting all my weight into it. It moves a few inches, and something scrapes against the floor on the other side. Something is pushed up against the door. I bang my shoulder against it, over and over again. All I need is to get it open just enough for Hadley and me to squeeze through. The moans get louder, and my heart pounds harder. I take a deep breath and ram my body against the door one more time, moving it another inch. Making it wide enough for us to get through.

"Come on!" I motion for Hadley to squeeze through.

Her eyes flit nervously to the large sign above the door that says *Emergency Room*, but she runs over anyway. She goes first, easily fitting through the small opening I created for us. It takes me a little more maneuvering—I'm not as thin as she is—but I manage to get through with minimal effort. I push the door shut behind me just as the zombies burst from the hallway.

A metal cabinet of some kind is pushed up against the

door. Hadley and I work together to move it back into place. I'm not sure if any of the zombies saw which way I went, but I want to be extra sure the door is secured. We grab a second shelf and push it over as well. I'm panting and sweating by the time that's done, but it suddenly occurs to me that I haven't checked out the room around us.

I spin around to face the ER, clutching my knife. It's eerily quiet, but even more surprising is the fact that it doesn't stink. Their scent always gives them away, and the smell in the emergency room is so faint that a person could almost convince themselves it isn't there at all.

"It's so quiet," Hadley says. Her voice floats through the ER, filling the silence and making me jump.

I nervously take a few steps. Something isn't right. This part of the hospital is too empty. Hadley and I walk forward slowly, scanning the rooms as we go.

"This is wrong." My heart pounds even faster as the sound of my voice echoes through the empty space. I'm on edge.

Hadley glances around nervously. "What could be wrong?"

"I don't know, but I don't like it. Let's get out of here."

She nods, and we take off at a full sprint. I pan my flashlight around and keep my eyes open, but it's obvious by this point that the ER is empty. But for some reason I can't quite pinpoint, that makes me even more nervous.

I follow the exit signs as we move through the halls. We pass curtained exam rooms and a couple reception desks, but no dead. There's nothing in here. No zombies and no bodies. It's like the place has been cleaned out. But I have no idea who would do it. Or why.

We finally reach the waiting room and come to a halt. In front of us is the exit. I can see the parking lot easily from where we are, thanks to a wall of windows. The area just outside the door is as clear of the dead as the inside is. Hadley and I rush out into the Nevada sunshine, stopping to look around and catch our breath the second our feet hit the pavement.

Once again, I'm struck by the fact that something is off. We're standing in the ambulance bay and the area is clear, but even more strange is the fact that it's block off by some kind of barricade. Cars and other debris are piled on top of each other, creating a fence. Blocking the way to the emergency room. The wall is six feet high, making it difficult—maybe even impossible—for the zombies to get into the ER. Someone went to a lot of work to create this barrier. I have no idea why it was done, but it seems to be working. There are dozens of zombies ambling around the parking lot in the distance, but none where we are.

"What the hell?" Hadley studies the structure with the same uncertainty I do before turning back to look at me. "We have to get out of here."

She read my mind. "I know."

We run forward and climb the wall of cars in front of us. My heart pounds and I keep looking back over my shoulder, waiting for someone to come charging out of the hospital. No one does though, and in a matter of minutes Hadley and I are on the ground on the other side.

"What now?" Hadley asks as the dead become aware of our presence and start racing toward us.

I glance around and try to catch my bearings. I'm not positive, but I'm pretty sure if we run to our right we'll be going in the right direction.

"This way," I say.

Hadley and I start jogging. She must be running low on bullets by now, but she shoots anything that gets too close to us. Most of the zombies headed our way are on the far side of the parking lot, so we're safe for the moment. If we can just hold out until Axl and Angus find us, we'll be in the clear.

Only a couple seconds after that thought goes through my head, a car turns the corner in front of us. I'd recognize the Nissan anywhere. My body relaxes, and I let out a sigh of relief. Hadley smiles, and I'm actually able to return the gesture. We're almost home free.

Tires squeal behind us, and I look over my shoulder. A white van approaches from behind, closing in fast. My heart skips a beat and I grab Hadley's hand, pumping my legs harder. I put every ounce of energy I have into making my legs work as I run toward the car in front of us. Away from the one behind us.

The Nissan is still at least fifty feet away when the van screeches to a stop at our backs. My heart nearly explodes when I hear the door slide open behind us. The footsteps on the pavement match the pounding of my heart, and I scream in frustration. He's so close! Right behind me! My hand grips the knife tighter and I spin around to face my attacker, swinging it through the air. He's a blur of black as he ducks and shoves me to the ground. My head snaps back and my body slams against the ground. All the air rushes from my lungs and my knife skids across the pavement. Hadley screams, but I can't figure out where she is because I'm too busy gasping for air. The man in black grabs a handful of my hair and jerks me to my feet. I scream when pain shoots across my scalp and down my neck. He runs, hoisting me up so my feet aren't touching the ground. I kick and fight, but I can't get free.

My head bobs and the world blurs, I can barely make out the Nissan when it screeches to a stop—it's so close. The doors fly open. Axl and Angus start firing, but the men in the van return fire. A window shatters right next to my head and the man carrying me swears before tossing me inside. I land on the floor right next to Hadley. The last thing I hear as they pull the door shut is Axl screaming my name.

Acknowledgements

I have been so excited and overwhelmed by the amazing reviews and feedback I've gotten for *Broken World*. Of course, I love the book, but the glowing reviews and enthusiasm of the fans has still blown me away. Thank you so much for loving this book so much!

As usual, I want to give a huge thanks to my three good friends Erin Rose, Sarah McVay and Tammy Moore-Brewer for loving this series and being overwhelmingly supportive.

To my editor, Emily Teng, who did such a great job. I'm so glad she does freelance so I was able to hire her to continue this series, and I'm looking forward to sending the third book to her very soon!

And yet again, thank you Robert Kirkman and AMC, Norman Reedus (Daryl Dixon), and every person who loves zombies as much as I do. Keep reading and I'll keep writing!

About the Author

Kate L. Mary is an award-winning author of New Adult and Young Adult fiction, ranging from Post-apocalyptic tales of the undead, to Speculative Fiction and Contemporary Romance. Her Young Adult book, *When We Were Human*, was a 2015 Children's Moonbeam Book Awards Silver Medal winner for Young Adult Fantasy/Sci-Fi Fiction, and a 2016 Readers' Favorite Gold Medal winner for Young Adult Science Fiction. Don't miss out on the *Broken World* series, an Amazon bestseller and fan favorite.

For more information about Kate, check out her website: www.KateLMary.com

Made in the USA
Columbia, SC
13 April 2020